HOUSE of
SCEPTERS

THE
FEHL
EMPIRE

CASP SEA

ZENURE

HEIT TERRITORIES

RA

LYNDEL

LORAN

BAHRA

★ TEHRAS

HERAT

TEHRASI

★ PARSA

EHLAKA ☆

CUIPSIN

HOSFURI

LA

★ KROKOLA

NURFINE

FEHLA-DA

FEHL
SEA

INDI

ALSO BY ANNE ZOELLE

THE SCEPTER SERIES

THE REN CROWN SERIES

LAYER TALES

ANNE ZOELLE

HOUSE of SCEPTERS

EXCELSINE≣PRESS

Art Credit:

Cover illustration @Eleonor Piteira
Scepter illustration @Eleonor Piteira
Scarab illustration – Modification of image from The Principles of Design by G. Woolliscroft Rhead, 1905
Shutterstock image components
Interior typesetting and design – Anne Zoelle

DEDICATION

To the usual suspects.

Mom and Matt, I couldn't do this without you. And I'll never grow weary of your red pens.

To Dad and S, for always being there.

To Barbara, Grace, Veronica, Sara, and Christie, for your endless support and encouragement.

To Tashie, for being awesome and taking this ride. You are a beam of endless light.

Thank you to Faith and Shannon for your great edits, and to Eleonor for your amazing art.

And to every reader who has sent me a note – thank you.

House of Scepters
Contents

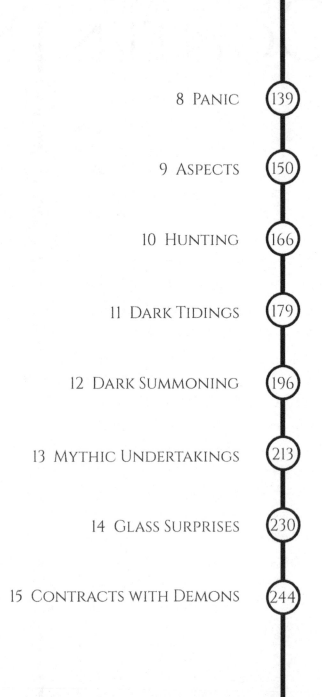

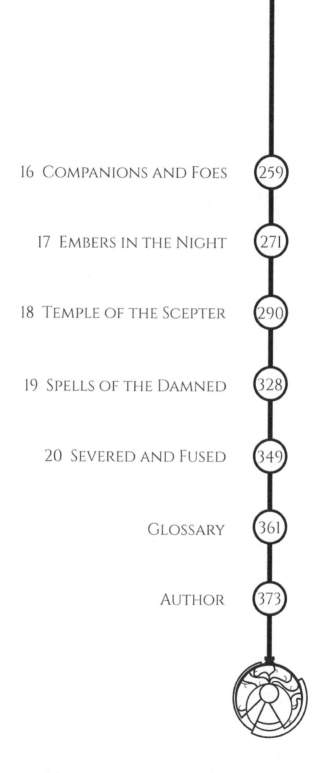

BOOK ONE

HOUSE of SCEPTERS

PROLOGUE

From the Scroll of Fehl, as written in the thirtieth year of the Fehl Empire:

When Sher Fehl campaigned to unite the tribes of the lower reaches, he was met with accolades and support from sovereigns far and wide who were tired of the unrest and chaos stemming from those lands. Even Tehrasi, the richest and cruelest kingdom in the Greater Medit region, saw the promise of unifying the chaotic lands that bled into theirs. They gifted Fehl with one of their prized gate scepters to allow him to maintain order of his newly conquered territories. But Tehrasi, ever wicked in its intentions, took something from the new ruler in order to show him *his place* at the same time.

Sher Fehl's mind churned with revenge, but the possibility of changing the world stared back at him from the powerful scepter in his hand—a scepter which would enable him to create five gates between his newly aligned territories and allow instantaneous travel between far-flung lands.

Many rulers were puzzled at the initial locations where Fehl chose to erect the five gates gifted by the scepter, and were even more baffled at the inconsequential tribes he chose to consume thereafter. When peace ensued and their kingdoms prospered, most lost interest. They paid little attention when Fehl rewarded lower-class magi with riches and glory, and less attention when he gathered very specific types of magic users to his lands. They ignored completely his proclivity for bearing children far and wide with the most dazzling and powerful magi in the lands.

What no one could ignore were the terrifying abilities he revealed—in both himself and his offspring—when he came years later for their blood drenched lands.

With little resistance, far too late for any kingdom to mount an offensive, Sher Fehl's hardened conquest spread through the entirety of the desert, forest, and sea lands of the sacred peninsula, and continued outward, creating an empire that would grow beyond the wildest of imaginings.

Tehrasi, the jewel of the Greater Medit lands—a kingdom that for centuries had withstood conquest and grown grossly opulent in the richness of its scepters—fell to Fehl's assault and revenge. The royal family was helpless to prevent the extinction of their line, but in death they managed a single, monumental victory against the new empire—they took the secrets of their powerful scepters to their graves.

When the Tehrasi scepters—and all the gates that had

been made from them—refused to answer to a new hand, only a mythical solution remained: to locate the scepter that could reset all the others. An instrument said to corrupt even the lightest of souls, a scepter that men would murder for and die to possess—the Scepter of Darkness would be found.

A THIEF'S VOW

NINLI
𝘺𝘺𝘵𝘺 ☼ 𝘬𝘬𝘬𝘷
TEHRAS, TEHRASI

"Do you understand the *power* we are discussing?"

Ninli ul Summora forced wisps of enchanted current to encircle her head-to-toe-wrapped, camouflaged body—keeping her back, elbows, and feet adhered to the exterior vertical stones of the second-highest palace turret while she listened to the men arguing vehemently inside the war room.

Nin forcibly relaxed the muscles in her shoulders and bent knees beneath the multi-layered spells and took a deep breath as she looked out at the capital city spread out below in all directions from the palace.

The long freefall that awaited a misstep on her part didn't make her stomach churn, but the conversation inside the palace did.

In Tehrasi, plots and politics always came back to the infernal scepters.

"With the Scepter of Darkness, you will hold *all* the power." False charm oozed from the voice of the head scholar and councilor, Crelu ul Osni, the Scholari of Tehrasi. "Even the emperor will be made to bow."

"I tire of your promises and your fireside myths."

The petulant voice made Nin curl her toes into the enchanted stones and adjust her position. She spun an extra layer of magic to keep her body adhered to the turret's exterior and grimly started weaving a revelation spell.

"It's no myth, Padifehl," Osni said. "The gates are failing, and your hold on this country will fail if the gates do."

"I sit on the throne of the jewel of the empire—*I*, Etelian ul Fehl, Padifehl of Tehrasi, ruler of the City of a Hundred Gates—and *nothing* will unseat me. I will execute every gatekeeper who fails. I will execute you, should you overstep further. You are only alive because of previous, false promises, Scholari, and I tire of you."

If Etelian ul Fehl, Padifehl of Tehrasi, were just a spoiled child, his position would be a problem. But he was a cruel, spoiled child, and his word was law.

"If your gatekeepers die, and if I'm removed, the last of the gates will crumble, for the scepters will be the only thing that hold such power any longer in this land," Osni said.

If Crelu ul Osni, Scholari of Tehrasi, were a simple scepter scholar, Nin might be empathetic to his concerns. But he was a traitor and his words were poison.

"Your gatekeepers will die," Osni said. "Then what will you do? The emperor grows weary of the failing gates—all our spies agree—and I will not be the only one punished. You will be whispered of in the halls of the Crown of Sunlight—what will your siblings say of your disgrace?"

"You *dare*. I will have your h—"

A flash of magic burst through the open stone window to her left. The flash forced her to squint painfully, but didn't stop her movements. She moved her fingers faster to complete the revelation spell. She needed to see the map beneath Osni's hand before he bled all over it. Osni played a dark game.

"Oh, dear, poor padifehl. Your *ceremonial* scepter didn't much like that attempt of yours," Osni said, voice darkly satisfied. In ten years, Etelian had never mastered the scepter he had grabbed upon taking the throne. "You need me still."

"You need *me*, Osni." The padifehl's voice was hot with rage. "Your scepter fails you, as well. I've *seen* it. That thief did something to you. Whatever you've been doing for the last decade holds sway no more. Your *use* is coming to an end."

"I am not out of tricks."

But Nin was darkly satisfied to hear the strain underpinning Osni's voice. Unlike Etelian, she knew how Osni had been powering the gates. Crystal and blood ripped from his possession three months before had ended a decade long masquerade. Without the blood he had stolen from the fallen rulers of Tehrasi, Osni's use truly *was* coming to an end.

Nin had made certain of it.

Three vials of blood remained—worn around his neck, disguised as ornamental spikes around the locket he held most dear. When the last drop of king's blood was shed, when true desperation took hold of him, she'd be there, waiting.

And she would rip that locket from his neck.

"The thief will pay," Osni promised darkly. "Failures can be wiped away with a single cast of the Scepter of Darkness."

"A *mythical*—"

"The Scepter of Darkness is *very* real. The man who holds the scepter that resets all other scepters to his bloodline will be the most powerful man in the world. The hand that holds it won't need any *tricks*. Think of it in *your* hands, Padifehl," the scholari repeated, voice dropping. "Think of what you could do with it. What you could demand from the emperor. Who of the imperial children would be raised in favor then?"

Nin's fingers itched insidiously at the thought of such potential power in her grasp, while her stomach turned at the thought of it in the hands of the men speaking. She forced herself to take a deep, silent breath and to complete the delicate spell she was weaving.

"*You* will have the power, and the emperor will recognize that worth," Osni stressed.

"Where is this scepter, Scholari," the padifehl said viciously, "that even the royal family of Tehrasi proclaimed a myth?"

"Of course they proclaimed it myth," Osni answered just as viciously. "It would have cost the Carres their two-hundred-year rule. But now..." Nin could hear the dark curl of pleasure as his voice dropped. "Finally, *finally,* I will have victory."

Nin curled her fingers around the finished spell. She would ensure that *never* happened.

Quickly securing additional wind strands around her waist, she let the revelation spell slip over the windowsill. She fished a crystal sphere from her belt and wrapped the tail of the enchantment around it, then let the threads on the seeking end find the map resting beneath the scholari's agitated fingers. Smoked wind blew the image of the room, figures, and map inside the crystal sphere in her hand.

Eleven positions were marked on the map. Eleven inbound chariots.

It was the absence of a twelfth marker that lifted a grim smile to her face. That was their chariot, then.

They had one chance at intercepting it. Once the shipment reached the palace, there would be no chance for subterfuge.

She clicked twice on the modified child's toy attached to the wrap at her waist, and lowered her headband insert with its two flattened spheres. She looked through the enchanted glasses. Roads spread in thousands of crisscrossing directions from the palace down to the hundred gates surrounding the capital city of Tehras—a city teaming with life and energy. Wind enchantments ferried spell-woven khursifas and their passengers along currents from district to district while mechanical conveyances freely navigated streets that had previously been held under the dark hand of the fallen Carre dynasty.

Colorful rooftops—a medley of old and new designs patched together across the city—spread in all directions, and light sparkled on metal adornments used to take in shared magic. A small flock of hand-sized dovedragons darted through the upper currents, testing the city's pest control forces.

Through the enchanted lenses, Nin could see everything except what lay behind the turret she clung to—and that view, too, was possible with a wisp of spelled wind. Twelve red lights traveled through the city on different routes—their positions glowing in the spelled glass.

When the empire had conquered Tehrasi, they had brought with them a bounty of new inventions and enchantments from all the lands they had claimed, converting the stringent, holy city of Tehras to one brimming with cosmopolitan advancements and delights.

A city that had once relied solely on strict, elite access to the gates that connected them to places near and far was now connected in a far greater way. Districts that had been far from each other as traveled by foot—farther than the coldest or warmest of climates by gate—were now mere ticks of the sun's path when traveled on wind streams that connected every part of the vast city with paths.

She clicked the instrument on her waist again while watching one of the red lights. *Position two, go.*

"The Hand has been increasingly active—five thefts in as

many days," one of Osni's aides said cautiously. "He has spies everywh—"

"I know," Osni said with dark pleasure. "I *want* him to try. He will be relieved of those hands, and I will know who is behind the hood and sash."

"You risk the scepter for revenge?" the padifehl demanded. She could hear Osni's aides whispering.

More fools, they. Osni would risk anything, *everything*, for revenge. She grimly pulled down her headband.

"Prize requires sacrifice." Osni's voice became maddened. "And I will have it all."

"*You* will have it all?" the padifehl said. "*I* will have it all. Rats and spies—I should kill all of you."

Nin paused at that, lifting her headband again with tight fingers and gazing into the glass sphere. The enchanted vision of the war room focused on the wall mirror and the displayed image of a man everyone in Tehras knew and feared.

She curled her lip at the padifehl's state of dishabille— eyes shot with the thin red lines of palmera ingestion, clothes half undone, a vicious set to his features, a woman unconscious on the floor at his feet.

Nin gripped her headband tightly, hatred overwhelming her.

The expressions on the faces of the aides and subordinates in the war room changed from dismayed to terrified. "We would never say anything," one tripped over himself to say. "We are keeping quiet until the scepter is found. The emperor and elite know nothing of these plans. Surely—"

"The scepter is the last chance for all of you," Etelian ul Fehl said, mouth viciously twisted in pleasure. "I *will* kill you if you fail to accomplish what you promise, Scholari."

Nin touched the cold, iron blade of the dagger at her waist. The Fehl Empire—or the Sunlight Empire, named from the crown that sat upon the emperor's head—had brought many wonderful things to Tehrasi, but they had left behind the scholarly rat who had served the royal family he murdered, and installed Etelian ul Fehl, second son of the emperor, upon the throne as Padifehl of Tehrasi.

Those two appointments, Nin would never forgive. And to wipe them from her country, she would do *anything*. A decade after a change in rule, Tehrasi stood on a summit. Anything could tip it—to the cruelty of the past or the progress and hope that Nin so desperately desired.

Until she could remove Etelian ul Fehl and Crelu ul Osni permanently, she would continue to disrupt the state of affairs in Tehrasi.

A shadow broke through the grove below, breaking Nin's dark thoughts.

"All in service of you, Padifehl, as my binding oath guarantees." The scholari's voice turned falsely obsequious— his greatest asset. "All for you, I can assure—"

Nin secured her goggles for flight, unsealed her upper body from the wall, and tucked the globe into the band strapped around her hips. She spread her arms, unsealed her hips and feet, and pushed off into a dive.

In the shadowed sweep of the palace banners as she dove, she watched the guards check their sand dials, eager to swap shifts and fly to the night bazaars.

The ground rushed to meet her, then enchanted wind did the same.

Wind encircled her and cast a reflection of the surroundings around her diving body. The ground rushed closer and she pulled her arms in sharply, using the momentum to flip herself. A gust of wind pushed upward, slowing her descent, and an unnaturally fast-moving object shot through the sacred grove of the palace on a perfectly executed intercept course.

Nin landed on the soft padding of woven linen and silk. A snakelike strap immediately wrapped up and secured her as the khursifa shot through the trees without pause. A steadying hand reached back, and Nin laughed in her sister's ear and held on. With the crystal sphere pressed between them, they banked hard right and swerved out of the grove and into the southern wind gust of District Two, nearly taking out five other khursifas in order to swerve and catch the east current to District Five.

Strips of linen rippled on the breeze as they caught a cross-sectional spell and Nin activated the fibers beneath them that Taline had painstakingly spelled and enchanted, reinforcing each with specific magic.

She paused momentarily as old memories infused her.

Scepters, power, horrid rulers, and secrets—revenge, intrigue, and erasing the legacy of Tehrasi…

You'll never wield my scepter, little maggot.

"You'll never cease giving me heart palpitations!"

Nin shoved old memories where they belonged and laughed at her sister's words, firmly gripping the liberation offered by newer, better memories—late-night, insane khursifa rides with people who would never leave you, no matter the misfortune of your birth.

"Stop enjoying yourself," Taline demanded over her shoulder.

Nin smiled and held on.

The wind from the crisscrossing traffic of flying khursifas brushed her cheeks. Imperial red and black banners trimmed in gold gently lifted in the winds along the streets. Enchanted lamps cheerfully dotted thousands of living quarters stacked five high on both sides of the street as the road sloped gently downward to one of the hundred gates that Tehrasi's capital city was famous for.

"It's a trap and you know it. You are sure the target is in play?" Taline asked.

"Osni hopes to accomplish two things tonight—revenge and triumph. Our target is on the board. The chariot from Nohr wasn't on the map."

"I knew it," Taline said darkly. "There was no reason for you to take the risk of going to the palace."

"Osni is confident that he killed everyone who knew the palace's eavesdropping enchantments, and it has made him foolish enough to think that keeping the Fehls out is more important than keeping out vengeful spirits of the dead," Nin said as they headed for the predetermined point and tucked the spying ball into Taline's pocket. "We'll take the chariot en route. Drop me on that roof there."

TALINE

The tap on Taline ul Summora's shoulder was her only warning as Nin dove from the khursifa, rolling onto a rooftop.

Taline resisted the urge to grab Nin again—her sister in everything but blood—and make for a gate instead. Resisted the need to leave this cursed city and find an oasis in the desert or a juniper house in the forest—to wrap Nin in thick cotton and create a quiet life away from the intrigues of the empire, the unabated guilt, and the harsh memories of the past.

She took a deep breath and did none of those things. Nin would be fine. She always was.

Taline took solace in repeating the litany. Nin had been fine when she had dragged Taline's broken body from a cage of fire four years ago—rescuing a nameless girl in need of help—and patched her up, giving her a home, a name in the empire's new naming scheme, and a purpose. Nin had been fine when she had single-handedly wrecked the scholari's estate with no casualties. She had been fine when she'd crushed the blood vials the scholari had been using to control the gates. She had been fine when she had rescued twenty civilian rioters last week from the padifehl's guards and prison.

She had been fine when she had—

Taline swallowed. Nin would always be fine. Taline had to believe that.

Taline kept her cloth-covered gaze on the younger girl sprinting across rooftops. She watched as Nin nimbly landed and rolled, drawing a hand along her midsection, turning her clothing from multi-colored-stone camouflage to black, as she slipped between the soft shadows cast by the bright lights of the night market.

Nin would be fine.

A thin white sash appeared around her black-clad wrist, trailing behind in the breeze of flight. A taunt. A mark. A statement. Nin wanted the scholari to know who robbed him this night—the person nearly single-handedly responsible for the mess the scholari and padifehl found themselves in.

Nin ran, her figure blinking between one position and the next, in a way no normal person could.

Taline gripped the spell-woven, reinforced threads of the khursifa. At times like these, it was hard to think of Nin as anything restricted by human physical standards.

As Nin ran, her fingers flashed. *Position two, clear.*

Taline banked and flew to the corner of the District Eleven bazaar, alighting on a rooftop. With a flick of her wrist, the khursifa was rolled and stored in an enchanted, cylindrical holster on her back that would recharge its spells. She processed the traffic above, below, and around her as she, too, added enchantments to change her own appearance—creating the stooped figure of a large man.

Horseless chariots—vehicles caught between innovations old and new—rolled along the sandstone roadway below, competing with pedestrians and magic-powered machines. They, too, would someday be obsolete, replaced by something grander—a mere stepping-stone between what once was and the brimming delights of the future.

It had taken a mere ten years to transpose the region from a tightly controlled city filled with ritualized bloodshed to one filled with the spellwork of the future.

Bitterness curled as she watched the horseless chariots. The horse masters had been driven to the dwindling interiors or farthest reaches of the empire, where the new enchantments had yet to spread, but on their way out, some horse masters like her father, clinging to the past, had done unspeakable things to stave the change—making others pay for their rejection of the future.

Taline had paid dearly.

She firmed her lips and shook the thoughts free as she always did when ghosts rose. She had a better life now—a better identity. And she had Nin.

A chariot with a red dot on its frame—visible only to those spelled to see it—turned the corner, rattling onto the sandstone thoroughfare. The chariot driver tapped his gold-tipped staff into the veins of power in the sandstone, tithing the trip through imperial enchantments and ensuring security measures would call the watch, if triggered.

Taline checked her softly spinning wind clock. Perfectly on schedule.

Position two, go.

The single guard on the chariot watched the streets through narrowed eyes as the driver navigated. Warded canvas hid the contents in the back.

As the chariot crossed the intersection, Nin's black-clad figure stepped onto the street and a wind-enhanced hole blew straight through the vehicle's center, separating the driver and guard from the vehicle.

The back half of the chariot erupted in wooden shards and a burst of coins from the weighted chests spilled onto the street.

People in the streets immediately fell upon the treasures and the armed guard leaped into action with scimitar and stave.

Nin slipped around the heap of riches and jabbed fingers into the driver's neck and back, carefully tipping his suddenly slumped frame to rest against a fallen box. She grabbed the folio from the heavy, leather satchel slung obliquely across his back, snapped the key from the chain around his neck, and brushed quick fingers across the man's temples.

He'd have nicer dreams and modified memories than those Taline would have given.

Never one to leave others to deal with her problems, Nin

darted behind the guard who was unabashedly stabbing civilians trying to gather fallen coins. She jabbed her fingers into pressure points in his neck and back in three quick movements. The heavy guard dropped to the ground like a sack of wheat.

Taline whipped out her khursifa just as a screech from the skies announced the arrival of the city's security forces.

A five-man unit of the city's elite airborne investigorii flew from their hidden perches, tossing specially enhanced khursifa spell fibers and halting flying traffic in all directions, as they dove upon the perpetrator below.

Taline dove as well, but instead of running to the best pickup position, her idiot sister remained at the scene, spending precious moments healing the fallen citizens the guard had stabbed. Five, four, three...

Nin's hand finally shot up and she leaped into the air, knowing that Taline would be there.

Taline grabbed Nin's hand and flipped her onto the back of the khursifa with a burst of wind—narrowly avoiding a collision with two of the investigorii, the stolen folio tucked between them—enchantments already activated to fling them to top speed. With her spelled hands, Taline gripped the front, reinforced strap of the khursifa and banked hard right.

She would *always* be there to grab Nin's hand.

The five airborne investigorii banked with them, their white khursifas appearing like rectangular, ivory eagles diving after small, dark prey.

The airborne investigorii were elite flyers—using the

spelled resources they had purposefully stashed around the city—sliding in from hurriedly sprung wind injections from the east and west to propel them closer.

Taline could have really used those precious seconds Nin had spent ministering to the citizenry.

"You can't save everyone," Taline yelled back.

"Drop me on the roof. Most of them will follow me," Nin said over the wind, with far too much manic enthusiasm in her voice. "They know which of us is the thief." Her white sash whipped in the wind.

"No."

"Come on, Tali, drop me. There are lots of places to disappear tonight." On the eve of a holy day, the people were spilling into the streets in greater numbers as darkness enfolded the town.

"You are going to get caught using your powers."

She could *feel* Nin's smile turn feral. "We'll see. Drop me."

Taline saw eyes watching from the candlelit window of an apothecary ahead. Saw those eyes catch on the white sash around her sister's wrist.

"Wait." Taline grabbed Nin's fingers.

Wearing the mark of the Hand was a risk, but...

An investigorii guard swooped down with a surprising injection of wind and reached for the cloth wraps around Nin's head. Taline swerved toward the apothecary's shop, then suddenly banked hard left as the door of the shop opened.

The edge of the opening cedar door brushed against her sleeve, and as they shot past, Taline caught the glittering eyes of the apothecary's assistant in the shadows of the opening door.

The door swung wide. The guard splatted against cedar, falling in a heap of woven white fibers.

The assistant exclaimed in feigned surprise and bent to help the guard.

Wearing the mark brought its own rewards.

Nin's laughter rang into the air around Taline, knowing Taline's enchantments woven deep into the khursifa edge straps would force the wind to swallow it.

Everyone thought the Hand was a young man, and it was within their best interests to keep it that way.

Taline banked left again. The remaining four followers banked with her.

A whisper of something slithered down the street. And suddenly candles lit in windows in quick succession, like a trail of birthing stars.

A line of abruptly hoisted laundry took out the second guard, wrapping him in clinging enchantments.

The third guard was dropped by a load of magic being emptied from a window into the stone gutter along the edge of the street.

Taline yanked the khursifa into Caszerby Alley, jumping two sets of designated wind drafts and slightly manipulating a third with her best weather spellbox to achieve the altitude required. Tweaking the enchantments was a dangerous risk— a windchaser would be on their tail soon and with active power in hand. The Weather Guild didn't approve of people exploiting their secrets.

Any powerful windcatcher could manipulate the paths, but there were consequences for being caught. A disruption in the winds was punishable by breaking the offender's fingers and losing a month's wages. Being caught with a khursifa that was created and imbued with magic to manipulate the winds and jump paths would cost her freedom.

Legal khursifas could be controlled and downed by the investigorii and had standard, set spells in their fibers and weaves to be used for inner-city travel only. Non-standard khursifas were only limited by the imagination and the city spells set up each night by the Weather Guild. Creating or owning a non-standard khursifa was strictly forbidden and harshly punished.

The guilds were harsh masters and guarded their secrets zealously.

Taline touched the bare skin at her throat. The farhani necklace tag she had removed earlier would proclaim her a Level Four healer, just as her full name did. It was thought that only a Level Seven trained in windmaking could change a preset windstream.

People gave little thought to what could be accomplished by a person who could duplicate spells perfectly given patience and time, or to what such a person could do with boxes, fibers, prepared spells, and the overwhelming abundance of magic from someone like Nin to power one's creations.

The first scroll Nin had stolen for Taline, teaching her how to do advanced spellwork, had been a gift as life-altering as the new identity Nin had given her.

Unlike Nin's under-proclaimed farhani level, Taline's was close to truth. If tested, Taline would register as barely powerful enough to do a tenth of what she had done tonight—catching Nin in her fall from the tower or giving Nin the pre-enchanted threads to put forth their plans.

Taline smirked and pressed a fiber on her belt, activating a preset spell filled with Nin's magic to whip up a tornado behind them, taking out the fourth man as Nin downed the fifth.

Nin had given her the power to be a reckoning force, regardless of the circumstances of Taline's birth and the crippling magic she had suffered under subsequent hands.

Screeching in the skies above, imperial reinforcements arrived in the guise of the head of the investigorii himself—Investigore Malik ul Malit—along with five elite riders and three windchasers.

Taline whipped the chase into the slums of District Eighteen.

They had to take care. With her preset enchantments, Taline was a force to be reckoned with *only* as long as she had everything mapped out. But if she made a mistake, the windchasers would be able to neutralize her without employing tricks.

She shivered in the sudden breeze. They couldn't afford to make a mistake.

⤙⤙ CHAPTER ONE ⤚⤚

A timely opening of a seedmaker's door ensured that the first windchaser would not remember the flight when he woke. A thrown bucket of slop took out the next.

It was always remarkable and rewarding when the citizenry of Tehras assisted. There was no designated group of citizens who helped them, but the community had pieced together quickly how the Hand could be "helped." Back doors opened mysteriously during chases, laundry was aired precisely at the right moment to encase guards flying hot through the streets, magic was emptied from windows to disrupt tracking spells.

Although most of the populace sung the praises of the empire openly and attended all oath and fealty festivals without a peep of protest, when it came to providing information to the scholari's or padifehl's troops, they were less helpful. Few regular civilians—even those who embraced the empire—liked the scholari, who was seen as a traitor and untrustworthy.

That the Hand's thefts against the elite left bounty in the laps of the lesser citizens only increased the aid the latter chose to give on nights like this.

Taline and Nin banked around the district's traffic circle, knowing more imperial reinforcements would be on their way. They had to ditch the skies for a drop point quickly.

Without her permission, Taline's eyes strayed to a familiar balcony in a shadowed section of the slums. An insouciant figure raised a glass—undoubtedly an expensive glass of fordenay—in a mocking salute.

Scoundrel.

She didn't bother gesturing back. It wouldn't be a kind one.

"Drop me," Nin urged. "I can feel your energy levels waning. Take either point three or twelve that I set up this afternoon and I'll meet you at home."

Taline headed for the ground. Nin wasn't wrong. Manipulating the wind enchantments around the city against people who did so for a living had drained her, and on a khursifa, she could only carry enough cached spells and boxes for emergency points and covering an escape.

Nin, who never ran out of energy or magic, would do better without Taline to protect.

The investigore and both windchasers immediately dove after them and six additional investigorii flyers appeared overhead, converging like small thunderclouds.

Taline focused on the entrance of an alley where they could separate their pursuers and use gate medallions to meet back at home.

By skimming the currents and light traffic in a street this far from the holy areas, and near two easily accessible secret points of travel, they were almost free.

Then a "helpful" bystander let loose an upward blast and the investigore tumbled from the skies behind them. Nin shoved the folio down Taline's cloak, then launched herself backward, turning her body in midair, hand extended.

"No, no, no," Taline intoned, yanking the khursifa

upward to turn around, a last cushioning enchantment pressed far too late to buffer Nin.

Nin's own burst of wind flew a moment too late as well, through the investigore's hair, as he slammed into the ground.

Nin slid across the ground in a forced crouch driven by momentum, then dove toward him while investigorii ravens descended in deadly fury.

It was sometimes hard to think of her sister as anything restricted by human physical standards, yes, but it was horribly easy to see the crippling emotions that ensured she would try to save *everyone*, with little regard for her own life.

Cursing, Taline manipulated the skies, depleting the last of her preset "special" spells to call down a whipping thunderstorm that spewed the diving hunters out in temporary blasts.

Nin passed a hand over the investigore's face and chest, and he heaved a breath, alive once more. A civilian crowd pressed in on the two of them.

Nin twisted quickly through the crowd and sprinted down the alley to the right. Nin wanted to help any who crossed her path, but at least she *did* understand the thin line she constantly traveled between freedom and captivity.

On their khursifas, the investigore's best enforcers were predators in the night, regaining their seats and pulling into perfect formation—narrowing in on their prey with deadly accuracy.

Taline admired their talent even as she activated the first

of her final set of spells and changed the patterns of the District Six winds.

Taline flew hard, banked sharply left, threw a masking spell at the thick stone jutting into the path, and tweaked the last wind enchantment, before ascending steeply up the building at the T of the street. Her fingers shook with the effort of using too much magic. The tweaked wind enchantment caused the final windchaser to turn sharply and give pursuit to the criminal manipulating the winds. But the windchaser was exercising more initiative than care and slammed into the hidden stone and slid to the street.

Taline crested the roof and dipped into the wind slide, diving into a steep descent on the other side before pulling up along the street that would deposit a traveler at the gate of Loran. She skimmed the street and curled one shaking hand around the edge strap of the khursifa. She rolled the woven mat with a flick of her wrist and landed at a full run—abandoning the route at the last moment and startling a small group of travelers entering the city from the mountainous province of Loran.

She skidded on the sandstone smoothed by foot traffic and spells, shoved the khursifa into the sheath on her back, then sprinted north, west, north, east.

She ran toward drop point three—one of the many alcoves Nin had carefully selected around the city—cutting a slice across her hand without pausing. Using a quick detection spell, she noticed her pursuers were out of visual range but gaining quickly. She'd have three breaths to escape. She whirled into the darkened space in the armpit of the alley and pressed her palm against the medallion that was inset into the stone.

She flipped through space and landed in a small oasis near the learning halls. Slipping through the palm trees, she used the last of her reserves to change her clothing as she walked—identity spells so much a part of her that they needed no preparation. Her black cloak was flipped to one of light brown patterns—an unexceptional woman heading home from a long day of work—and her khursifa and sheath were enveloped by a large workman's bag. She let a layer of magic wash from her features. Three more changes to her face and clothing were completed before she reached their home.

She took her time, carefully changing only as she moved around corners and slipped through shadows. Caution was needed over carelessness and panic. The gate medallions were spelled to destroy themselves upon completion, but it was never smart to bet against advancement. If someone ever guessed how the Hand disappeared and discovered a way to trace the point of disappearance, they would be in deep trouble.

Being caught as the thief would mean a loss of a hand, at minimum. Being caught as a magi who could move bodies through space would mean a lifetime of caged, enforced servitude. Nin would be a pet in a gilded cage.

Gatemakers were rare, and once identified, they served their rulers—celebrated and confined—or they were exterminated in the streets as monsters by fearful zealots.

Taline would never allow either to occur.

Awash with grim thoughts, Taline took an extra two routes through the increasingly tight and shabby streets of their home district, just to make sure no one was in pursuit, then slipped silently inside their tiny fifth-floor home.

Chucking the folio on the table, along with her khursifa and sheath, Taline checked the wind sphere Nin had tucked into her pocket.

Inside the enchanted sphere, the moving image played of Crelu ul Osni igniting the papyri sheets on his desk and his aides cringing against the walls. "I want that thief's hands! I want him drained of every bit of power. I want him *hanging* from his neck at the Sacred Gate for all to see."

Etelian ul Fehl's sprawled visage in the mirror behind the scholari made her insides freeze and her breath grow short. She closed her eyes and forced herself to inhale deep breaths and think of other things.

It was the fifty-second year of the emperor—the tenth year since Tehrasi had been forced to accept a new calendar that started at the emperor's birth. Her name was Taline now, followed by a lot of census-identifying words until Summora was reached—the family name she had eagerly embraced with both hands. She had a life as a healer's assistant. Her wrists were free of chains. The wall her fingers were touching was simply textured instead of the elaborate lion imprints of the palace's master suite—crisscross, crisscross, crisscross...

She opened her eyes on the last deep breath and let her gaze drift slowly back to the sphere.

"And what body part should be removed from *you* this time, Osni?" the padifehl said lightly, his poisonous, perfect features warped by the rounded glass. Her pulse leaped in learned terror without her permission—Etelian ul Fehl was ever light before he was cruel, as were all the children of Emperor Sher Fehl and his favorite wife. "Not just your hand, I think, should the thief get the scepter."

Osni snarled and signaled to one of his underlings with his replaceable clay hand. "Let him try. The temple isn't protected by secrecy alone. Tonight was a ruse that failed, but no matter. Anyone who seeks the temple will die. I hope he tries."

The darkness in Osni's features was overwhelming. The Hand had cost him control of the gates and sent him into this deep downward spiral.

The gates had been flickering more each day for the last three months—their power stretched between those last vials of Carre blood he wore—the blood of the last Carre king. It wouldn't be long now before they failed entirely.

"I will enjoy watching you die." Etelian ul Fehl's words lingered, as he disappeared, leaving a blank mirror behind.

There was something strange about Osni's expression for a moment. Something almost like triumph. It didn't sit well with Taline. Osni had nothing to feel triumphant about.

"You, like all of those who sit a throne, forget who holds the true power," Crelu ul Osni, Scholari of Tehrasi, said darkly to the blank wall. He turned to his subordinates. "Find that *thief.* I want his *blood.* I want him dead."

"The temple—"

"A second set of documents will arrive tomorrow, then the day after, and the one after that. There are destruction and explosion charms on all of them. I'd like to see the thief try to capture any of those shipments. I will extract the location and its secrets from the temple source myself. The documents were a ruse that didn't pan out because the investigore is weak. The Carres, for all that I wish them into an eternal Sehk-ridden underworld, knew how to run a city with fear."

Taline touched the folio, but didn't unwrap it, listening to the ongoing threats emanating from the scholari while she stared at the blank mirror behind him.

"If only I had more activated vials..." Osni muttered darkly.

But Crelu ul Osni had no ability to obtain more. Nin had made certain of that. Made certain to extinguish the remaining blood supply of the Carres from Tehrasi.

Only Nin's entrance through the window forced Taline's gaze. Nin ducked in with a wide grin, but her grin dwindled as she looked at Taline. Nin approached carefully and looked her over for injuries with quick, sharp brown eyes. Taline motioned at the folio on the table then the sphere, still in her hand, in explanation.

"The folio is ensnared," Taline added unnecessarily.

Nin looked at the sphere for long moments, then muted the scholari's voice with a slow wave of her hand. "Of course it is. That's not why you are upset."

Her fingers rested on Taline's before taking the sphere

slowly from her fingers and setting it on the table. "Better or worse than the last one?" Nin's warm fingers wrapped around Taline's again, slowly chasing away the cold. Nin never looked away.

"Better." She let Nin's warmth envelop her. "We should check the trap spells."

"I wrapped the folio in a stasis spell and surrounded it with a pocket of air from the Telb Mountains. They can't find us and nothing can detonate. We have time. And I have you." Nin squeezed her fingers gently. Taline accepted the comfort with greedy breaths.

When she was finally feeling equilibrium, she looked at the folio.

Nin's gaze followed. "Don't worry. I didn't read them without you."

The last of Taline's tension drained in a huff. "You are just full of wit."

Nin smiled and pulled forth a pocket of barren landscape from mountains leagues away to fill their living room. She reached for one of the small, contained null fields Taline had painstakingly created just for this type of activity and flipped it into her hand. "Do your no-magic, oh creator."

Taline activated the small null field around the folio while Nin stayed far from its reach. Taline stepped into the pocket landscape with the wrapped folio and went to work, picking apart spell threads and redirecting frozen currents. The spells were easily deactivated in the null field until nothing was left to connect them to a trigger.

Taline deftly removed the traps while keeping the preservation enchantments—delicate work that required precision and no magic. As opposed to intuitive, overpowered Nin who had never had to live or work without magic, Taline was used to having hers stripped—was used to having to use cleverness instead of power.

Inside the folio were hand-coded logs and directions. The logs detailed the travel land markers to the "Temple of the Scepter" and displayed information about the temple and its surrounding area.

"Well?" Nin asked, with a cursory glance at the materials, gaze quickly focused back on Taline.

"Exactly where you said it would be," Taline murmured, following the path of coded words and clues to the indicated endpoint—an easy feat when you already knew the endpoint.

The tension in the room increased. The Scepter of Darkness was a myth, the story of legends, and Taline was used to Nin looking amused whenever they looked over the scepter maps treasure hunters sold.

The steady stiffening of her sister's spine this time was quite different.

"Well," Nin said lightly. "It looks like someone finally found it."

Taline watched her closely as Nin gazed at documents she couldn't read, as if searching for an answer to a question she didn't want asked.

Taline didn't know how to fix the wounds beneath such carefully feigned nonchalance. She wasn't sure it was something fixable at this point. They both had soul-deep wounds camouflaged beneath so many other layers. They were two broken pieces that fit together.

Taline didn't know how to soothe the deepest fear of the person she held closer than blood. But she knew how to momentarily deflect her insecurities.

"You nearly got caught tonight." Taline eyed the sphere on the table. The wind would record for another hour, saving the contents inside—a spell she had devised based on a complete set of Sand family incantations they had discovered. "You risked much by saving the man who already has suspicions about you."

Nin silently stripped her night gloves from her fingers. "The investigore is merely doing his job. I'm not going to let him die on my account." The tension in her shoulders eased a fraction.

"He would have our hands in a basket and the rest of us in chains. Then he would hand us to the scholari, who would personally skewer everyone we know."

It was an old argument—well-worn like the handwoven rug in front of their door.

Nin sat heavily in her favorite cushioned chair and pulled off her boots. "The investigore is not the villain. The scholari and padifehl are. When those two fall, we will need the investigore and his investigorii in place."

"Others will—"

"I must trust that there is good in the empire." Nin looked at the documents, then the sphere. "That exterminating the rot in Tehras will be enough. That having a check on those in power will be enough."

So much for deflection.

"We are seeing the effect our thefts have on the elites," Taline acknowledged. "Two hundred gold pieces on our head—whichever head is holding the sash when caught."

"The more bounty they put on us, the more effective we become."

"The elite will still be in power, even if the scholari and padifehl are deposed," Taline pointed out.

"But if the library is established, the ranks will change," Nin said decisively. "The entire populace will be lifted by progress and knowledge—to help when vocations are replaced—and to cultivate and instigate creative solutions and advancement. Hope. Those who want the old traditions back, like the Festival of Blood, can be convinced to embrace solutions where thousands don't have to be sacrificed *and* the resulting magic is *better*. If we can place one of the scholarly princes on the throne—"

"More than likely we will get a politically minded one," Taline said with grim certainty, the argument old. "Or a warrior, if we go too far in our rebellion. Or another son of Nera—Aros, if he finally prevails."

Aros ul Fehl, the eldest of the emperor's innumerable children, was constrained by his tainted birth, though. Tainted by the possibility that he had a Carre father, not a Fehl one. For Nin, a Carre on the throne was the stuff of childhood nightmares. Even Kaveh ul Fehl—the head of the empire's armies and the terrifying nightmare of enemies and allies alike—would cause Nin less unease as padifehl.

The latter would never be a possibility, fortunately—everyone knew the "Nightmare of the Empire" never strayed far from the continuously expanding battlefronts he ruled with his living shadows. But the former...Aros would ever be a problem. It was not a secret that he wanted Tehrasi.

"Then we take care of that issue when it arises. We have to think positively. There are other imperial children with promise. Ones who have adopted Shiera's ways." It was an even older argument—Shiera, the Padifehl of Cuipsin was beloved by her people, and Nin was forever lamenting that Tehrasi hadn't been blessed to get her as padifehl. "Or we could make a play for Simin or Baksis, neither of whom have been assigned territories."

"Baksis, second or third best of the imperial children at every skill—you are the one who said he could be a vengeful leader."

"Or a *moderate* one. My experience has yielded examples of both. It just means we need a superb negotiating position," Nin said, ever trying to see the sun. "One where we can scrutinize and control the choice of the Fehl on the throne."

"Negotiating positions aren't your strong point," Taline said pointedly.

"I beg your pardon." But Nin looked reluctantly amused.

Taline's hand hovered over the documents. "The scepter won't be in the temple."

"Not in the temple, no," Nin said. "But..." Her gaze

drifted to the documents again. "But the key is," she added in a softer voice. "A relic that, once activated, will unlock the true location of the scepter. I need you to tell me what they know about it." She indicated the sheets.

"Nin—"

Nin's gaze dropped. "Osni is clever. And single-minded. Death holds no concern for him. With enough manpower, he will unlock it. Eventually. And if the scepter is secured by Osni..."

It would be Carre dominion all over again. No one could wield the scepter without going mad.

"If—"

"We won't unlock it. We will just take the key."

"But—"

"It will be well. Even if the worst came about, even with the scepters under their complete control, the Carres were defeated," Nin said lightly, reading Taline's expression. "There is no such thing as a fail-safe when the scepters come into play."

"Nin—"

"Taline, if Etelian ul Fehl and Crelu ul Osni secure the Scepter of Darkness? If *Aros ul Fehl* does?"

Taline already knew the answer. "Can you get to the key?"

"Yes."

Taline met Nin's gaze and let it communicate her own answer. She would assist Nin until the day she could no longer raise her head. But once they embarked on this path...they would be entering a new game—a game that would put Nin's secrets at risk.

Nin said nothing for a long moment, gaze dropping unnervingly to the documents before she looked back up with fierce eyes. "Yes."

Two days later, they went to the temple and stole what was inside.

MIGHT OF THE EMPIRE

KAVEH
ZENURE

Kaveh ul Fehl strode into the foreign banquet hall, black cloak flaring and writhing in the air. Ifret wound purposefully and visibly around his collar like a dark asp—the corporeal shadow dismissive of the games played by her less advanced brethren who were clinging to the edges of writhing darkness at the hem of Kaveh's cloak. Fresh from the battlefield, she was far more interested in showing her teeth of dripping shadow in the bright sunlight.

Conversation ceased immediately, and Kaveh processed the uneasy gazes of those seated at the long stone table, as each touched upon the demon at his neck and the red, bloodstained clothes beneath his cloak.

Kaveh had no patience for cowards.

Sher Fehl, Emperor of All He Touched, dominated the head of the long table, watching with the rest of the room as

Kaveh advanced. The emperor's expression showed the charismatic ease with which he beguiled nation after nation before consuming them and moving on.

In the opulent halls of an about-to-be-conquered Zenure, where a peace treaty was being shaped, his father was at his most charming and gracious. Only when the gazes of Zenure's nobility were frozen upon Kaveh did the emperor let his eyes glitter with the ever-present bloodlust that flowed beneath.

Kaveh tilted his head in acknowledgment of his father as he strode the length of the banquet table laden with sumptuous, culinary delights. The enchanted tuffets of Zenure lifted and fell around the table with the bulk of the Zenurian ministers too lazy and overfed to move on their own. Enchanted cushions carried fools who were too used to political solutions and wealth.

"Gentlemen, we intend for you to retain your culture, religions, and traditions," the emperor said, continuing the interrupted conversation as he looked to the Zenurian king with a charm that was second nature. "We seek to have you join the Sunlight Empire in the best of faith. Unlike your neighbors in Heit, who chose not to join us in good faith, I have no doubt that you will choose more wisely. I have called forth the highest commanding officer of our forces, the Imperator General, from the battlefield in order to show you what you will gain."

His gaze moved slowly back to Kaveh at the use of

Kaveh's battlefield title. As if hypnotized, the rest of the table followed suit.

Most looked away just as quickly.

"Of course, Your Imperial Majesty," the King of Zenure said, visibly swallowing as he looked to the end of the table where the Crown Prince of Zenure had been placed to the left of the emperor's head seat. "However, we do have concerns about a military presence. No offense intended toward the Imperator General."

He sent a quick, constricted gaze at Kaveh and, more specifically, at the living shadow encircling his throat.

Kaveh had done this song and dance many times. It was one of his least favorites. He preferred to be on the field, surrounded in darkness and honest bloodshed. But he understood the reason for his presence—for those who perhaps doubted the stories about him—and for the delicate dark control that was, at times, needed to sever an enemy.

He met the few Zenurian gazes that were strong enough to meet his coldest stare. The only benefit to this game was that, unlike his thirty siblings who had been raised as diplomatic political pawns, Kaveh did not have to be pleasant.

He looked at the six brothers currently present: the eldest, Aros, ten years older than Kaveh's twenty-two, to the youngest, Limil, just grasping his full powers at sixteen.

In Sher Fehl's empire, power, use, and blood mattered, not age. Each child had a purpose, predetermined by maternal line, and cemented when their powers awakened.

He wondered which one of them would be placed within

the newest padifehl position being created, gaze passing over the middle two. Simin, at twenty-six and as the eighteenth blessed child of Sher Fehl, would do well on the Casp Sea with his ability to shape water to his will, his calm bearing, and the strong relationships he maintained with the other half-siblings near his age.

Baksis, at twenty-seven, had passed on all padifehl positions previously offered to him, and doubtless he would pass on this one as well, waiting for whatever it was that he secretly desired. Perhaps two territories that could be ruled together. Close in age and raw abilities, Simin and Baksis were an undeniable duo at court and outside of it. Their emotional connection was an exploitable weakness that Kaveh did not understand, but it was a point ever in their favor that thus far they were powerful enough to keep such partnership intact.

Simin would do well here, but so would a few of the other siblings who had been blessed and were in line to lead an imperial province.

Zenurians leaned as far from Kaveh as possible as he passed, making him reconsider his thinking. No, Simin would do better with the Axšaina Sea countries which Kaveh planned to focus on next. He rarely concerned himself with his countless siblings, but Simin and Baksis were two who had always looked him squarely in the eye. They deserved to rule people of equal strength.

"Concerns. I see," the emperor responded pleasantly to the Zenurian king, then turned to look at Kaveh as he neared. "Kaveh."

"Father." Kaveh tipped his head deferentially and slowed his pace.

Tension rose around the table—fear escalating at the sound of his voice and deference. A show of respect from an apex predator increased tenfold the power to whom he deferred.

Each blessed child had a special, recognized skill that the emperor manipulated like a surgical blade where needed, and Kaveh, as the thirteenth blessed, had been raised to be exactly what each person innately sensed—a cold-blooded killer of unparalleled ability.

A few shaken faces around the table looked at the emperor in new fear, as if Kaveh's regard made a difference. Fools, to think that the emperor was not the most dangerous man in the room.

"We were just discussing terms with our new friends and they have expressed concern with the skirmish occurring on the southern front." The emperor smiled. "Where does the north stand?"

Flicking the edge of his cloak, Kaveh lifted the orb the nestled shadows had been hungrily encircling. Without breaking stride, Kaveh tossed the crystal sphere carelessly to the table, forcing it to roll loudly along the marble until it struck a platter of fish. Glittering, enchanted sand rose and fell within the orb depicting shifting warriors, walls, and agonizing death—a battle record enchanted by one of the imperial scribes.

CHAPTER TWO

The Zenurians winced and tensed. It wasn't their kingdom depicted, but the scene was a clear warning.

"The Heit forces have been crushed," Kaveh said, "and the king's court will surrender within eighteen hours. We have poisoned their wells, nullified their wards, and barred their gates. They have nowhere to flee except Death's door."

The emperor smiled, watching the sand-enchanted recreation of the battle from his position at the head of the table. The emperor was ever charming to countries like Zenure who folded immediately, but the empire was ruthless when resistance was encountered.

Everyone knew it, so the countries who chose not to heed the warnings earned their outcome.

"Excellent work, as always. I look forward to visiting our northern forces in their victory, Imperator General." He motioned and an enchantment pushed the Crown Prince of Zenure—and everyone else on that side of the long table—down one position.

Kaveh inclined his head and sat at the left hand of the emperor. Beside Kaveh, the crown prince leaned unconsciously away. Fatuous and weak.

Intolerable, that this kingdom had gone without a change of ruling line for a hundred years. It was for the people's best that they would be ruled by the empire instead.

Perhaps it would be best to simply end the line here even? Kaveh allowed a wisp of shadow to crawl and curl lazily around the Zenurian prince's throat as the prince shakily reached for his goblet.

"Con-con-congratulations on your victory over the Heit forces, Your Imperial Majesty and Imperator General," the Zenurian king said, somewhat desperately, from the other end of the long table. His fingers unconsciously touched his own neck as his gaze watched the deadly shadow dance across his son's. Reality had finally settled in. Few had seemed to understand that when the emperor made the seating arrangements, he had already won. Having an heir sit close to the emperor? A bloody tactic wrapped within false esteem.

Kaveh did not need to be sitting next to the prince to kill him. If he chose, Kaveh could kill everyone in the room before they knew they were dying. His presence in the seat next to the prince just made the prince's death...so much more apparent.

"We will, of course, be grateful to your military presence while combining our territories," the king said hastily. "I see that now. Let me show you our taxation reports."

Kaveh released the shadow from the prince's throat, and it slithered back into the sleeve of his robe as he lifted the goblet in front of him. Baksis and Simin, who were strategically positioned closer to the Zenurian king's end of the long, banquet table, tracked Kaveh's movements for a moment before turning back to the conversation that required their level-headed discourse.

They had always looked him in the eye, but neither was negligent in keeping track of threats. Kaveh would always be a threat.

Kaveh checked his drink for poison as he lifted the goblet

and accepted the political tedium that was to come. That the Zenurian king had given in so quickly to a threat against his heir and volunteered to discuss finances said all that it needed to.

Negotiations such as these always started with finances—countries and tribes hoping to buy their way out of total annexation. The need for Kaveh's presence would wane as the emperor used his charm over his might to quickly impose his will in a way that made it seem that both sides had won.

With his duty complete, Kaveh turned his attention to the man across from him, seated at the right hand of the emperor.

Reclined in his seat, loosely coiled like the viper he was, Aros' gaze was covetous, questioning, and vigilant as it always was when he looked at Kaveh. Watching—always watching—with that avaricious gaze, plans circling in his cold eyes.

Kaveh stared impassively back—he held little regard for his eldest brother's future motives and plots—but the Zenurian prince next to him choked on the meat he was shakily shoving into his mouth, reacting to the dark pleasure reaching across the table from the eldest imperial prince.

Kaveh was used to making people gibber—being choked by one's own shadow tended to provoke that response. Aros, although not as physically intimidating, was a ruthlessly effective emotional manipulator, and he displayed a charm that provided a thin veneer over his merciless and sadistic nature.

Kaveh glanced at the Zenurian prince and idly considered

killing him again. If he had been taken in by Aros's facade, it just showed the depths to which the Zenurian line had sunk. Shaking uncontrollably, the man went sickly pale at the examination. Disposing of him would set back negotiations for a minute or two, but the pool of remaining humanity would be strengthened.

Kaveh looked at the spread of too-rich foods. Luxuries that made men listless and foolish.

He let his shadows slide around the floating tuffets. Soft men "left in charge" grew softer with their fingers in succulence. He could kill them all before they knew the kapper they had just swallowed was their last.

There were endless frontiers still to be conquered and he should be moving his soldiers forward and securing and expanding the empire rather than wasting his time here.

Kaveh reached for the plate of figs and dates, ignoring the sumptuous feast of heavily dressed meats and pastries. He idly considered how many pits it would take to kill the Zenurian prince by shoving them down his throat. An interesting thought to stay the tedium.

Ten? Thirteen?

He ran a quick, standard poison detection spell on the date in his fingers as he idly planned the table's demise. The ones who had promise and fire in their eyes would be spared. But the others... He would start with the Fehl ambassador, who was seated to the right of Simin. The ambassador was a man of simpering notions and no ideals. And Simin had never liked him anyway.

Simin raised a brow, reading Kaveh's expression, and Kaveh let his cold gaze wander to the next man, a Zenurian councilor. Sweat immediately beaded across the councilor's brow and his eyes swiftly lowered. He would be dead before the moisture reached his cheek. The next Zenurian met Kaveh's gaze, though he obviously found it difficult to do with the way he shook. He would live.

A deliberate cough from his eldest brother had Kaveh's gaze sliding back to Aros.

Aros's gaze fell to the date in Kaveh's hands, then back up, eyes glittering maliciously. Kaveh impassively let a deeper detection spell slip from his skin to the fruit, then a third, before he pressed the pitted date between his teeth and sliced through it without taking his gaze from the firstborn.

Fifteen. He could squeeze at least fifteen dates down Aros's throat.

Aros's mouth slashed into a smile.

"Your terms do Zenure justice," the emperor said with the political warmth only he could attain, bringing Kaveh back to the negotiations. "I doubt we will have trouble."

"Excellent, Your Imperial Majesty. We look forward to joining the empire and standing under the Crown of Sunlight."

Kaveh slowly separated the fruit of another date while the conversation drew to a close; the Zenurians simpered and his father charmed, until finally the "negotiations" ended and the Zenurians rose.

The Zenurian prince stumbled free of his overly plush

tuffet in his haste. Kaveh, bored of the man's uselessness, didn't bother turning his focus away from the plate, but let Ifret have her pleasure, writhing and hissing like a shadow asp from around his neck.

The prince staggered from the room in terrified flight, not bothering to wait for dismissal.

"We require your banquet room for an hour more." The emperor smiled charmingly, as the prince's actions flung the doors open. "We must discuss other matters, before we leave."

"Of course. Take all the time you need, Your Imperial Majesty." The Zenurians simpered and bowed as they quickly backed away, leaving the emperor, seven Fehl princes, the emperor's five favorite councilors, and three gate delegates from imperial provinces to the room.

With a motion of his finger, the emperor flung the doors closed and pulled the remaining attendees to his end of the table.

"Kaveh," the emperor said.

Kaveh's shadows slipped free of their binds. The wraiths slithered out and wrapped around the table, the chairs, the columns in the room, the domed ceiling—joining with the shadows in the room and finding all the crevices and hidden enchantments. Small puffs of hellfire and brimstone lit around the room as the shadows snuffed out each eavesdropping spell, before crushing each person connected.

In a distant corridor, someone screamed in agony—the

intensity of the sound skipping along the stones all the way to the grand hall—then another scream followed, then a third.

Kaveh lifted another date as the information from the shadows fed back to him. What a worthless country.

Kaveh's abilities were public knowledge. A worthy spymaster would have known better than to attach himself or any magi of consequence to an eavesdropping spell—the life-force of the spell was too integral a part of the connection and meant certain death when his shadows...ate them. If they didn't have healers to resurrect their dead spymasters quickly, that was also to their discredit. Such lack of awareness and planning said a lot about the ease with which the Fehls had enveloped this country already.

Kaveh tilted his head at the emperor to indicate the room was secure.

"Excellent." All feigned humor dropped from the emperor's expression. "Governor Nunde, tell me why Lyndel has stopped gifting our supply lines with magic?"

"It's Tehrasi, Your Imperial Majesty." Nunde's eye flicked to the delegate from Tehrasi. "Their gates flicker and fail, affecting us all."

"Rumors you use to protect your own greed," the delegate from Tehrasi accused. "The gates—"

The delegate from Tehrasi was cut off when the emperor raised his bejeweled hand—onyx and opals flashing.

"Be careful with your words, Crelu ul Osni," the emperor said with an insouciant curl of his fingers in Kaveh's direction—never taking his gaze from the delegate. "I traveled ten gates from the east yesterday. The deplorable state of the gates is not *rumor*."

Kaveh negligently flicked his own finger at the visual command.

Osni bent and clawed at his chest with his one good hand—wrenching at the shadows abruptly squeezing his body. They pulled him forward and Osni's cheek smacked against the table along with the garish locket he always wore, while his clay-crafted left hand scrambled across the surface, trying to gain a hold where his natural flesh one could not.

"I allowed you to continue your desperate game far too long amid continuous rumors and hints of malfeasance," the emperor said. "Thinking that a cockroach had enough regard for self-preservation to locate a solution. Now, tell me, *Scholari*, why I should leave you with any abilities or life-force when this council is adjourned?"

Kaveh watched the man writhe. Crelu ul Osni bled with the silver tongue he had used to betray the Carres, his former rulers.

When Osni had betrayed the royal family of Tehrasi, he had sealed his own fate. It was a fool's notion to trust a traitor, and Sher Fehl was no fool.

Betrayer and oathbreaker, and therefore not worth the air he breathed as far as Kaveh was concerned, Osni had one critical skill that had kept him alive. With the entire royal family dead, Osni was the only one who had known how to run the gates and scepters of Tehrasi.

Kaveh switched his gaze to his second-eldest brother,

Etelian, Padifehl of Tehrasi, the Fehl in charge of Tehrasi. It was little secret that even a decade later the leader of one of the richest territories in the empire had little knowledge of how his kingdom worked.

The emperor's decision to put Etelian on the throne...a decision by a cunning and intelligent leader, but one made in *emotion*...had been as much a learning point as any for Kaveh as to the dangers of attachments.

Any other blessed child would have been a better choice, in Kaveh's opinion. He cared little for any particular imperial province, but Tehrasi had too much power in the gates that connected a quarter of the world together to be ruled by someone incompetent. But Etelian was untouchable as the favorite child of the emperor's favorite wife, and Kaveh obeyed all of the emperor's decisions.

Still, Kaveh wondered how Etelian would spin this failing. Everyone had noticed the waning of the system of gates, which relied far too heavily on Tehras, the City of a Hundred Gates, the capital city of Tehrasi.

Unsurprisingly, Etelian stared at Aros—expecting his brother to come to his aid, as their shared mother always demanded. But Aros feigned disinterest in the whole affair, watching with only the slightest curl to his lips as Osni writhed.

Osni pulled uselessly at his chest—his lifespan diminishing in torturous breaths with a movement of Kaveh's finger. "The gates...simply...need...an...influx..."

"Then where is this influx? You stated you knew how to

keep the gates running smoothly and *forever*, Osni. You assured me of this after the entire royal family you so *diligently* served was mysteriously slaughtered."

"Need...more...time..."

The emperor clenched his fist and Kaveh released the shadow. The shadow slipped back under the table to curl into his hem.

"You've had years. Years of borrowed time." The emperor raised his hand, and Osni was lifted off his feet, choking as the emperor's power gripped him around the throat. "I dislike deception. And I won't tolerate betrayal."

As the emperor squeezed his fist, Kaveh could see the emperor's unique magic stripping layers away from Osni—stripping into an unbreakable lock and rendering him less and less of a magi. Level Seven, Six, Five, Four...

Kaveh ate another fig.

"Please," Osni choked out, feet scrambling vainly for a perch that would stop the pressure and the agony of his power being ripped away. "The...Scepter...of...Darkness..."

Osni dropped to the floor. The attention of the entire table shifted at those words.

Most interesting was the way Etelian stiffened and Aros smiled.

"What tale do you now intend to spin, Scholari?" the emperor asked. When calm, the emperor was at his most deadly.

"We located a temple," Osni gasped, trying to regain his breath. One look at the emperor's face, though, made him hurry despite his pained breaths. "With markings identical to the scepter archives."

"And? We would not be having this discussion about the failure of the gates, if you had found the scepter that resets all scepters."

How the scepters were activated and renewed was the piercing secret the Carres had taken to their graves. The royal family of Tehrasi had died with their knowledge, although Osni had successfully professed that as the widower of a Carre-bound gatemaker, he possessed it.

It had been a gross failing to execute any member of the royal family without obtaining the knowledge they possessed. But then only the brother of the king had been meant for execution.

Lined up in the great hall, the spell that had been intended to kill Jisarek Carre alone—an execution twenty years in the making by the emperor—had encompassed *all* the Carres and their servants, killing every one of them. No one had definitive *proof* who had linked the spell that had killed all those enveloped, but it took little thought to deduce who stood most to benefit.

Kaveh had been twelve at the time, a silent, shadowed killing hand observing at the emperor's side, ready to torture whichever Carre was brought before him first.

He had witnessed the intense satisfaction on Osni's face as all the Carres had dropped dead, souls ripped out so they could not be resurrected. At the time Kaveh had not understood the ramifications of what was happening and its implications for the future.

But the emperor had and his rage had been swift. Only Osni's display of being the last remaining soul who could wield several of the Carres' famed scepters had saved the man—though it had cost him his left hand.

It had been a greed-filled mistake lining the royal family up in order for the emperor to get the maximum pleasure in revenge over Jisarek for the kidnapping of his first and favorite wife. It was a mistake that had stuck with Kaveh.

The strategy-driven emperor had given in to an emotional need for revenge on a grand stage, and he had paid for it. Jisarek should have died, but the rest of the Carres should have been kept alive in adjoining cells without access to their powers. They should have used them against one another, and if no bonds existed between and among them, they could have been used as canvases for the torture they would experience should they not cooperate.

An important lesson learned. A mistake that Kaveh would not make.

The Carres had taken their secrets with them in death, but the legend of the Scepter of Darkness persisted—first in myth, and now in desperation—that there was a way around the Carres' hold on the scepters that controlled the gates. That they had, in fact, used one scepter to power all the others to their bloodline—that there was a scepter imbued with the power to replace the Carres' hold on the scepters, long ago hidden away.

"The temple has been found. But we—"

"Was that before or after you lost the documented location to your persistent thief, Scholari?" Aros asked nonchalantly. "You were distraught over a Tehrasian criminal, according to reports."

Etelian went completely still.

A bead of sweat slipped down Osni's cheek. "I assure you, my men—"

The emperor held up his hand, and Osni's teeth clicked together.

"Let me see if I understand." The emperor rolled a date between his fingers, then let a suddenly elongated nail slice slowly through it as it turned, halving it neatly around the pit. "You found directions to the temple that legend says contains the location of the Scepter of Darkness, then allowed such a document to fall into someone else's hands? A map to locate and use the scepter that can reset every gate in Tehrasi—and every gate that has ever been touched by a Tehrasian scepter—including the one given to me before the Carres became our enemy? The scepter fully under my control? And such a map is now in someone else's hands?"

A ripple of unease ran through the room. The shadows under Kaveh's cape swirled faster, scenting the blood that would be spilled. Osni would not be leaving intact. *Etelian* might not be leaving intact.

"I'm certain the temple sits untouched, Father," Etelian said, for once no lethargy to be found. His usually perfect skin was clammy-looking and slick. "With the number of traps reportedly involved, there is no way a two-fehltan thief could gain access. And we nearly have him in our custody."

"Etelian," the emperor said with the silkiest of voices. "Do such things normally occur in your country without your knowledge?"

"It was to be a grand surprise, Father. The scepter. A most glorious offering to you. The Hand—an unexceptional thief—is merely a Tehrasian brigand," Etelian added unhelpfully, obviously panicking. "He will easily be brought to justice."

Osni winced visibly, and Kaveh narrowed in on it even as a twitch from the emperor called Kaveh's attention.

Something strangely dark and odd ran through the emperor's eyes. Kaveh set his mind to finding a connection that would illicit such responses from both the scholari and the emperor, but not from Etelian.

"This problem ceases to amuse me." The emperor coldly examined Osni and another level of magic ripped from the man with a whimper. Once taken, only the emperor could give one's abilities back.

Having one's ability stripped away was an invasive torture that was never forgotten. It was among the rarest of powers, and one that no child born of the emperor—even as exhaustively as he sired them—had managed to fully manifest. Only Etelian had attained the slimmest manifestation of its powers.

The emperor had used his ability only once on Kaveh—peeling away five of his nine levels before restoring them. It had been a test, not a punishment, but Kaveh had never needed a second reminder.

"He, this *Hand*, usually steals academic texts and family heirlooms," Osni spewed. "Sharing it with the riffraff—"

"Do you think I care for the lost knowledge of Tehrasi's elite?" the emperor said, tone calm and deadly. "If I did, you would have brought this to me before now. If Tehrasi's elite loses its societal control over the commoners, that is their problem. What concerns me is the continued existence of someone who has obviously made it a point to disadvantage the empire. This *Hand*."

Osni kept his head lowered, not meeting the emperor's gaze. And Kaveh slotted his sire's emphasis on the name into memory. Only one recollection fit the situation.

The Carre king had made a taunt as the execution spell had hit him—as he'd realized his own impending death—*"My hand, the hand of Tehrasi, will hold the scepter when your time has come."*

A Tehrasian brigand calling himself the Hand— coincidence or a deliberate taunt made by a common thief? Had a palace warrior or cleric escaped the chained spell that had taken out most of the palace's inhabitants?

"The padifehl and I are hunting the thief. We have—"

"You will desist immediately," the emperor said without waiting for Osni to finish. "Give Kaveh every piece of information you've obtained. He will deal with this *thief*."

Kaveh didn't pause in the motion of retrieving another

date as he pushed down his displeasure, denying himself the luxury of visible annoyance at the assignment.

Shadowshapers were the ultimate assassins, but considering his skills were infinitely more useful on a battlefield, he was seldom assigned such menial tasks. Assassinations were insufferably boring—the hunt usually beyond dull. A useless, menial task, and likely fruitless in the promise of finding a mythical temple and scepter.

Might as well seek the Eternal Spring, while he was at it. Sehk-damned Osni. Sehk-damned Etelian.

"Father," Etelian said. "It is unnecessary to—"

"Be very relieved that I spare your brother for a week to fix your deficiency in this matter, Etelian. You will do better moving forward."

The second-eldest prince's expression pinched at his father's rebuke.

It was little secret that Etelian was apathetic in matters of state. The running of Tehrasi was done by others. Etelian controlled the social structure and elite with a ruthless hand, however—and for that, he maintained his assigned rule.

Kaveh cared little for what Etelian did, so long as his brother was nowhere near the front lines. Etelian was as disappointing a combatant as he was a human. His most unique power—the ability to strip a few power levels for a few hours while freezing an opponent in temporary, crippling pain—was a lackluster facsimile of their father's. To elite frontline fighters who could decimate a hundred opponents with a single blow and were able to fight for days, sparring against Etelian was a waste of time. Etelian had enough power to strip an assassin of his goal but place him in a room with twenty decent enemies and no outside aid, and although nineteen enemies might die, the twentieth would succeed.

It was a pity no organization had pitted more than five against him at a time. So far, Etelian's largest success had been staying alive.

Living in his gilded apartments, savoring his earthly delights—so long as Etelian was out of sight, he was out of Kaveh's—and the emperor's—mind. Much like Osni, Etelian could get away with much so long as the *gates worked*.

The front was Kaveh's prime directive—the expansion of the empire, improving imperial technology, and spreading their ideals—and consisted of direct, brutal engagement between equals. Others mopped up what was left behind. And apprehending this "Hand" was a mopping task, if ever he'd heard one. But the empire would be stalled in its tracks without the gates.

He understood why he was being assigned. He let none of his displeasure at the task touch his expression.

Etelian did not. "Father, we will have the scepter within the week. Kaveh isn't necess—"

"You will be silent," the emperor said more severely than he usually spoke to the overindulged, favorite child of his favorite wife. "Aros, you will accompany Etelian and the scholari to Tehrasi. Get the gates working and the governing forces in line. Kaveh will deal with this *Hand* brigand and regain what you've lost."

Aros inclined his head, while casting a layered look Kaveh's way. "My men can take care of the thief as well as find the scepter. There is no need to involve the Terror of the Battlefront in the hunt for one man."

"Kaveh will have it done sooner," the emperor said dismissively. "Get the gates working smoothly again, Aros. That is your task."

Aros nodded pleasantly. "Of course, Father."

Kaveh played with the fig in his fingers and wondered whether Aros had a hand in this matter. It would be like Aros to play Etelian, Osni, and a two-fehltan thief from the shadows for amusement. But toying with the emperor was another matter entirely. Playing the emperor required *many* far greater maneuvers—and a base that was already in place.

A myth with the promise of unlimited power in hands that could wield it: it was not hard to guess what lengths men would travel to secure such a treasure.

And it was no secret that Aros wanted Tehrasi, which he considered his birthright. If Aros secured the scepter...

Jisarek Carre's abduction of Nera, first and favorite wife of Sher Fehl, thirty-two years ago had cost Aros any possibility of being the imperial heir. Jisarek would ever be whispered as his father, due to the timing of his birth. The emperor, powerful even then, had tried, but was unable to hush the whispers. Only blinding revenge had satisfied.

Thirty-two years after his birth, and with the empire increasing to unheard of size, Aros was still whispered to be of non-Fehl blood, and therefore was still denied the only throne he desired. Etelian's legitimacy was certain, so he had been taken from the throne he had been first placed upon and placed upon Tehrasi's throne instead. Nera was ruthless in securing the best territories and most powerful thrones for her children.

The councilors and generals had argued that keeping Aros from the throne was best for the Tehrasian populace, a kingdom finally relieved of its bloodthirsty rulers. The rumored spawn of Jisarek Carre on the throne might provoke revolt.

Sometimes Kaveh wondered whether the emperor himself used his generals' arguments as an excuse. If he, too, believed his eldest son would turn on the empire and embrace the insidious roots of his rumored birth should he sit upon the throne he wanted so covetously.

Aros had turned down every other throne offered to him, seemingly content to remain as the emperor's right hand in all diplomatic matters. It disconcerted the generals to have Aros so close to the imperial throne. It was an open secret that they thought he was trying to use his position as a stepping-stone to the imperial throne and that they would ensure another took the position instead.

But Kaveh did not care overly much about the court gossip. The emperor would live for a long time.

Talk continued over the state of the empire, quick summations that tiptoed around the real threat losing the gates would have on the imperium.

Finally, the emperor waved his hand. "Wait for us outside. I need a word with my commander."

Baksis and Simin had their heads together, speaking quietly, as they walked from the room. Etelian and Osni fled quickly, glaring at each other. Aros was the last to leave. The eldest's eyes were calm and collected as he cast a final, loaded glance at Kaveh and the emperor before the doors closed behind him.

Kaveh did not wait for a signal from the emperor before sending out his shadows again.

He did wait until the room was fully secured to air his displeasure. "A fairy-tale relic at such a critical time—"

The emperor held up a hand. "I need you for this task, fairy tale or not."

Kaveh let his shadows slip back into the depths of his robe, pressing his annoyance down with them. He nodded shortly. "It will be done."

A small, real smile curved the emperor's lips for the first time that day. "I know. That is why I've given the task to you, even though it is like sending a dragon to catch a sheep."

It pointed further to the emperor being unnerved by the name of the thief—or as unnerved as the emperor allowed himself—because there was no way he would be sending Kaveh to take care of the problem otherwise, scepter or not.

"You believe the information to be real?"

"I believe that the Carres took the knowledge of how to renew the scepters to their deaths. Osni has eked forth the last dredges of power from the gates with whatever failing gambit he put into place, but that feeble effort, too, is dying. But I know that the ability to wield the scepters wasn't intrinsic to the Carres' bloodline alone."

No. If it were, Aros would have been wielding them long ago—something the emperor would never admit aloud.

"They need to be specifically keyed. I have given Aros the task of getting the gates and scepters running, but it is a false task on its own. We *need* the Scepter of Darkness to exist. And Osni believes it is real—his lies are truth in this. I will allow this last game."

Kaveh acknowledged the statement. "Osni is a liability."

The emperor smiled grimly. "One that I will set Aros to squeezing. Then we will dispose of the scholari in turn. Osni knows he has outlived his usefulness. He will try to gain the Scepter of Darkness and key the rest to his own bloodline in order to remain relevant."

"And Etelian?" Kaveh asked casually.

The emperor tapped a finger against the table, mouth firmed in displeasure. "I could not, and cannot, deny Nera the prize of so rich an entail for her son." For her legitimate, favorite son. "The elite have a firm grip on the economy and Tehrasi continues to produce. We will allow things to continue until they become a problem. I will control the scepters, Etelian will sit on the throne, and others will rule the financial sectors from behind."

"Aros plots." It would be better to give him Tehrasi and let his plots wind within his own kingdom.

"I'm giving him the entirety of the Medit principalities when you are through collecting them."

"He will refuse that throne, like he has all the others."

"He won't. He will rule the Medit Sea and all its resources—a throne far greater than even Tehrasi. A throne rich with boundless resources. And the warring states will keep him quite occupied with secrets and plots. If he succeeds, he will be a challenge even to me."

A throne with enormous resources and excellent geographic position, but it was not Tehrasi. And that was what Aros wanted above all. It was redundant to say so, though. The emperor knew.

"He is simply testing his bounds." The emperor waved his hand dismissively. "He will come around when he sits a far greater throne. As to the gates, we will blame the problems on Osni and this Hand, then get rid of both. I will make certain Etelian knows what is expected of him henceforth." He narrowed his eyes on a faraway target—mind always moving. "If we lose control of Tehrasi and our own scepters, we lose control of the expansion."

"That will not happen," Kaveh assured him.

"The shift columns must be powered. The gates must remain open. There is nothing more important than that, right now. I know you have little interest in Tehrasi or our other conquered lands, but the future of the empire rests in the hand that holds the scepters."

"We can conquer without the scepters." The gates made conquest easier and faster, but they weren't indispensable.

The ability to plan, war, and siege were necessary, no matter whether a gate was available or not. Caravans would be a nightmare, but relying on a single strategy, like gate travel to move entire armies, led to failure. "We conquered Tehrasi at their full might."

"Through great planning and exploitation of weakness. And we built our conquest on the back of the scepters, even so. We cannot allow anyone else to possess the Scepter of Darkness. If we do not possess it, no one can."

Kaveh tilted his head in acknowledgment. "Yes."

"Anyone who has seen information on the lost scepter must die. Anyone who has heard *rumor* of a temple or map must be exterminated."

"Of course."

The emperor called the gazing ball that held the memory of the Heit's defeat to his hand. "If indeed the myth is true and it is the scepter that can reset all others of the Carre line, we will have all that we need. Nothing will stand in our way."

Kaveh nodded.

"Kill the thief. Get the scepter."

Shadows curled through Kaveh's fingers. "It will be done."

DREAMS OF HEALING

NINLI

TEHRAS, TEHRASI

Nin washed her hands in the provided basin, while Taline packed up their supplies and released them from the summons that had brought them to this newly blessed household three hours before.

The yells and squalling cries of earlier were gone, leaving a lovely peace behind.

"Thank you." The older woman smiled and looked at her daughter, who was hugging the newborn babe up to her chest.

Nin smiled at her. "It was my pleasure. A birth during daylight is always a delight. I'll return in a few days to make certain the healing is progressing. Call the guild if anything goes amiss, and they will send someone right away."

Afterbirth care was something this household would have little trouble with, though, and the baby would be in experienced hands.

CHAPTER THREE

Nin didn't lose her smile as she and Taline trudged out of the house near the top of the city, in the long shadow of the palace. Nin loved delivering babies, but if her farhani necklace showed her true power level, she'd never be allowed to do such mundane tasks. Deliveries had long become something more than penance for Nin. The delight, the emotion, the hope in bringing forth new life was exhilarating. Little compared.

And with her skill being superior to the task, things rarely went wrong. With all the extra power running through her that was unnecessary for a regular delivery, she'd figured out how to speed things along, coaxing the body to naturally release a babe more swiftly, and for the baby's system to be fully in synergy to the task. She could cut a delivery time in half, sometimes by three-quarters even for a mother's firstborn.

She'd gained a reputation for easy deliveries and was requested often. Though delivering babies did little to help her life's work, on another level, it kept her sane.

Registering as a Level Nine magi would get her squirreled away for testing or placed at the side of the emperor or one of his most vicious offspring. *Never.* Never would she allow herself to be placed in that position again.

The first nine years of her life had been rife with death, power, and tyranny. She had determined to do far better in her second nine. Not to be consumed with the thirst for power and vengeance that was bred into the bones of all who had lived in the shadows of the palace. As she approached twenty, she was finally feeling her stride.

In addition to all the other benefits, delivering babies kept her illegal nighttime activities in check, and made the activities more rewarding—protecting the future, building a hall of knowledge to ensure that those born even to the lowest of circumstances could have a chance at a better life.

And the network was nothing to scoff at. She had made inroads with households all over Tehrasi. Their gossip chain was unrivaled.

A raucous caw heralded an enchanted crow as it broke through the mist. Nin's farhani warmed in connection and the delivery construct of the crow swooped low, then broke into fragments that fell and formed into a summons in her hand.

Taline groaned at her side. "I swear, this entire city is going to be overrun with babies soon."

Nin smiled. The birth rate was a good indication that Tehrasi was recovering. And though the empire had brought with it its own problems to replace issues that had plagued the previous kingdom—unlike the Carre rule, killing children wasn't one of them.

The imperial mark that formed on the summons caused her to lose her smile. Opportunity and tension coiled through her, wiping away her pleasant lethargy.

"What is it?" Taline asked, sensing Nin's tension.

Nin handed her the summons to read.

Taline stiffened, then a grim smile pulled her mouth

upward. "The palace? A good opportunity to duplicate another entrance ward."

"I can—"

"No, you can't."

Nin didn't want to accept the statement, but she knew it was truth. Her mind didn't work like Taline's. Even before the injury that had made reading a laborious effort, Nin had been an intuitive thinker—things came to her while she was doing them. She could replicate spells and enchantments in the middle of a fight that she'd never be able to set to ink. But Taline...even with far lower levels of magic than Nin, Taline was a scribe. All she needed was to be shown a spell once, and she could replicate detailed instructions on papyri, even if she could not infuse them with power.

But Nin could power anything within the walls of the city gates, and that included Taline's spellsheets and boxes. Together, they made an unbeatable combination.

Nin wrapped her magic around the summons. The summons accepted Nin's magic and disappeared.

As they walked, Nin could feel Taline laying additional concealment wards over her face, increasing the disconnect between Taline's real features and what people would see. She then turned her magic to Nin—putting in just enough of a suggestion to the magic to make Nin incredibly forgettable.

The scroll Nin had stolen for Taline, giving instructions on altering physical appearances and light sensory manipulation, had proved priceless.

They began the upward climb toward the palace, readying

themselves. It was one thing to flit through the grounds in the dark of night and quite another to walk exposed in the daylight.

One street before they arrived, a flare of power caused them both to freeze. The second scepter in the temple grove next to the palace blazed brightly—a scepter that could be seen from nearly everywhere in the city.

The blood drained from Taline's face. Etelian ul Fehl was back in residence.

"Go," Nin said, as casually as she was able. "Go talk to the windcatchers about their guild accounts. I'll catch up with you in a few hours."

"But we need—" Taline's breath was skipping.

"There will be other calls," Nin said. The prince wasn't one to stray outside his sumptuous quarters, but it wasn't worth the risk. "This is a Level Five assignment. I can handle it with minimal deception."

They were registered by the guild as a team—healer and assistant. Taline trailed Nin on her rounds, and as a four and six designated by their farhanies, together they could pull off a proficient seven healing level and accepted those levels of calls.

The massive benefit to their deception was that while Nin was healing patients using her own powers, Taline was using visual enchantments, making it appear that she was helping Nin, when in fact she was copying house and warding spells. When they were called to lower economic areas without useful spells to survey, Taline used her time to construct mechanical wonders and create spellboxes for the guilds.

Taline was only a Level Five, in reality, just a single level higher than what was stated on the imperial registries, but she had the unique ability to create containers and boxes that could contain Nin's magic and use that magic at another time. When in possession of such a container, Taline could use Level Nine abilities for the short duration allotted by the spells.

Their deception would never have worked if they weren't outright lying about Nin's level, and if they hadn't circumvented the imperial oaths that were mandatory under the penalty of death. Nin's unique connection to the city allowed her to break and reconnect oaths that ran through the city's temples.

Their deception allowed them to hide in plain sight.

And if on some days Nin took a clone of Taline with her when responding to easy calls while Taline worked at home, there was a reason that they were continuously overlooked as having any connection with the Hand. They couldn't be in two places at one time.

Nin started a clone enchantment.

"No." Taline took a deep breath. "I saw the summons. We are to treat someone in the servants' quarters." She smoothed the Healing Guild's navy, utilitarian work scarf draped around her frame. But Nin detected five additional spells that Taline had worked into the fabric—a testament to her fear.

"Tal—"

"No," she said grimly. "I won't live in fear of him. And we haven't recorded the entrance wards at the palace. Any spell in our control improves the odds of your success when you decide to stupidly scale the palace walls or creep through the halls."

"Tal—"

"Nin. Stop speaking."

Nin could feel her sister triple-checking the spells laden through her farhani, making certain that her identity was hidden beneath. Then, she added a headscarf that further obscured her features—facial characteristics sealed behind additional layers of magic and henna dots beneath her clothes.

"Let's go," Taline said, chin raised.

Nin didn't even want to think about what was going on behind her sister's suddenly steely facade.

Nin gripped her satchel as they approached the back palace entrance indicated on the summons. Taking a deep breath, she pressed a finger against the red acacia wood.

A stern, older woman opened the door and looked at her. "Come."

The wards parted. Through their bond, she could feel Taline grab the last whispers of the wards and wrap them into the seal around her wrist to study and inscribe later.

Nin signaled for Taline to fake an illness. She had captured the day's wards and didn't need to stay. But Taline shook her head.

"Follow me." The female head of staff frowned sharply at their delay.

The woman led them onward through a maze of halls. Nin kept her gaze locked on the back of the woman's shawl, only allowing her eyes to move in certain segments of the hall—and not letting her gaze stray to her sister.

It wouldn't do to pretend too much or too little interest in her surroundings. Nin already knew them well.

It was not a good thing to be noticed by the palace staff. It would be worse to be noticed by those of the upper floors.

Their patient was in a bedroom underground in the servants' quarters. A swarthy, but kind-looking man held his arm against his chest at an unnatural angle.

"Fell from a tree," he said, abashedly, as Nin started delving with her power.

Nin smiled at him. "Not a good place to lose one's footing."

"Assuredly not," he said with a semblance of cheer. "They needed a bit of a trim." He rubbed the back of his neck with his free hand. "Can't let age wear me down."

"Never." She eyed the groundskeeper's aging, jovial face. The Grounds Guild near the western gates was looking for a man to manage a team. Perhaps she'd leave the slip of paper requesting excellent candidates.

"But now that you are here, I can be trimming trees again by dawn. Our in-house healer was recalled for the week because of a guild matter."

"Mmmm." Nin knew this because Taline had made

certain the paperwork showing that Healer Amura wasn't up-to-date on the newest embalming techniques had made it to the guild head's desk the week before. The gambit they'd done during Amura's palace absence had already been completed, but a second opportunity to gather information was never to be ignored.

The man looked at the farhani tag around her neck. "You're a six? Healer Amura is an eight."

Nin smiled at him. "Together, my sister and I equal a Level Seven. But even alone, I can handle your broken arm."

"Course you can!"

Taline stayed silent, laying out all the supplies Nin would need in motions too precise to be necessary. The groundskeeper was a Level Five earthkeeper. He wouldn't be able to detect the way that Taline was collecting intel from the room and grounds while pretending to do nothing but busywork.

"You work together often?" He indicated the two of them.

Nin nodded. "The guild pairs different healers, but once a rapport is established, we often are sent in the same pairs or trios."

Most of the healers in the guild were Levels Four, Five, or Six. Anyone registering more than a six was considered rare in any field. But healers could combine their powers to perform greater feats.

And some healers specialized in treating ailments, increasing their own power level in more focused ways. Most in the guild were satisfied that Nin simply had an affinity for delivering babies that allowed her to perform beyond a Level Six's ability during difficult delivery circumstances.

It had taken a bit of artifice for them to be a pair that was rarely split. Lying about one's abilities and familial relationship made it easier. Sympathies in magic was still an art, not a science. Family members were usually a default for sympathy, and Taline and Nin were marked down in the registry books as sisters.

"For this ailment, though, I don't require assistance."

"My girl wanted to be a healer. Ended up in the kitchens." He waved a hand forward. "Darn good cook, though."

Nin smiled at him and touched the guild amethyst stone Taline had unwrapped on the table, then her own healer's tag at her throat, and let the combined healing contract spell touch the man's palm. He accepted the spell, his magic opening to hers as per the standard healing contract.

Permission granted, she reached inside and gathered the life-force in his arm and directed it to work with her power to seal his bones back together and manage his pain.

A dozen heartbeats later and it was done. Nin looked surreptitiously at Taline, who gave an infinitesimal nod. She had gathered all that she could.

Nin let go. "There you are. How do you feel?"

"My headache's even gone," he said cheerfully. "Healer Amura doesn't bother."

Nin smiled. "Well, I won't tell, if you don't."

"May Sehk-Ra's blessings be upon you, Healer."

Taline was already rolling everything back into place.

They were walking toward the exit when the head female servant blocked their path.

"There's another...incident...we need you for," the woman said in distaste.

Nin tried to relax her shoulders and keep her eyes off her sister. "We will need to clear any visits with the guil—"

"No. We will pay you directly."

"The guild—"

"You are a healer. You have taken an oath to heal. There's a girl in an upper suite with broken bones. You fixed the groundskeeper fast enough. You will fix her."

Upper suite? Nin wet her lips. That meant the royal floors. "Your healer—"

"Isn't here," she bit out. "Will you leave the girl to die?"

"No, of course not." Nin used a soothing voice. "My assistant must return to the guild, however. She—"

"Doesn't need to yet, and will accompany you," Taline interrupted smoothly. "It is my oath to help as well."

Nin stiffened, but shrugged. "Of course."

They headed upstairs to Etelian ul Fehl's rooms. If there were ever a time to be both terrified and exhilarated, this was it.

MEMORIES OF HORROR

NINLI
THE PALACE OF TEHRAS

Although Osni had kept his own areas under the "unbreakable" eavesdropping wards that the Carres had loved, the Fehls had systematically changed every entrance ward to the palace—and all the wards on Etelian ul Fehl's private areas were of Fehl origin.

Gaining entrance to the guest or master suites was something that had been entirely out of their reach without wholesale slaughter of the entirety of the palace's guards—a task far beyond their abilities or intentions.

The girl slumped on the sheets, however, made her rethink those intentions. Her injuries were all too familiar.

The tension in Taline's frame was so tight that she looked as though she might break. Nin hurried to the girl while Taline activated their spell bag.

Osni was a hairsbreadth away from having everything ripped from him. Seeing him lose everything would be its own revenge.

The padifehl, however.... His comeuppance, though harder to bring about and unforgivably further in the future, would be far more satisfying.

The initial examination was almost unnecessary. Nin had treated injuries like these before.

Catching the attention of the emperor or any of his wives, children, or commanders was never something to be taken lightly, just as it had been with the Carres. Many sought favors, but it was a double-edged sword to be in the eye of power. Those rewarded could be cut down as quickly as they rose. And the penalties for falling were far more severe than the rewards for rising.

Power ruled the empire, and as such, women with power were given a status level near to that of men. However, if there was one unspoken rule in the empire for women, it was *never* to catch the eye of Etelian ul Fehl, second-born son of the High Imperial Majex—the emperor's favorite wife—and untouchable in the eyes of the empire.

Nin looked at the girl on the bed, then at another girl watching from the corner. The deadness in their eyes spoke of a certainty that their abusive circumstances would not change. The girl in the corner looked away, eyes focused firmly on the window, lips quivering.

If ever there were a man to be assassinated...

But for all his lack of adding anything positive to the

world, Etelian ul Fehl was hard to kill. He had inherited a portion of his father's ability to drain anyone attacking him magically and a monster's innate ability to protect itself from threat. For all that, he was too self-absorbed to be a fighter. No assassin had ever succeeded in killing the man, and plenty of broken women had tried.

Another of the emperor's children would have to be the one to do the deed. An overwhelmingly powerful one, like the thirteenth blessed or the first. She had been waiting for Aros to do it for years now. Aros on the throne of Tehrasi would only be possible with the death of Etelian.

"Well?" the head servant said impatiently.

Nin couldn't look at her sister, but she could feel her tension and terror.

Nin closed her eyes. Her fingers hovered and skimmed over the girl's wounds and internal injuries.

"Broken bones. Asphyxiation. Blood wounds," Nin said softly. "I'm skimming to determine the order of repair. It will be a moment more."

Damage to her lungs and throat, a broken wrist, two fractured ribs—the girl could recover from all those injuries with a few carefully learned swipes of Nin's magic. No healer could argue that the girl would need to accompany them elsewhere in order to be repaired. If only—

Nin's fingers slowed. There was a reaction blotting the girl's skin that showed the effects of light poisoning. Palmera poisoning.

Such visible effects meant that the girl had no tolerance

for the more potent form of the drink that was regulated for upper class consumption and entertainment. Susceptible to its effects, the girl would quickly grow more ill the more she consumed until she passed out. It was not an abnormal reaction to palmera—Nin had seen it in many others. It was considered a test of manhood to conquer the palm sprig drink. Palmera-induced calls were a standard post-festival slog. Nin carried a potion to treat it.

She could give the girl the potion and fix her light poisoning at the same time that she fixed her injuries. It's what a healer would be expected to do.

Instead, Nin grabbed a palm sprig from her medicinal pouch. She felt Taline's gaze snap to hers. Nin curled the sprig into the cup of her hand and let her will work, hiding the threads of magic beneath a steady flow of Level Six healing that she let flow to fix the girl's ribs and lungs.

Taline released a flurry of spells that were little more than show, but they drew the servant's gaze away from Nin. The head servant wouldn't be as easily deceived as the groundskeeper.

"Her wounds are grievous," Taline murmured, wrapping her fingers around Nin's arm, as they did when they wanted to demonstrate more power being used.

"She is fine. You will fix her and be gone." The woman sneered. "She is the padifehl's current favorite."

Nin stared at the stuttered rise and fall of the girl's chest and didn't look down at Taline's fingernails cutting into her arm. The padifehl's favorite... If they didn't patch the girl up quickly and leave, the scrutiny could prove their undoing.

Anything other than healing the girl would lead to questions.

Nin pressed the palm sprig against the open cut on the girl's thigh, then mentally *pushed*. The girl jerked immediately, as if someone had restricted her airway—which was exactly what Nin had just done by inducing her allergic response.

Taline's fingernails scored deep, crescent-shaped moons into Nin's skin, but her magic didn't stop.

"Ferra bless her," Taline said, voice thready. Give her a death chase through the streets, and Taline was in her element. Give her this... "There's something else wrong..."

Nin pushed aside all fear and let her mindscape narrow in on the mission they had just accepted, and all that it entailed. She let the new state overwhelm her mind until it was all she knew.

"She is bleeding internally." Nin frowned at the servant, flicking her wrist to pull the sprig up her sleeve and out of view as she moved her hands upward. "And there is something inside her, as my assistant noted. Like a worm..."

The tension from Taline coiled tighter, but she moved with the gambit, and Nin felt the wisp of visual enchantment that her sister had mastered long ago slip onto the girl on the bed. Thin lines of black formed on the girl's skin.

"Yank whatever it is free and patch her up," the head servant demanded. "She will live with the pain of a stomach ailment."

Nin nodded agreeably and pressed her hand—and the remaining palm oil upon it—against the cut closest to the girl's heart. The girl jackknifed on the bed. Red lines shot across her chest, then under the wisps of Taline's enchantment, red lines turned black and spread in all directions.

The head servant gasped. "What in Ra's name—"

Nin flew from the side of the bed, crossing her forehead in the sign to ward off evil, and Taline gave a shriek, throwing herself to the side—where a number of manuscripts were spread across the sideboard.

"The Stygian pestilence!" Nin backed away, drawing all attention with rapid signs of her fingers.

The head servant pushed Nin forward roughly so she could lunge backward through the door. "Get rid of the girl! Guards!"

The guards ran inside, then just as quickly tried to stumble back out, pressing against the other to get through the door first as the girl jerked and shuddered. The spiderwebbing on her skin turned charcoal.

A spear appeared in one of the men's hands and it took all Nin's control not to react with magic.

"No! You'll release the demons!" she yelled.

The man dropped the spear and stumbled, bumping into Taline, who was cowering over the manuscripts, fingers quickly flipping pages beneath her hunched upper body— never one to let opportunity pass by.

Nin looked at the girl on the bed and let a pained grimace overtake her expression. "I...I think I can contain it."

"Do it! Do it!"

Nin approached the girl with feigned reluctance and twitched an encasement spell with her finger.

The girl abruptly went rigid, her face a rictus of agonized death.

"It's taken her!" Nin pulled out a shred of linen and flipped it into a sheet, while maintaining a false sense of terrified distance. The shroud quickly covered the dead girl and she had strips fastened around her in less than twenty beats of the heart.

"What are you doing?" one of the guards asked nervously, their gazes never moving from Nin and the deceased, plague-ridden girl.

"Stifling the possibility that the pestilence can hook into those near her." Nin let the relief that she couldn't yet allow herself seep into her voice. "The chance of contamination is gone as long as she's within these wraps. Did..." Nin let a terrified look overtake her face as she reached for the first fastener on the shroud. "Did you need to examine her?"

The guards tripped over themselves, pushing Taline farther into the sideboard and toward another small stack of manuscripts with their uncontrolled movements. "No! We saw her die. Her heart stopped. Verified. Verified! Just leave. Take her. We'll tell Madame Forsa."

They had verified nothing. But they would never report that. Just like they would get a completely clean script of health from another healer within the hour and simply thank their gods that they had escaped a death they could not be resurrected from.

The other girl who was dressed in luxurious garments in the corner, though... For someone who had looked close to breaking apart mere minutes ago, there was something shrewd narrowing her wide eyes. Her thousand-year-old stare said she knew that the shroud-covered body was not dead. That something was off. That she knew they had done something to the girl.

For all that she had looked as if she'd rather be anywhere else moments ago, it was never easy to guess how someone in such a circumstance might react. Desperation could force many different paths. Of all the times Nin had come closest to being caught, it had always been due to someone so embroiled and entangled that they couldn't see any other way out.

There were those who rejected the notion that they could be free of a bad circumstance. And sometimes those most desperate clung harder to any bit of control and sought to control others in their shared misery. If the girl thought to gain favor by turning them in, they would likely have to fight their way free of the palace.

Nin waited.

"How?" the girl asked finally. The unfeigned sorrow as she looked at the girl on the bed made the tension inside Nin relax a measure.

"Pestilence." Nin waited for the girl's gaze to connect

with hers again. "It's a terrible thing. Unrecoverable. And it activates in the span of a moonrise. All of you should remain here tonight and be checked in the morning. The madame will be told that those who have had contact with this girl will be held in isolation in this room," she said, without breaking her gaze. "And be removed upon the morrow, if they show signs."

The girl said nothing for long moments, swallowing hard, eyes returning to the body of her friend. "They'll kill us, if they suspect."

There were two ways to interpret the girl's words—if they suspected the other girls had the disease, or if they suspected any fraud.

"Yes." Taline moved forward and let her hand rest against the dead woman's shrouded shoulder.

The girl swallowed again, but something in her eyes shifted as she looked at Taline—seeing something there. "How many?"

Taline's gaze never wavered. "However many contract the disease," she said slowly.

The girl's lip wobbled, but she nodded.

Nin kept her magic stable as fierce elation replaced the tension. They could *do* something positive here.

"Someone from the guild will be by in the morning to check. Someone who will ensure that only those who are *infected* are removed." Nin made the sign of the moon on her palm. Those who gave the sign to the healer would be removed. It would be up to this girl to identify those who would choose to play the deadly game.

The girl nodded again, hope mixing with terror.

Madame Forsa returned, demanding they leave with the body.

Touching the appropriate symbol on her bag, Nin activated a stasis-and-removal spell on the body—floating the shrouded figure in front of them as they descended to the ground floor. Like most advanced magic in Tehrasi, it was a preset spell that was keyed to the guild and specifically allowed for healers on duty.

Taline "cowered" behind as Nin marched.

Three streets away from the palace, Taline's form straightened, her shoulders rounded back, and she drew alongside Nin. "There will be consequences."

"Yes."

"Your plans—"

"We weren't leaving her there. We aren't leaving behind anyone who wants to escape."

Taline continued moving forward in her steady, strong pace, but her expression was tortured.

Nin stopped and slipped her palm around the back of Taline's neck. She pulled her sister's forehead to hers, keeping their gazes connected.

Taline swallowed and nodded, tears in her eyes. Her gaze moved to the shrouded girl on the pallet. "He'll get more."

"Yes."

"It won't stop."

Battlefield losses meant that members of the losing side could be conscripted to build, dig, and enchant for the winning side for a term of years—and wartime alone saw a threefold increase in such activities in each country—but girls like this came through "gifting." A parent or guardian could gift a dependent to a citizen of the empire—and such gifts to the elite, especially, were paid for in return by increased status.

Etelian ul Fehl never wanted for gifts.

"Every girl is there because she was given to him by someone who had the ability and authority to do so."

Every time she thought about Etelian ul Fehl's household, she wanted to torch it to the ground.

And Nin would be lying if she said she held no plans to end Etelian permanently, if they couldn't take him down another way. It would be the last act she'd undertake, but there would be grim satisfaction in her end.

It was a dangerous path to decide who lived and who died. She knew intimately the darkness such a path could bring. But if Etelian couldn't be deposed another way, she would accept the consequences of making that choice.

"We will stop it," Nin said.

"He will never change."

"No. But we will force the change."

She would do as she must. She had never thought she would live to see nineteen. And if she could take out Etelian ul Fehl and Crelu ul Osni after making certain Tehrasi would be in good hands, she would take it as her destiny.

"Nin?" Taline looked at her worriedly.

Nin patted her hand. "We will ruin him so thoroughly that the light of judgment will shine upon him and he won't have the power of Tehrasi to support him. A circle." She made a sweep with her finger. "A completed shape that will allow us to sleep at night."

A completed shape that she would undertake fully once she was certain she could do so without bringing vengeance upon those who depended on her.

An end that would bring her sister peace.

The body chariot intercepted them en route. Taline looked at her grimly, then turned and continued on foot to another district to await the swap.

Nin stepped into the driverless chariot and activated the spell on the handrail to drive to the nearest embalmer. She didn't have much time. She held a silver coin and concentrated, then slipped it beneath the shroud. The chariot rocked to a stop in front of the plain door of the establishment.

The embalmer looked at the shrouded body in disinterest and motioned for Nin to activate the spells showing death and cause. He rarely checked the bodies himself. He only cared for the gold that made his business run.

Once she placed his payment on the table, he levitated the girl's body to the rollers, then pushed it into the incineration chamber. With a slide of a lever, the door sealed.

Nin touched her farhani, then the bracelet cuff around her wrist, and activated the sister coin beneath it.

Flames lit the incineration chamber, leaving behind nothing but ashes a moment later.

The embalmer marked the disposal on the sheet and

waved the ashes away with a spell. Nin bowed her head, murmured a quick prayer for the deceased's body and soul, then murmured her gratitude to the embalmer.

Making sure she wasn't followed, she quickly made her way to a very specific house, satchel clutched in her hands.

Her tension released as she heard the soft murmurings in the antechamber, indicating Larit and Qara had answered Taline's summons.

She entered the healing room to see Qara ul Polingsa and Larit ul Polingsa lean their foreheads briefly together, ever in synergy, exchanging some communication special to only the two of them. Even their tones were complementary—burnished golden rays preceding dusk and the deepening dark twilight right after.

Something squeezed in Nin's chest, aching. She looked at the body lying in the middle of the room.

The stasis charm on the displaced girl had been removed and her chest was rising and falling at regular intervals. Nin's magic moved over her, looking for lingering wounds. She'd patched only the most severe of her wounds at the palace. Larit was an excellent healer, though, and had already fixed the rest. Bonded as she was to Qara ul Polingsa, one of the elite of Tehrasi, they'd both obviously figured out what was happening when a body was transported from the crematorium to the room where their circle hid those in need.

Nin exchanged a look with both women. "Thank you."

Qara nodded. Larit gave her a sad smile.

"Taline is gathering the necessary documents, new

identification, and farhani tags that this woman will require," Qara said.

Qara's bearing was regal, as always, but her gaze was compassionate. She might dine and coolly converse with the richest in the country, but she was what Nin wished all the elite to be—intelligent, caring, and kind. And brave, most especially—for she risked her position near the top of Tehras's social and political structure repeatedly to help Nin and Taline.

"Thank you. Again." Nin felt the last of her tension release. She looked at the body on the bed, healed and breathing easier. Tomorrow the girl would become a new person, starting a new life.

"One of Etelian ul Fehl's," Qara said.

It wasn't a question. Nin nodded grimly anyway.

"And the rest of his current crop?"

"Tomorrow," Nin answered.

"You take great risk," Qara said, gaze piercing. "Both of you—though I know who leads this madness."

Nin closed her eyes. She hadn't been strong enough to push Taline away after the older girl had glued herself firmly to her side. Nin was used to people she saved and healed finding new lives—leaving quickly, with genuine gratitude, but ready to move into a new existence. Taline hadn't been like the others...her new life had wrapped firmly around Nin's.

Nin hadn't been strong enough to push Taline away four years ago. She definitely wasn't strong enough to do so now. And if her goals had shifted somewhat to encompass Taline's past, muddying up all the other penances she had determined to pay, that was on her.

"I know." She opened her eyes and fixed her gaze on Larit, who had long held the secret from the rest of the healers that Nin had powers greater than a Level Six. "This is putting you both at risk, too. I'm sorry."

"I'm not," Larit said simply. Qara nodded sharply, as well. "But we can't save every girl like this, Ninli."

Nin focused on the intricate clasp of the supply chest. "I know."

"Do you?"

She looked away.

"You have to decide your course. Is the library your ultimate goal? Bringing knowledge to the masses and saving your people? Is it setting Tehras free of the blood rituals that have soaked our past? Or is it revenge?" Qara hammered. "The two of you have gathered enough materials for the whole of Tehras to acquire new occupations—to stay ahead of the shifting, progressive landscape. What will happen to those plans if you are caught?"

"Never put your power in full sight. For you just encourage someone to steal it. To steal your secrets. We must guard our power and secrets close. Never share your knowledge, your skills. For what will you be if everyone holds the same power?"

"Nothing," Nin whispered in response to the memory. She looked at the recently stolen documents at the end of the table containing the secrets of four of the top families in Tehras and would soon also contain the manuscripts Qara was "donating" from her own family. Qara would maintain her grip on the outraged side of the elite at the same time that she forwarded the library's aims. "For you will carry it on. I will be publicly put to death, a traitor, should I be caught, but the library plans will live on. Through you. You are the future of Tehrasi, Qara. You will be the change. You, Larit, and all the others."

Nin and Taline had ensured that path through the dispersal of the manuscripts and documents they stole and duplicated.

"*You* are the future, and you are not a traitor." Qara grabbed her shoulders. "But you are slipping, losing your grip and focus."

"Keeping too hard a grip on anything just makes it slip away faster." Nin had learned to let go.

"Ninli, you don't have to let go." Qara's full lips firmed. "But you are slipping. You aren't being as careful as you used to be. You find too many causes. You are scattering your focus. You are making yourself vulnerable."

She knew it was true. "I can do nothing else."

It had been easier when she saved people and they left— leaving her behind. The ones who stuck around...they always made her attachment to their issues overtake her own long-term plans.

Nin grew attached far too easily. And she had so much to make up for.

Qara's eyes softened. "I know. But should you maintain your current pace, you will be caught, and you will take Taline down with you. You risk her freedom, too, in the advancement of revenge in her name."

A collar, an unbreakable farhani, a gem buried beneath her flesh—less kind than an executioner's spell. People with power did terrible things, and the list of people who would wield her was too terrible to contemplate.

There had always been a time limit on Nin's freedom and life.

But for her beautiful sister...

Taline strode into the room and frowned at the tension, gaze moving suspiciously between the three of them. Nin pulled herself upright.

Only a little longer. She was *so* close.

"I have documents and new tags," Taline said, still frowning. "And with a few small facial adjustments, this girl will blend in with those born to Indi. There is a gate opening to the country tomorrow and she will have a pass."

"And the others?" Larit asked.

"I keep a dozen sets of documents and tags in reserve, just in case. They won't be as tailored, but we will fix that over the next few days. There are more tags for Indi, if they want to stick together. And two relocation possibilities in Nurfine."

"You can't keep doing this," Larit said, seemingly testing Taline's responses now.

Taline stiffened. "We have located what we need to finish our plans. There will be no need to do this again."

"I don't want to bury either of you."

"Nin's too tricky to be caught."

"Tali's too smart to die," Nin said with a lightness she didn't feel.

"If you keep trying to save everyone, you will be unable to save yourself."

"We'll just have to make certain that we are not caught," Nin said lightly. She couldn't let them be harmed.

She rubbed at her chest, trying to free it from the sudden constriction, and smiled quickly at Taline to reassure her.

They were so close. She would focus more. Play it safer. Break more imperial oaths in order to make additional sets of fake identity documents for Taline, Larit, Qara, and all the other women and men scattered through Tehras who helped them from the shadows.

Somehow.

Traitor, the same voice of memory—her father's—spit.

"Yes," she murmured. But she would fix her father's mistakes.

Just a little longer...

Everything was going to work out.

She would make it so.

SHADOW OF THE HUNT

KAVEH

TEHRAS, TEHRASI

Shrouded beneath a hooded cloak, Kaveh reined in his magic and stepped through the flickering gate from Fehlaka, the imperial capital, to Tehras, the City of a Hundred Gates. The capital city of Tehrasi loomed upward in the winding, bustling streets leading to the palace and temple at the high point of the hillside town.

Arches made of stone and magic ringed the encapsulated town, offering protection and opportunity, flickering different exit points on a ten-minute schedule that the Gatekeeping Guild encoded.

If only they were true gatekeepers instead of glorified spell pinchers filling a role, Osni and the bloody scepter problem would have been a flea to be squeezed. If only they had a *gatemaker*, who could create gates and not rely on weak tools. With a gatemaker chained to the emperor—they'd be unstoppable.

Headed toward the palace, Kaveh stepped past the gate egress, barely sparing attention to the bustle around him. His working shadows swirled, hidden, beneath a reinforced layer of a plain traveler's cloak. Beneath the cloak, he smoothed a hand down Ifret's back as the shadow reoriented to a different city. Even at noon, Ifret was able to connect to the shadows of a city quickly, then pass their secrets to her master.

Kaveh's outward appearance was no more than that of a legitimate traveler who, having passed through the gate with ease, wished to go unnoticed. Gaining a travel pass was a far more laborious effort than hiding ill intentions.

A few people glanced at him askance, but the gazes were of a curious and wary nature directed toward an unknown, hardened traveler, rather than the utter terror that would have occurred were he walking unmasked. He'd grown immune to the fear and had little patience for artifice, but he prized efficiency, and the most efficient solution required hiding, waiting, and striking.

He strode the active streets full of colorful shops, civilians, and traveling vendors.

People naturally moved from his path, even with his identity masked. He never bothered to shut off the battlefront mentality of motion, where every movement held purpose. In a civilian crowd, hooded and with his magic hidden, smooth and deliberate motions cleared him a path as readily as on a battlefield.

Active morning shadows of the city licked at his feet to taste him, then rippled out to spread the news among their kind.

Despite his legal entrance, he picked up human followers quickly—the investigorii quick to identify potential threats coming through the gates.

Between his fingers, Kaveh flicked out a carved wooden disk brimming with magic. Five followers abruptly broke away, leaving only one trailing behind. The imperial disk permitted the holder complete authority. The single follower maintained a respectful distance and kept others away; then he, too, turned back as Kaveh entered the ring of buildings at the city's center near the Temple of Sehk-Ra.

Aros was waiting in the almond grove, gazing contemplatively at the nearest temple scepter indicators that stretched into the sky.

The indicators encircled the acropolis that contained the palace and temple. The highest was keyed to the emperor and would light only when he set foot in the city. The second-highest scepter was lit to indicate that Etelian, Padifehl of Tehrasi, was in residence, and the third, for the scholari, was lit as well. The other scepter indicators in the ring—all dormant since the Carres had died—decreased in size until the shortest was adjacent to the one keyed to the emperor.

The actual scepters that were tied to the indicators stood inside the palace, but like their indicators, they, too, remained dormant.

Having the Scepter of Darkness would alleviate the problems Tehrasi's waning scepter and gate magic had caused the empire over the last ten years.

Aros sat on a stone bench and looked at the unlit scepters in narrowed contemplation. A stack of papyrus was piled next to him. He didn't look Kaveh's way when Kaveh stepped from the waning morning shadows.

"As chamberlain of the palace, Osni used the weak, ceremonial scepter he possessed at the beginning of his coup to key three of the least useful scepters—ones that are celebratory alone," Aros mused. "He uses the third scepter to pull people to him from around the city in showy displays of fake power. It has always been clear what the man deems important."

"Osni is a dead man walking." Kaveh moved to the bench and the papers there. "I care not what he deems important."

Aros tilted his head. "Perhaps. Or perhaps he will prove useful in the end. His motives are superficial. As are our brother's. How Father could think to give those two fools the richest jewel outside of Fehlaka, I'll never understand."

Kaveh was used to Aros's moods, and contemplative was the eldest at his most dangerous.

"One day your plots will end with Father's fingers around your throat and your power drained to his palm." Kaveh lifted and scanned the pages Aros had brought, noting reports, times, locations, and other gathered information.

"Don't be boring, Kaveh. I'll think you champion Etelian."

"Only if it ends in your death as well," Kaveh said, just as dismissively.

Aros's cold mouth turned up at the edges. "And that is why you will always be my favorite of the pitiful flock we call kin."

"Don't let Nera hear you say that."

"Please, brother. If Mother could get her hooks in you, she'd have done it years ago. But ever the challenging thorn, you provide so few ways to control you. If only you'd been born when I was permanently in the palace. I grieve the circumstances of time."

Aros had been away when the third wave of children, of which Kaveh was a part, had been born. A hugely missed opportunity for Aros, who dominated the first two generations.

"I would have sacrificed all of the others to make brutally certain you were loyal only to me. Or if you'd been born ten years later," Aros mused. "Of course, if I'd been ten years older, I'd have taken your mother for my own."

Aros touched the deep welt that scored his waist beneath his clothes. A gift from Irsula of Denz, Night Terror of the Lands of Sand and Mistress of Shadows—a scar that would never heal. A marred patch on otherwise unmarred skin.

Aros's fingers pulled along the scar—a familiar and calming path for his fingers to travel that Kaveh had seen him practice many times before. "Missed opportunities, alas. Father lacks the ability to control the woman he caged, though he succeeded gloriously in binding her single spawn."

"You court death."

"Always," Aros said with an equivalent casualness that was feigned on both their parts. "The Mistress of Shadows is the jewel upon which all rests."

"Angry with Nera again, are you?" Kaveh asked casually. Nera hated and feared Irsula. Her firstborn's obsession with Kaveh's mother was therefore a card that Aros strategically used.

"She continues to be an impediment to getting rid of Etelian—a move that would serve you and me both."

Kaveh knew these games—though no one other than Aros dared play them around Kaveh. Aros was always careful. So long as he wasn't caught, Aros could do anything he liked to the rest of the princes and princesses, but Etelian....Etelian was off-limits.

Nera was as power hungry as her first son and as lecherous and attracted to shiny things as her second, but she differed from both in her fierce loyalty to those of her own blood. She celebrated her children's malice as long as it was outwardly flexed. She brooked no malevolence between those she'd spawned.

"Still magically bound not to kill him?" Kaveh asked. Nera had tried to get the oaths to her children extended throughout the imperial lines, but the emperor had put an end to the practice when it had become apparent that an executioner among them would eventually be needed.

Kaveh had no restrictions to his oaths.

"The restriction is beyond irritating. But I came to see

quickly the gift it clearly is—to let Etelian become the spoiled, vain child who never matures past his own vices and desires. So *very* easily led—both Etelian and all those who surround him, who are so easily influenced after Etelian's many shortcomings."

If there was one thing Aros actively encouraged, it was Etelian's narcissism—his base values, self-interest, and cruelty.

"If you want to rule here through him, I care not."

The emperor couldn't give the empire or Tehrasi to Aros, so he gave the richest plum beneath the empire's canopy to Nera's second child. A boon. That it was the only plum Aros wanted, was doubly a knife in the gut.

"Etelian is easy to manipulate, and as such, quite boring. There are larger things to seek."

"The emperor will never give Etelian rule over the whole empire."

"Of course not. We know where the empire will go." Aros looked at him through half-lidded eyes. "I had considered pitting you against Etelian once, but you consider Etelian beneath your notice."

"I consider all of you beneath my notice," Kaveh said, looking through the last document.

"Yes. You are my favorite for many reasons," Aros mused. "But you are wasted anywhere you are not brutally conquering."

It was the one thing they held in agreement.

"Where's Osni now?" Kaveh finished the page and

motioned to Ifret. The corporeal shadow leaped from his shoulders and swiftly slithered into the palace. Kaveh rarely set foot in the Palace of Tehras, and the shadow would map all that had changed since the last time Kaveh had visited.

Aros leaned back on his hands. His sharp gaze followed Ifret's path hungrily. "The scholari is scurrying through his rooms, hoping he doesn't cross your path."

"And Etelian?"

"Currently destroying the south wing," Aros said languidly. "Every single one of his latest bedmates was stricken by the pestilence and led away to slaughter."

Kaveh looked at him sharply. "There is pestilence in the palace?"

"Contained. Magnificently contained." The right side of Aros's mouth twisted up into a smirk. "You missed the absolute reckoning the Healing Guild had to perform to clear everyone left in the palace. Outside of the women themselves, only two servants were plagued—both of whom were slated to be executed for trying to protect the first woman to die. The two servants were killed by healers in their cells this morning and their bodies removed. No more pestilence to infect anyone else in the household. *Magnificently* contained."

Kaveh didn't need to hear Aros's cold amusement to understand. He went back to reading the documents in his hand, disinterested. "I take it the 'savior' has been exterminated and the women are being returned."

"No, no. Dear Etelian would undeniably be having less of a fit, if so. Every cremation was carried out and accounted for in precise, unquestionable ways. The Healing Guild should be celebrated for their skills."

Kaveh couldn't remember the last time he had heard Aros so honestly entertained.

"Either someone is trying to undermine Etelian by taking away his toys or trying to save him by clearing real dangers," Kaveh determined, uninterested.

"And you thought this visit would be dull."

"It is. I care nothing for these types of games."

"A true pity." Aros smirked. "You have come for naught then. Etelian and Osni assure me that the investigorii have the location of the thief's lair and that they have the map to the scepter—that there is no need for either of us to be present."

Kaveh didn't pause in his flip through. "Serendipitous timing."

"Exceedingly. Osni sent a squadron of adventurers and thieves this morning to secure the scepter."

"Did you note where they were going?"

"Perhaps."

Kaveh let the bait slide from his shoulders before it could attach. He knew Aros. And that Aros hadn't followed meant there were avenues of higher interest elsewhere for him. Whether Osni had found the true scepter temple or not would be verified elsewhere. Kaveh would find and interrogate the Hand—and all those who led to and from him—to determine the real truth of the temple from the thief's bloodstained lips.

"You should really play the games, Kaveh dear."

"I leave them to you." A lie if there ever was one. Kaveh left all games to their father.

Kaveh held little love for the siblings who obsessively stalked the political arenas. What spewed from their mouths never matched the expressions in their eyes. And they plotted against their father, mothers, and one another instead of serving the empire like the warriors, the scholarly, and the civically minded imperial children.

Aros smiled, as if he knew exactly what Kaveh was thinking.

"At some point the front will be at an end, the battles will all be fought and won by you, every country in this world under our rule, and you'll have to exist inside of the empire like the rest of us. How will you do that, Imperator General?"

"I am unlikely to escape the fate of most commanders on a decades-long battlefront. I'm certain my death will please you greatly when it occurs."

"It will make things easier for me, certainly. You have so *little* weakness to exploit otherwise," he said contemplatively. "Finding points to apply pressure to is an ever-laborious chore."

Unlike Aros, whose points were easy to find. But few survived pressing them.

"Only the emperor is held dear to you," Aros mused. "It is your greatest shield, your lack of care for others. We are alike in that, though only you will feel the need to avenge Simin or Baksis when they are slain—maybe even a few of the more bookish idiots and your generals—but, even then, it would be out of a sense of duty rather than true rage. Not even the death of your magnificent mother would truly touch you."

"How is your wound, Aros?" Kaveh asked calmly, flipping the last pages. "Still unhealed? I've heard shadowburns are excruciatingly painful and that hers remain unabated until they consume the recipient."

Aros smiled and touched the side of his stomach. "Held in stasis in its place of honor, as always. Irsula was wasted on our father."

"Mmmm. Nera is certainly happy for the waste. And Etelian, favorite that he is." No one had any question that Etelian, perfect of face and weak in character, was Nera's favorite, not Aros or any of the other, lesser siblings born of Nera and Sher Fehl.

"Now Kaveh, everyone knows the emperor's favorite, and it's not Etelian." Aros's eyes glittered.

Kaveh didn't take the bait. "Etelian will remain on Tehrasi's throne, no matter what you wish."

Aros smiled sharply. "That is my problem to deal with, as always. You just find the thief."

Kaveh scooped up the papers and turned.

He felt the shift, the anticipation, and flicked three shadows in the bushes to intercept the ceremonial dagger descending rapidly toward the back of his neck.

He didn't turn to see the aftermath. He didn't need to as the shadows provided him eyes.

Aros laughed as he pierced the two shadows strangling

his arm and the one around his throat, flesh burning beneath. With his enchanted sunlight dagger, he ripped them away in a spray of gray mist. But even with his toy, he couldn't stand against the multitude that Kaveh could call.

"You shouldn't turn your back on me, Kaveh," Aros said lightly, feral pleasure in his eyes.

Ifret was already bounding back, and Kaveh let the shadow slip around the outside of his cloak. "I never do, Aros."

Kaveh strode away without looking back.

~*~

Kaveh read through the documents on the Hand. Public humiliation of the scholari and padifehl, destruction of property and secrets—those things made sense. Some of the thief's other exploits didn't add together, however. The public works? Deliberately getting the public on the thief's side, maybe. Deliberate or not, it had become a good tactic, and had been employed frequently by the thief, if the number of times random bystanders helped the man was any indication.

But the instances outside the capital city—there was little that would aid the thief in helping a farming guild in Rhedes. A specific instance of helping someone the thief knew could explain one incident. But there were lists of jobs the thief had done across the empire. Either this was a long con to enlist future help, or the thief was on a mission to spread knowledge outward and to bring more back to Tehrasi.

Combined with the goal of taking out the scholari and padifehl, though, it didn't make sense. Spreading knowledge was in alignment with the goals of the empire. The emperor was a proponent of progress and prosperity. The elite of Tehrasi, less so, admittedly, but why would a common thief care about such things?

No, he was dealing with a not-so-common thief who stole documents detailing the whereabouts of the Temple of the Scepter, then "lost them" again.

If Kaveh's orders were simply to kill the thief, he would have started with the first thief he saw on the street and worked his way through to the last one standing. However, obtaining the scepter was the primary goal, with information retrieval coming in a hard second.

He needed to make certain he captured the right villain from the start and used the correct way to apply pressure.

Ifret wound around his neck, then down his arm, as hungry to be back on the battlefront as he was.

He could still kill this Hand and backtrack his identity, then kill everyone he had contact with until the scepter whereabouts were in his palm. But a modicum of patience ensuring that the first assassination was the correct one would reduce the overall time spent on this Sehk-Ra damned endeavor.

Once the thief knew he was being hunted by Kaveh, a new set of variables would be put into play. Kaveh couldn't let that happen. The faster he got the information, the faster he could determine whether the scepter was fact or myth—painted legend or whispered relic.

If Osni had the real temple's location and found the

scepter while Kaveh was finding the thief, Aros would take care of the scholari. Kaveh wasn't blind to all the reasons Aros was in Tehras when the emperor usually tried to keep his eldest from the soil of Tehrasi.

~*~

The Hand was silent during the first three days of Kaveh's vigil. Kaveh's boredom and inherent frustration with being assigned this tedious task was only alleviated by the promise of the extermination of a defeat that had bothered the emperor since the death of the Carres.

He slid through the shadows as a man and woman whispered below.

The lack of movement by the thief wasn't unexpected, according to the whispers in the streets. The man in the mask was an opportunist—but an opportunist the citizens were far more able to anticipate than Kaveh had expected. They even had an entire group name for those wanting to give assistance—the Fingers of the Hand.

"The Fingers posted a note that odd omens have coiled in Tehras. Demons roam the dark corners. The portents swirl in odd directions. The Hand will need help."

"What do you think it means?"

Kaveh thought it meant that they were both traitors. He sent a wisp of shadow to lightly score their farhanies with shadow tears, as he'd done to the last five dozen traitors he'd tagged. There'd be plenty of time to send cleaners around the city after the thief was taken care of.

He was here to rid the city of a specific rot first.

"Probably just an increase in investigorii attention. It won't matter. The Hand can do anything. He can fight, heal, control the winds, the wards, the seas—he is everything and no one at all. He can disappear at will and reappear wherever he desires."

Kaveh highly doubted it. Though the skill wasn't outside the realm of possibility, magi who could open ripgates were exceedingly rare. There weren't any gatemakers currently alive—they would have been chained to service immediately upon showing their powers. Even the lesser desired magi with gatekeeping ability were snatched up quickly for their ability to manipulate gate coordinates in established gates without needing extensive artifacts to aid them.

"A master of weather, earth, and trickery. A myth, a legend," the man murmured.

It was inconceivable that a man would be skilled at so many things. Therefore, it was far more likely that the man had created the legend around himself.

"I'd make him a legend." The woman leered. "He just needs to visit my chambers and remove his disguise."

Kaveh had figured out quickly that there were many citizens who arrayed themselves around the Hand, yet no one had offered a name or hinted at a description to the shadows. Hired hands, or opportunistic aides.

Traitors. He stroked the shadow that had marked them. They'd meet their deserved ends with a single signal when this affair was done.

"Sway your hips in his direction tomorrow," the man said.

"There's a shipment of scripts going out tomorrow night through an eastern gate. The Polingsa manuscripts. He won't let those slip his grasp."

"The Polingsas' warding enchantments?" The woman's eyes grew fevered. "We will all know the spells within them soon, then."

The man nodded. "The Hand is always generous."

She frowned. "But an eastern gate? I heard tell that the Hand might have need of aid in the western districts after sunset tomorrow but before midnight. A number of devotees plan to head there at dark's descent."

"Two tasks in one night, then." The man shrugged. "The Hand is a marvel."

Kaveh hooked shadows to the woman's hem and the man's sandal. The waiting would be over soon.

He hoped the Hand used his last day well.

Bazaar Movements

NINLI

Tehras, Tehrasi

The softly flowing banners of the District Seven bazaar blew steadily overhead, propelled by the blistering breezes of the desert sun. Nin and Taline made their way slowly through the marketplace, blending in with the crowds and stopping from time to time to sample wares and purchase goods. Crows dove between the khursifas crisscrossing the main paths, sending small, darting shadows between the flickering shade cast by the khursifas—small bits of relief from the hot sun in a district that sat between two sets of weather spells.

At this time of year, the heat was nothing new, but the strange feeling of being watched was. There were no investigorii actively working the area—Nin knew the feeling of their magic. The Hand was still being actively sought by the investigorii for crimes that had been committed, but their presence had diminished drastically with Osni's need to leverage forces for the assault on the temple. The city's main strike force was hunting for the scepter, leaving behind only the regular patrol.

It would be remarked upon as strange if the Hand *wasn't* seen going after the Polingsa manuscripts. And Qara had put too much effort into getting her family's manuscripts in the open—it would be suspicious to change anything now. Nin knew that some of the investigorii would be hiding in wait—the investigore wasn't a stupid man. But they could be easily avoided with one of the many plays Nin and Taline had readied. There should be nothing to cause this feeling of unease.

Nin tried to shake off the pressing feeling of danger as she stopped to admire a lovely caftan, pulling the collar of the garment toward her. It was the day after the dark moon, and that meant deliveries would be expected. She leaned closer and softly shook a bundle of papyri from her sleeve and into the sleeve of the caftan she was admiring. They'd been waiting to deliver that bundle for a week now, and it felt good to finally get it into circulation.

Her fingers moved to the next garment on display while Taline haggled with the shopkeeper in the stall to her right.

"I don't know..." Taline hemmed.

"Try this one, young miss. The best honey in ten kingdoms." Other customers rummaged through the baskets around them as they swapped jars.

"In ten kingdoms?" her sister replied dubiously.

Movement to the other side had Nin shifting her gaze. A woman without distinguishing features grabbed the caftan that Nin had concealed the papyri in, as well as the garment next to it. Nin let a small smile curve—the local farmers needed new production options that weren't "gifted" by the elite, and the information contained in the scrolls would let them move forward on their own terms.

She stepped out, moved to the next shop, and slipped the next batch of scrolls into a decorative urn.

The elite had grown fatter in the ten years under the empire. The empire had brought riches and astounding advancement, and those in the best positions to receive the technology had done so with alacrity. Those without the resources to pounce...had been forced to scrape by. The elite had quickly figured out how to own the new progress and control the supply lines before the knowledge became readily available to the masses.

Nin was just making sure the masses had the same opportunities.

Her gaze drifted back to the stall where Taline was still haggling, but at the same time moving her deft fingers over the ceramic jars.

A sleight of hand from Taline, and a slip of papyrus was tucked beneath the honey pot. "Very well. Not this one, though. A smaller pot would be lovely." Taline withdrew her coin purse.

The man grabbed the larger pot, tipping it toward her with one hand. "Are you certain?" he asked, as his other hand swept the first pot, retrieved the note, and slipped the paper beneath the counter.

"The smaller one, please." Taline smiled.

The old shop owner turned a little pink even as he gruffly produced a smaller jar from behind the shelf. No one was immune to her sister's smile.

Nin planted another set of papyri enchantments for basic mechanical wonders into a satchel in a third stall, then moved on to the luxury fabric and accessory stall next in line.

She let her fingers run softly across bolts of beautiful fabric imported from Indi, Moru, Odryssa, and Punt, the four corners of the vast empire. An array of sensual textures and colors spread before her, from delicate silks in every hue to luxurious winter furs and soft, pliable leathers. Fabrics seamstresses would use to create gorgeous garments for any climate, from the southern edges where the desert transitioned to thick forests of humid rain and predatory animals, and from the temperate coastal regions to the harsh snow-covered mountain ranges.

Moving to the rear of the stall, where accessories were displayed, Nin's questing fingers ghosted over a decorative, expensive satchel and slipped a set of Heka slates into it.

She then touched a delicate, bejeweled headdress with its attached blue silk veil. Lorsali would have loved it.

Lorsali carefully arranged the beautiful blue and green silk glittering with jewels—setting off her lovely amber eyes, her deep glossy brown hair, and impeccably maintained skin. She glowed like the vast colors of the beach on the Medit Sea with its rich multi-colored sand and jeweled tones.

Nin reached out to touch the silk and Lorsali batted her hand away.

"Begone." Lorsali drew kohl along the underside of her eyes—making them stand out even more. "I don't care about what power they think a mongrel like you will be able to wield. Or what your eyes mean. You are a repellent tool—like that shadow monster boy the Fehl upstart wields. I don't want your greasy fingers contaminating anything. Four princes and the sons of five governors are attending the Gate Festival, and while the prince of Zenure is handsome and pliable, the governor's son from the Mining District is said to be beyond divine. With two million people in attendance, it is imperative to craft a presence. A smart woman desires many options on the groom's side of the temple's marriage staircase, but for her to be the only one on the bride's."

Nin stared with hungry eight-year-old eyes at the blue silk—so vibrant that the dye must have been made by the goddess Gripna herself.

She found herself wanting such beauty with a fierceness she didn't understand. Wanted to look like the princess before her, who knew how to arrange herself to best vantage even in a sea of millions. Wanted to look like her, for just one single moment.

It would be a terrifying thrill—the idea of being stared at like people stared at Lorsali. One moment would be more than enough.

"It's beautiful," she whispered to herself.

Lorsali looked her up and down. "Only on one born to wear it. No use setting finery to dirt."

"Are you going to buy it?" Taline said, shaking Nin out

of her trance. Taline looked at her with a half-amused, half-exasperated expression, a full shopping satchel slung over her shoulder. "Or are you going to stare at it longingly until it follows you home?"

"No. Of course not." Nin let her fingers drop and smiled ruefully. "Could you imagine me in something like this?"

Taline frowned. "Yes. What's to imagine? It's sitting right there next to your head."

"No, I meant..." Nin shook her head. "It reminded me of someone. That's all."

Taline's eyes narrowed and she looked at the garment, then back to Nin. It was a look that never boded well for Nin. "You are allowed to wear pretty things."

"Yes, of course." Nin took her arm and maneuvered them out of the colorful stall. It had been their last stop.

"You are allowed pretty things," Taline repeated more forcefully, digging her heels in.

Nin smiled. "I have you. Nothing is prettier."

"Nin."

"What need have I for such finery? I'm hardly likely to attend a cassirie."

"You could. Indi has a masked festival every fourth moon cycle. The padifehl there is said to throw the most sumptuous of affairs." Nin could hear the longing in Taline's voice. "We could sneak in...pretend we belong."

"Go to the next one." Nin gently tugged at the cuff of her sister's sleeve. *Find a new home with all the comforts that should be yours—belong in truth...* "Bring me back a gazing ball of all the delights."

One day Taline would leave. It was the inevitability of all Nin's companions—that they would one day leave. That they *should leave.* For their safety, she wanted them to go, for she knew her own end.

Before Taline came into her life, the inescapable loneliness had been softened knowing that those she had rescued were all safe, living under new identities—most of them still working toward a common goal, just in safer locales with new, less-colorful lives.

She still wasn't certain what she had done to deserve Taline staying at her side for so long, but even after being together for so many years, Nin regularly updated documents with three identities for Taline, for whenever the moment came that she would leave.

"You will come with me. And we will have a splendid time."

Nin smiled. "Someday."

"You pay for others' sins." Taline's voice was harsh and distressed.

Nin looked away. "Of course I don't." She tugged Taline under an awning as they reached the edge of the next district, where rain was pelting in a torrent of manufactured lines.

They ducked between the many patterned tarps pulled above the alley to protect the bazaar from the strange combination of weather enchantments the stormbrewers and sunchasers had decided to cast today in the three surrounding districts—full sun, oppressive heat, and torrential rain.

The Weather Guild catered to all types of businesses in the districts, so on off-days, when the perfect climate was not in store, other solutions had to be found.

That was one thing that had *not* changed with the empire—people and businesses squabbling to push forward their own interests. It had perhaps even increased with the streamlining of the enchantments and the overwhelming advancements they had brought with them.

"Nin, I'm seri—" Taline stopped dead in the street before the man who stood blocking their path.

Nin smiled tightly at Investigore Malit, head of all enforcement in Tehras, as he stood in full dress regalia between the deluge on one side of the street and the blazing heat of the other, steam rising in the middle to curl around his body.

"Ninli al Six el Healer il Tehras ol Gomen ul Summora." The investigore was a tall, taciturn man known for being both scarily competent and rigidly married to the law. It wasn't the first time she'd been so addressed by him. "And Taline al Four el Healer il Tehras ol Gomen ul Summora. What a pleasant surprise."

"Full imperial names today, Investigore?" Nin tipped her head. "And here I thought that we'd come to a less formal agreement after your nephew's birth. I can't say that I know what temple you took your oath in or where you were born or what your professed power level is, though you do have a fondness for the Gomen district's house of worship, so I'll give it a try. Malik al Seven el Investigore il Tehras ol Gomen ul Malit?"

"Tehrasia, actually."

"Ah." She nodded. "The royal temple. A lovely place, I'm told."

"I'm sure," he said somewhat dryly.

She smiled. She never regretted saving him when they tussled in the streets, even when extensively questioned later.

"Where were you ten nights ago, Healer Six Summora?"

He ignored Taline completely, which was for the best as she was inching something from her sleeve. Nin stepped in front of her to block her sister from the view of the head of the investigorii or any minions he might have hiding in the bazaar.

"Ten nights ago? Goodness. Let's see. I was out. So was Taline. On visits. The life of a healer is one of constant movement."

"Visits to patients? Which ones?" He flipped open a canister filled with delicate machinery.

Nin stared straight at the investigore. "The Lendowez family. The Meydehs. The Calipsines. Core and Timón ul Smothen. Two men passed out in the streets—one in the center of Yerl, the other in Bypen District. You can ask the streetwatchers there."

"I have a feeling each will have a grand story of how much time you spent there and the lives you saved." He stared into the canister, checking her oaths. He'd find no answers there, though, not for the questions he really wanted to ask. "And not that you were opening doors or throwing waste magic in the streets."

She tilted her head. "As you say, Investigore. Neither of us are followers of that brigand."

He flipped the canister shut. "I'm certain you healed those people. Probably for nothing more than the meal you may have consumed to maintain your healing strength. And I'm certain you didn't spend your full night doing so. Just as I'm certain Healer Tenzig will have a story to cover all the other bits of time needed for accounting."

"You seem to have all your answers then. Are we free to return home now?"

"Healer Six Summora. Healer Four Summora." He tipped his head. "Do stay in tonight."

He turned and strode away in precise, military strides. He'd been a young captain of Tehrasi before the empire had taken over, then risen quickly in the imperial ranks under their efficient system of enforcement and merit.

"He thinks us minions." Taline's voice was a mixture of delight and disgruntlement. "How many people did he interrogate before getting to us ten days later?"

"He relies far too much on logic, but he's a good man, underneath his disciplined facade. He'd probably champion the library himself if everyone volunteered the information and agreed to strict rules of comport inside." Nin grinned, then frowned as she inched the translated weather schedule from under her sister's arm. "The spells have been set by the Weather Guild to storm in Arcadie this eve? All night?"

Taline nodded sharply, gaze moving restlessly around the thinning crowds. "The perfect setup—and the Weather Guild scheduled their monthly meeting for this eve. It will last until the morning hours—since two thousand harping insults take time to exchange—and they use their best spells against one another as they argue. The manuscripts are in a district on the other side of the city from the guild, however."

"Lovely. We can even tell the investigore truthfully tomorrow that each of us were nowhere near the other site."

"Let us drop one task. There's an ill wind." Taline looked to the distance beyond the falling curtain of rain. "I don't like splitting up this eve. We can get the weather enchantments another time."

"They have patched all that you wrought through the city ten days ago, though. We need to know what enchantments they plan to implement next."

Of the two tasks planned for the eve, the one that required observation and recording skills was tailor-made for Taline with her diligent scripture and perfect recall—an in-and-out task made for a ghost. As to the manuscripts, Nin was best suited for any physical or intuitive task—or anything that could go pear-shaped. Because of her background and the way her power manifested, she could get out of almost any trap she found herself in.

Taline frowned at the sky before they entered their building and ascended the long, winding stairs to their rooms.

"Farsa, Meran, and Sari are in tonight, if an emergency occurs." Nin locked their door behind them. "And the caravan route is the same."

Taline turned her frown to the spread documents on the table. "I don't like that part either. Promise me, no rescues tonight."

"Honestly, it's as if you think I rescue every orphan off the street."

"You do."

Nin rolled her eyes, then leaned over and planted a kiss on Taline's cheek. "It'll be fine. Let's give the investigorii a bit of fun tonight."

~*~

Later that night, right before they set out, Taline finished translating spells from fifteen handwritten slips of papyrus, and set parameters for others as she worked, painstakingly setting triggers to spellboxes, then setting them aside so Nin could power them.

In between powering the boxes—something she could do without conscious thought at this point—Nin stared at the totem, tracing her gaze down the carvings, but keeping it far from reach. They had been careful not to touch it more than was necessary, and only with reinforced gloves. The Carres had loved their poison traps as much as they had loved their festivals of blood and sacrifice.

The marks on the totem were deliberately made to confuse. Only when inside the temple with the totem in hand would the correct path be revealed. Slotting the totem into place and providing the correct key sequence would reveal the antechamber beyond. The totem needed to be manipulated inside the temple—so removing it from the temple rendered it useless.

Her mind went to the bloodstained hall containing the totem. How many had died trying to retrieve the totem or to enter the sealed antechamber beyond before they had admitted defeat and turned the information over to the empire?

With the lure of such a prize, the halls of the scepter had been filled with blood—blood that seeped into stone cracks to further sustain the enchantments that fed themselves in a never ending cycle.

Only tricks gleaned from a dark childhood in the palace had allowed her to secure the prize inside. She now held the totem, the key to locating the scepter, in her hands—it need only be fitted in its final lock.

It need only be fitted in place...and she could retrieve a scepter she could wield. A scepter to key all others.

She stared hard at the relic and tried to shake the dark, curling thoughts.

The totem held no dark power of its own, but the enticement of its master could almost be felt reaching through the ceramic. With effort, she looked away, concentrating instead on Taline.

Her sister was strong. So strong. In the temple, gloved and with a small jar of stolen magic, stolen clay, and a stolen ink-dispensing reed, Taline had painstakingly duplicated the totem, adding tiny modifications. Anyone who had seen it from afar would think it authentic, but if they tried to use it as a key, they would be in for a nasty surprise.

Meanwhile, the real totem would be kept safe.

Taline reached forward and pulled a cloth over the top of the totem, hiding it from Nin's view, and giving her a careful look. Taline patted her hand before returning to her spellboxes and translations. Nin allowed herself a deep breath, broken from the spell.

Nin brushed her fingers across the back of her chair where the veiled headdress from the bazaar was carefully draped over the wood. Taline had disappeared for an hour before dinner and then claimed no knowledge of how the beautiful piece had appeared on Nin's favorite chair.

Love, hope, and new memories to overshadow the old.

Nin touched the delicate fabric of the headdress and felt the first stirrings of true hope. Maybe there would be a future not overshadowed by her past.

She lifted her tools, slotting them carefully into place around her belt sash. Nothing was going to go wrong tonight.

121

CAGES IN THE NIGHT

KAVEH

TEHRAS, TEHRASI

Kaveh stoically watched the thief steal the expensive manuscripts designed to lure him in, then watched the man make fools of the investigorii sent to capture him. He watched the way the man moved.

The citizenry intervened three times when a move was made against their folk hero. The thief didn't need the assistance—flitting quickly and smartly through the streets—but help was readily available.

If the thief weren't a traitor, he'd make an excellent imperial asset.

Kaveh learned three things from watching the man. One, the thief made every effort to keep others from being harmed—he had a strange sense of duty to the citizens and even the officers sent to apprehend him. Two, he was intensely chaotic. As noted by others, he displayed a wide range of skills, but none of his famed spellboxes had been used when, in at least two instances, doing so would have proved helpful. Furthermore, the thief had missed two written signs that had been expressly engraved to assist him— one at a baker's shop and the other at a cowlmaster's.

And lastly, to account for his knowledge of where an opponent would land—or a strike would fall—the thief either possessed the collar of a luck demon or he could absorb knowledge from the city itself.

A sad waste of a superior skillset. In another life, Kaveh could have conscripted him into his shadow army. Instead, the thief would die ignobly in an alley tonight.

Kaveh followed from the shadows as the thief picked his way carefully through back streets, manuscripts tucked securely under his shirt.

True efficiency would have been swallowing the slender man in darkness and forcing the entirety of his guts through his nose, but—and it was why he hated tasks such as this—securing knowledge and acting in overall secrecy bested expeditious removal.

Interrogation would reveal who else needed to be removed from the world of the living tonight.

But if watching the thief had shown him anything, it was that the man wouldn't have stolen documents detailing the location of the Temple of Darkness, then done nothing with them. He'd bet half his shadow army that if the temple existed, the thief had already been there.

And that was why secrecy trumped efficiency. Rumor of any kind about the temple or its contents needed to be squelched before it had a chance to gain traction.

The thief, and everything he knew, would simply cease to exist tonight. And whatever knowledge—or stolen temple items—he had would be revealed before he took his last breath.

Kaveh waited for the thief to enter an alley free of bystanders, then he folded the alley into shadow—masking and caging it from outside view—and leaped.

The thief threw himself to the side and shoved three tightly pointed fingers upward, as if he could feel Kaveh descending upon him, or read Kaveh's killing intent.

He really would have made a good addition to his ranks.

Kaveh shoved the reaching fingers to the side with a palm strike against the thief's wrist and pulled a shadow around the thief's small neck.

The thief twisted with the movement—trying to deduce what had wrapped his throat—and another set of fingers struck Kaveh's side, sending debilitating magic through his system and shutting down embalming point three—his liver. Kaveh directed a shadow against the strike point automatically, then looped and pulled the shadow taut around the thief's throat.

The shadow abruptly snapped tight and knotted only itself—a noose without substance between its threads.

The thief landed in a crouch on the sand and grime floor of the alley three paces to the right of where he *should* have been, his neck free of restraint. The man's body was tight with awareness and shock.

Kaveh felt a real curl of interest despite the mundane nature of the task. He narrowed his eyes as the slipped shadow merged with its brethren writhing en masse at his feet. He couldn't recall the last time he had to make a second attempt at a shadow wrap.

He called a brace of shadows to curl over the figure at the same time he halted the foreign magic trying to invade his liver. "What did you find at the temple?"

The thief shifted a foot into a stance Kaveh was familiar with—he was going to run.

A predictable and dull response.

His curiosity receded. Likely, the tedious nature of this assignment had made Kaveh sloppy in attaching the shadow to the thief's throat. Kaveh flicked his finger in disinterest and five shadows from the brace shot around the thief's wrists, ankles, and throat, pinning him to the writhing wall like a stuck insect.

Kaveh stepped forward, thoroughly bored once more. Sehk-damned Osni. Sehk-damned Etelian. "The temple—"

Fingers jabbed sharply into his arm—mysteriously *freed* fingers. Agony twisted the tendons and lit his nerves on fire. His boredom vanished, and only reflexive action born of experience saved him from further injury. Ifret slipped from his neck—poisoned shadow spewing from her mouth.

He could feel the spike of terror from the thief, who twisted under the hissing onslaught and darted to the other side of the alley, still penned in by the dense, corporeal gloom Kaveh had created for the interrogation.

Kaveh placed his hand against Ifret's head, halting the thief's certain death. They still had to get informa—

Taking advantage of his attacker's hesitation, the thief dashed forward, jabbing Kaveh's other wrist. Agonizing flame *scorched* beneath his skin, as if his blood had been set to boiling.

How *interesting*.

He smiled and his scorched fingers shot out to grab the thin stalk of the thief's neck. He lifted the man, ignoring the excruciating pain radiating through his wrist. The thief dangled, strangling, in midair for a split second, surrounded by writhing shadows and the firm grip of a hand capable of dealing death. Then Kaveh's fingers crushed into one another—fingernails scoring his skin—as the throat he had been strangling disappeared, along with the figure it was attached to.

He turned slowly.

The thief was crouched on the ground two paces away, shaking his head in disbelief—as if he'd expected to find himself farther away.

An ability like Aros's phasing?

Had Aros sired a bastard who shared his powers? Aros was careful and had no children as far as Kaveh knew, but Aros played a deep game. And it wouldn't be the first time an imperial child had been found on the streets. It wouldn't even be the hundredth.

Thirty-one-year-old Etelian had a fourteen-year-old bastard among his countless spawn strewn across the empire. It was physically possible for Aros, a year and a half older than Etelian, to have one running the streets as well. The thief was small enough to pass for fourteen, and the streets raised the young fast.

The thief launched himself forward, fingers brushing Kaveh's midsection. Kaveh felt his lungs being compressed, but he absorbed the pain and whirled with the figure's motion, using his clenched fist to knock the lunging thief into the wall. Shadows reached up to secure him more firmly, but once again the thief transported himself to the other side of the alley, as if he had used the shadows themselves to move.

An interesting ability, but it was obvious from the entire interaction that the thief wasn't a fighter—that he was accustomed to using tricks and a well-known landscape— because he was reacting to the strikes, unnerved, not using techniques that had been practiced for use against a trained killer.

Kaveh tightened the perimeters of the shadow cage, pulling the walls closer and throwing his forearm against the other's chest, pinning him to the wall.

It had been a long time since he'd done anything *other* than annihilate an opponent on the field of battle, but he hadn't forgotten how to inflict pointed amounts of pain. He snapped the thief's left wrist and used the shadows to crush both of the thief's ankles, hobbling him.

"Let's try this again." He read the movement of the

fingers above the thief's broken wrist and released Ifret instead of defending as the thief made a last jab—fingers barely moving under his pinned arm. The corporeal shadow attached to the jabbing fingers and spit around them— reversing the spell that was emanating out. The thief's body slumped forward with shuddered waves of pain—his own spell working against him.

No—*her* spell.

Kaveh felt the slight curves moving beneath his arm, heard the breathy exhalations of pain and adrenaline, and absorbed the details Ifret was sending about the makeup of the thief's magic and physical state. Not quite like Aros.

Interesting.

But ultimately pointless. Even if she was Aros's—which would be the slightest bit more interesting than one in the long line of Etelian's bastard children—he had information to gather, and the world was better off without another of Nera's line. He grabbed for the tendrils of oath that bound every citizen to the empire—that each citizen swore to, and that tied them to the empire in good standing—to force her to answer truthfully to whatever he asked.

There was nothing to grab.

He narrowed his eyes at the thief. "Oathbreaker."

As a favored son of the emperor, Kaveh had sworn fidelity to the fewest oaths possible, yet the ones that he affirmed, he believed in fully. The Hand had no oaths upon her with which to manipulate or identify—or to honor.

Getting rid of imperial oaths was impossible—but so too

was having none in the first place in a land sworn to the empire.

The figure made no response. She *did* disappear from his grip, though—one moment there, the next moment gone—which was far more of a surprise.

Kaveh braced his hand against the wall and turned slowly, surprise spiking into an interest far more intense. Phasing was a more gradual process—one he had trained Ifret to negate. What she had just done had not been a gradual phase.

With her crippled fingers and wrist curled into her chest, and her ankles unable to support her, she dropped to the floor of the alley, striking five points in rapid succession on the stones with her working hand. The shadow cage retreated, and reality pulled back around them—making the very air swirl into a vortex. Only the absolute control he had over the shadows draping the entire alley allowed him to maintain the cage, pulling it back into the form she was trying to break.

Very interesting.

He pushed from the wall and stalked slowly toward her. "By itself, the penalty for breaking an oath is death."

Her fingers worked fast, jabbing at her ankles in bright flares of healing blue, and she hopped up into a standing crouch. Holding herself in ready position, trying to read his next move, she slapped her broken wrist against her hip, enveloping it, too, in healing blue.

He didn't usually play with his food, but for the first time that night, he considered his next move.

If he wanted, he could suffocate her within the shadow

cage—could thickly constrict it around her and squeeze until her insides turned out. Her ability to slip from individual shadows wouldn't save her from a cage of them.

He knew she understood the danger, too, from the way she held herself on the balls of her feet, and in the way the movement of her head gave away a hidden, but darting gaze.

She was smart enough to know how to remove imperial oaths, and she had some ability to travel. She'd been able to slip from his physical grasp, but she was still in the cage. "Popping" wasn't rare, though it was still rather unusual. But creating the beginning of that vortex... It almost looked like the start of a ripgate.

If he pushed... Well, he'd get an answer either way.

Ifret wrapped his hand and he let the other shadows shape into monstrous forms on all sides of the cage.

"What did you steal from the temple?"

She crossed her arms in front of her in an X and the full force of a Level Nine sunlight spell lit the area, sending the converging shadows scuttling back.

He narrowed his eyes. Few magi could fight the shadows. It could be that she had access to a relic that produced sunlight. Or, it could be something else.

But she could only dodge and deflect for so long. Her last bids at freedom only meant that the fight would last another thirty seconds.

He raised a shadow to overwhelm her from behind. She jabbed it, and it dropped. Another jab made the next in line drop as well. Neither shadow rose again; they lay like blank spots in the landscape.

Silence encompassed the alley as they both stared at the fallen shadows in disbelief.

She was the first to recover and didn't hesitate—hacking through the cage in a flurry of motion.

His curiosity piqued, overtaking his initial goal, and he strode behind her as she broke through—sending shadows to nip at her heels and bite at her throat—seeing what else she would do, then shoring up the openings in the shadows she defeated.

He tipped his head. With each of her responses, he learned more. Unwittingly, she was helping him make the cage stronger. He hadn't realized that was even possible.

It was midnight, and the entire town was now cast in shadow, and as they moved from the alley, she began darting around and trying to keep the civilians out of harm's way. It was a tactic that would get her killed. Casualties were a part of war and it was stupid to give oneself such weaknesses.

He briefly considered grabbing two of the civilians and holding them hostage. However, he hadn't been so intrigued by anyone in a long time, and the outcome of this fight, no matter how narrowly amusing, wasn't in question. He could afford to indulge a bit.

He wrapped himself in the connected shadows between them, and exited the shadowed mass in front of her instead of following behind.

He let the woman hit him in the shoulder, deadening his

right arm again, but bringing her closer. Kaveh whipped the shadow around her torso and yanked her chest against his, pulling the mass around them like a sandstorm of darkness, tightly encasing them in enough darkness that even Aros wouldn't be able to escape.

"Too slow," he whispered down into her masked ear, a smile curving his mouth inside the swirling mass of writhing shadows.

He could feel her panic in the connection from her skin to his as he slid his fingers beneath the long, hooded mask and around the soft skin of her slim throat. Victims telegraphed their emotions when shadowtouched, and skin to skin, there was no way to escape having thoughts leak through. But the thief should have thought of that when she decided on her traitorous path.

Escape, escape, must use it, can't, must, can't, Ta—

A blast of sound emerged from her mind, then another. He squeezed, pulling his fingertips together in a clawed shape, and her struggling body stilled as all the shadows of the district circled them in death's embrace. There was nowhere to go anymore.

Nowhere, must—

"That's right," he soothed as a shadow slipped from his fingers to form a full collar around the skin of her throat. "It will be over soon. Now tell me what I want to know. Tell me quickly," he whispered, "and I'll only kill you instead of you and everyone you hold dear."

Terror, unsurprisingly, flooded her thoughts. But terror

was boring; more interesting was the resolve that hardened every other emotion.

Must, rang out.

A single hand sign against his chest was the only warning he had before she disappeared—one second held against him; the next, nowhere in sight. The freed air whirled gently around him in direct opposition to the sudden maelstrom within. The shadows that had been caging them dropped, then shot out in a flurry, like crows dispersed suddenly.

Kaveh shot them in all directions, searching.

Any lingering boredom disappeared with the tremors in the ground and the single coil of wind she had left behind.

He smiled slowly. There was only one type of magi with that ability...

He released Ifret, and the shadow shot off, forming figure eights too fast for the normal eye to see and marshaling all shadows in the surrounding neighborhood blocks. But the girl was nowhere near, the remnants of her power slipping away like sand in the wind.

A heavy beat started in his chest as he straightened.

He looked at his fingers—at the wrapped shadowy tendrils that swirled into place around him. How long had it been since someone had escaped his grasp?

He closed his eyes and reached out to the shadow he had slipped around her neck.

She was running on a rooftop. She was shooting a spell to someone on the ground, yelling in her mind—*go, run, flee, danger, Ta—no!* Then she was grabbing at her throat, and the shadow was violently expelled.

Magnificent.

He wrapped himself into darkness and rode the shadows to her location.

There was no one on the rooftop where she'd dropped the tracking shadow, but a black-clad figure with a distinctive white sash was sprinting through the street below. He recognized the area. It was the location of the second job mentioned on the streets—did the thief think she could still complete her second task? He dropped through the darkness, then shifted in front of the figure—spinning her around and lazily throwing her against a door.

She felt, strangely, the tiniest bit taller, and curvier. The white sash had been blowing in the breeze, but it suddenly surrounded her, lengthening—as if she were calling for help.

The breeze was snuffed beneath the shadow cage he erected. This time he made certain it was a complete cube.

She pushed against the shadow wall, trying to flee, then scrabbled back.

He took a moment to examine her posture as she froze in a state of shock she should have been accustomed to by now. He could see her physical terror but couldn't read her thoughts—there was no lingering emotional connection from the shadows he had attached. Strange. She had expelled the shadow, but in such proximity, a remnant should remain.

Even the emperor couldn't rid himself fully of one of

Kaveh's shadows in the span of a minute. Another oddity to add to the growing list.

"Now then. How did you accomplish that interesting little travel maneuver? I'm curious enough not to torture you immediately."

She struck out in a more conventional strike than she'd displayed before—a better strike from a trained fighter's perspective—but far less interesting and far less effective than her more unconventional previous approach.

He easily parried the attack, not even needing to shift his feet.

"If I wanted to kill you straightaway, I would have already."

She struck out again. It was almost clumsy—overly panicked. He frowned and blocked the attack.

Kaveh could beat conventional fighters with both arms removed.

He was interested whether she would try the same maneuver to break through the barrier, or whether she would show her tactical strategy once more, knowing that he wouldn't raise the same type of barrier twice.

But the thief barely looked at the barrier, other than in terror, before fighting against him directly—flinging handmade spellboxes that might immobilize another opponent, but that his shadows easily swept aside. He was finally seeing her famed spellboxes, but it was as if she'd learned nothing.

Within three more deflected strikes, he found himself flirting with boredom again.

Where was the creativity shown before? The unexpected thrill?

Dispassion descended as he countered another blow, allowing the fight to continue on her side, to see whether she would convert styles again. He knocked her back.

Dispassion quickly shifted to annoyance. The interaction in the other alley had been a blip, then. Or there was nothing left in her and she'd been using spells embedded in her clothes instead of inside her veins.

She'd used a gate medallion, then, to get here. How dissatisfying. Gate medallions were rare, but could be found for the right price.

He reached forward with a shadow-gloved grip to strangle the thief, rip the information from her, and end the game.

The air shimmered at his side and his reaching hand closed upon a fast-moving wind. The faintest brush of silk shifted against the back of his fingertips, throwing his arm off course as another figure shot between them.

With the barest remnants of his previous shadows expelling around her, the second figure pulled the first against her chest and both disappeared into the sandstone as they hit the ground.

Gone.

Dispassion broke beneath thrill once more, and he nearly laughed aloud as the pieces of the puzzle aligned. He sent his shadows in an exploratory outward burst out of habit, though he expected they would find nothing this time.

A third Hand would be even more unlikely than a second.

He could feel somewhere far away in the city—the last remnants of his shadows dispelled. The shadows whispered a moment later that the figure that had dropped their brethren was gone.

He looked at the spot where one dark figure had become two of similar size. Two women donning one role.

Of course. The mismatched patterns and abilities made into myth made complete sense now, even above the whirlwind of styles the first had displayed. He reordered the previously documented interactions in his mind, breaking them neatly into two columns of behavior and movement.

There were two of them. Maybe even more than two. Masquerading as the same person. And the accomplices who were sometimes mentioned—likely they were accomplice to the other.

Same size and body shape—or spelled to be that way. But *similar* enough, at least, to avoid detection when they weren't next to each other.

That no one had realized the Hand shifted identity was either a gross oversight, or a zealously guarded secret of the community.

And both were female. He'd stake his life on it.

The second one was of no consequence.

But the first...

He smiled. The first...

She had appeared in the middle of his shadow cage, then disappeared again with her partner. No gate medallion could do that.

A traveler, a gatekeeper, maybe even a gatemaker—an art so rare that it was frequently thought lost, and the reason that the Scepter of Darkness was so desperately needed.

But no art was ever truly lost. Since the deaths of the Carres and the Barrinis, it had only been a matter of time before another with the ability would rise outside the strict controls both families had kept upon anyone born with such power. The emperor had contingencies in place for just that occurrence.

And a collar.

Energy strummed through him and Kaveh smiled.

She had come for her compatriot. *Loved* her compatriot enough to reveal weakness.

Bait easily exploited.

He shifted priorities. Information and the scepter came first. But he'd be hunting to capture and chain now.

Easy enough to find the thief, now that he had the feel of her, oath or not.

He twisted into the shadows with a smile.

PANIC

NINLI

TEHRAS, TEHRASI

"Sehk, Sehk, *Sehk*."

Nin backed Taline against the most well-lit wall in their bedroom, scanning the shadows on the other sides.

She had only the vaguest notion of how shadow travel worked, but she was pretty sure that he couldn't pierce the twelve places of light she had jumped them through before returning home.

Still heaving from the rush of terror and pain, though, she pressed Taline behind her and waited for him to appear in a burst of malevolent shade.

"What...*who*?" Taline clutched her from behind. "It felt like all the air was disappearing around me. *How...what?* And, *Nin*. Nin, you *moved* us."

"He was going to kill you." Nin ripped off her hood, panting loudly, trying to gain air. She felt claustrophobic, suddenly, the air stifling around her like the cage of his shadows.

Sehk-Ra, she had felt his killing intent—his *annoyance*—through the shadow remnants that had stubbornly clung to her.

"He was going to kill you," Nin repeated, hand shaking.

"He *saw* you move us," Taline said, voice shrill.

"I *know*." She gripped her hood tightly to her chest. "There was nothing else I could do. I'd already fought him. Neither of us could beat him in a fair fight. We couldn't beat him in an unfair fight!"

She'd gone to warn Taline directly, because if he had found *Nin*, he would undoubtedly have intel elsewhere.

"But he *saw*—"

"I *know*. And his surprise was the only reason we escaped." The only reason Taline was still alive. Her hands shook. Whether he would have resurrected Taline to interrogate her elsewhere didn't matter. Nin would never have seen her again.

Taline slipped around to face her and Nin slumped against the wall.

"Who is he?"

"I didn't see his face. He wanted to know about the temple. Didn't even ask about the documents. He used the shadows against me."

"An illusion of shadows," Taline corrected forcefully. "He made an illusion of shadows around me, backed by a hidden field."

Nin closed her eyes and let her head hit the wall before opening them again. "That cage was no illusion. He is a shadow manipulator."

"He made it look like he was *using* shadows," Taline corrected, expression unable to grow more alarmed, though the muscles in her face were giving it a go.

He'd been *playing* with Taline before he'd grown annoyed and decided to end it. She'd seen it on his face right before she'd opened a ripgate at his side and grabbed Taline. He had been toying with Nin, too—of that she was sure. And wasn't that a terrifying concern.

Nin jerked her head in the negative. "They weren't for distraction and artifice. Not like an assassin making a showy death play due to a malicious customer's demand. That man...he used the shadows—made them do his bidding. I stunned two of them. One bit me. One bound me."

She shuddered and checked her throat for the fourth time. She had scanned Taline immediately after the first jump and in the third. But he hadn't used the shadows directly against her sister. That was the only thing that had given Nin enough time. Taline was a good fighter, but whoever the man was, he was way above either of their skill levels.

They trained for defense and evasion, not offense and assassination. Neither of them desired to be front line fighters and previously had no need to train for such fighting. Not that they would have been given that training by the empire—neither of them had the build or temperament to enlist.

That man, though... Nin had never felt that level of skill

and killing intent mixed with a truly undeniable amount of ennui—at least at the beginning of the fight—not even from Rone, who hid acute bloodlust beneath a charming, lazy facade.

She had been a dwarf beetle beneath his boot.

"The only ones I've heard with that ability are the Shadow Prince and his mother. But she is caged, and he would never be skulking in the slums of Tehrasi." Taline looked troubled, though. "Unless..."

Nin closed her eyes. "Unless the emperor sent him."

Taline made a strangled sound. "*No.*"

"I couldn't see beneath his cloak, so I can't confirm it, but..." Eyes, dark as night beneath a new moon. An overwhelming feeling of death, strength, and power—so much power. Nin shivered.

"If he *is* the Shadow Prince..." Taline ran a hand over her coiled plait of hair, loosening it with shaking fingers. "Sehk, only Aros would be worse."

No. Aros ul Fehl could be bought, for a *very* steep price—and Nin had made sure to carefully investigate what that price would be.

The cold and ruthless thirteenth blessed prince, on the other hand, cared nothing for anything they could offer. He was singularly loyal.

"*Whoever* he is, he thinks the Hand has already been to the temple."

A dangerous extrapolation to make, and a person with a killing intent like that...

"You need to run," Nin said distantly, letting her eyes slip closed. "Larit can make it look like you caught the plague. A healer slipping away after treating pestilence is a tidy solution. Qara will get you to Hosfuri with the other girls."

Taline reached out and grabbed her arm hard. "*Both* of us need to run."

"You know that will not work." The assassin would have had to realize there was more than one person playing at the Hand. Removing one of them from the field of play would work, though, and it had to be Taline. She wouldn't let Taline be interrogated.

Nin started to initiate the plague spell. It had only been a matter of time, anyway. It was truly a tidy solution. Taline would be free.

"No, *no.*" Taline ripped the spell from her. "Absolutely not."

"Tal—"

"I'm *not* leaving. You *know* I'm not."

"You—"

Taline bared her teeth. "I don't think so. *You* need my cooperation for a plague gambit, and I will not be giving it."

"We need—"

"Players who are desperate enough to play at the Hand and can disappear quickly? *Agreed.* And both Gantre brothers are available this week."

Even Taline's hasty solution couldn't cover her inherent distaste of the men. The Gantres would do anything for a price. Taline had never approved of the "anything" part of their parameters. Nin and Taline had made *especially* sure never to have contact with them without a disguise in place. The Gantres would sell them out to the empire faster than a hot wind whipping over the dunes.

"We can't use them—"

"The gold crescent spellbox they've wanted since the Loh theft will provide sufficient motivation for one of them to appear as the Hand tomorrow night—with simple and quick objectives and *no deaths.*"

"That they might face the Shadow Prince himself isn't worth *any* fee." Nin would not set anyone up for death.

"Such a challenge will likely make the job more desirable to them," Taline said darkly.

"They won't win." And Nin was starting to think that neither would she win with Taline.

They might truly have to run. She tried not to let relief mingle with her despair. The relief just secured the notion that she was a terrible person. There were still things she *owed* Tehrasi.

"Then I'll tell them they need to run as if their lives depended on it, if they see him." Taline was already scribbling glyphs over a sheet of papyrus. "We will set up residence elsewhere for a time. Qara will get us papers. We'll get clearance for a gate by week's end, or we will—"

They wouldn't have a week. The assassin who had chased them would find them again. Soon.

She looked at Taline as her sister continued to murmur. What was their best play? Was it time? She touched the handheld looking glass on the table, afraid to view herself looking back.

You? You will never wield my scepter.

Nin shoved those words back into their dark place. She covered the looking glass with her hand. Hubris to believe there had been time to play. Time stood before her, waiting for her to grab it.

Her fingers curled around the *Ritual of Three Moons* scroll and she took a deep breath. "I will retrieve the scepter."

The tip of Taline's reed stuttered across the papyrus. She stared up at her. "Nin, if you touch the scepter—"

"I know." Nin rubbed a thumb along the scroll, then put it in her day pack. "But it can't stay where it is. We run with it. We destroy it. And if we can do neither—it is the ultimate negotiation tool. We can get rid of Osni and Etelian for good."

"But *you*—"

"We could force them to put Baksis in charge," Nin said, rolling quickly over Taline's half-formed words. "Or even move Shiera as padifehl. We could use it to win."

"But you can't—"

"We could win."

"The emperor will then have the Scepter of *Darkness*."

"Better than Crelu ul Osni."

"*Nera* will never allow Etelian to be unseated," Taline stressed. The most favored wife of the emperor wielded great power, especially where her favorite son was concerned. "You said it yourself years ago. That is why we've been—"

CHAPTER EIGHT

"For the Scepter of Darkness, much can be leveraged."

Taline tapped agitated fingers against the desk. "Getting the scepter is a plan—*except* for the fact that you can't read, and I can't decipher the glyphs quickly enough to aid us in the temple. We only secured the totem because of your previous knowledge. The scepter is an entirely different matter. We'd need to engage a treasure hunter."

Nin's expression didn't change.

TALINE

Taline knew immediately where this conversation was going. "*No.*"

"He will do it," Nin said simply. "He knows we will pay, and he knows scepter lore better than anyone besides Osni and me."

They had the totem, but it would have to be placed in a designated spot in the temple's antechamber to be deciphered. And physical circumstances ten years ago had made it so that Nin's brain...could no longer process written text.

Rone ul Valeran, interpreter of a thousand languages and puzzles, treasure hunter extraordinaire, would have no trouble deciphering that which her sister and she could not.

"*No.*"

"We need him."

"He's a scoundrel."

"He'll do it."

"I don't *trust him.*"

"I know." Nin's fingers wrapped her wrist. "Will you leave me to this quest? Start a new life elsewhere?"

"*No.*"

Nin nodded. "You choose to accompany me to death instead. But I will fix things so that won't happen. I have been...avoiding the end. We need Rone. And despite wanting nothing to do with the empire, the challenge of the temple will appeal to him. He will take our money. I can check the gambling dens in Cla—"

Taline slammed her reed down, ink splattering everywhere, and growled. "He's running through Vanichrest this week."

Nin blinked. "Vanichrest then," she said easily, letting go of any question of how Taline knew his location. "It shouldn't be hard to find him there. One only has to follow the gamblers and admirers to find the indolent phoenix in the center."

Taline grimaced, picturing his ridiculous hair—thick sections of blond and red vying in a ceaseless war for untamed control—and icy-blue eyes ringed in hard brown circles.

The Valerans were known for their hair, their ice, their power, and their complete domination of the northern countries bitten by seasons of snow and frost.

As a girl of the desert and heat, she shuddered at the thought of living in unending cold.

Valeran's face and charm ensured he had endless admirers. Charming and indolent, few saw the cold power and darkness beneath the veneer until it was too late.

And Nin, for all of her street knowledge and instinct, saw him as one of her lost, wounded birds—and when it came to her birds, she lacked the survival instincts not to trust them.

"*I* will get Valeran." Taline's voice darkened. "You'd just give in to his demands with no assurances."

Nin tried vainly to keep a smile from her face. Taline was fiercely glad for it and willing to play any role if it removed the look of desolation Nin had worn mere moments before.

"Madame Yates is due to go into labor by dawn," Taline said. "It will take you perhaps half an hour to usher the third Yatesling into the world. No one will blink if I'm not there."

They had been waiting for the rune to activate—the one Nin had placed on the Yates matriarch, to chart her progress. The levels indicated birth that night, and Nin's birth seals were never wrong. It was half the reason they had decided to do multiple Hand tasks that night.

"We must move quickly. I'll contact the Gantres," Taline said grimly. "At a minimum, we can allay suspicion for a bit longer. We'll also need to cover our absence." She started scribbling. "Croupa," she murmured, adding it to the list.

When she looked back up, Nin was looking at her fondly—but beneath her forcibly relaxed exterior, she was strung tighter than a lyre.

"Clean up our items at the guild. Better for everyone around us to be honest in their surprise."

"Yes." Nin closed her eyes, the weight of the world reaching up and wrapping around her once more.

Taline gripped the reed and moved it across the page.

She would protect her sister from the world by grabbing it by the throat, if that's what she had to do. And she knew where to start.

ASPECTS

RONE

VANICHREST, TEHRAS

Rone ul Valeran knew she was there—could sense her before he saw her, even disguised as she was.

What was the untouchable Taline ul Summora doing in the slums of Vanichrest, one of the darkest districts of Tehras?

Nothing for his benefit.

He ignored her long shadow and tossed the first round of dice, raising his eyes only as he lazily placed his second bet.

Tight wraps of black and emerald encompassed her form. No skin-revealing clothes for Taline ul Summora, never, and yet the wraps of black and emerald did more for his imagination than the scantily clad women draped over the patrons at the most expensive table in Vanichrest's core. He'd never seen a lick of skin below her chin or above her wrist, but neither did she wear the voluminous cloths of the matrons. She knew better than to adorn herself in anything that could be snagged by eager hands.

When she condescended to appear in his presence, he was always pleased to partake in the view.

Eyes hidden beneath her hooded cowl, her lips tightened, as if she could read the way of his thoughts. He dropped his eyes to the table with a smirk.

A prickly, delightful package he would never unwrap outside of the safety of his mind. Taline ul Summora wasn't an easy, meaningless discard. She meant trouble and bad luck.

She slipped soundlessly toward the door with a lithe but commanding grace now that she knew she had his attention.

He admired the view for a moment, made his bet—always bet on pain when a Summora turned up—then picked up the dice with fortune fluttering in his mind and tossed them.

Double bones. Death. The Summora luck continued its streak.

He swiped in his winnings, accompanied by an overwhelming groan from the table.

"Leaving so soon, Valeran?"

He gave a single nod. "Fortune ticks time."

"Better luck to the rest of us," one of the regulars said, laughing in decent humor with most of the table.

But one man's eyes narrowed as Rone rose. The man had been growing angrier as Rone continued to win while the man steadily lost. Rone gave the man a slicing grin and a wordless invitation and warning—if the man wanted to lick the ground tonight, Rone would be waiting.

Rone collected his weapons at the door—short staff, knives, picks—not that the establishment had disarmed even half of what he had on him.

Taline appeared from the shadows as soon as he stepped outside—a slip of a demon following in his wake with soft footfalls.

"I need to speak with you, Valeran."

Trouble. This woman had been trouble since the moment Ninli ul Summora had dragged her broken body in from the street and nursed her back to health. Trouble since she had turned down Ninli's offer to assume a new identity far from Tehrasi like all the sane ones did, and instead had taken a place at Ninli's side. Trouble, because unlike all the other doves Ninli had saved, this one had *never* left. She guarded her savior like a dragon guarded a gilded crown and expected all who Ninli saved to do the same.

Taline had been a troubling thorn in his side for the four years he had known her.

"Well, Your Highness, that won't be much of a hardship," he drawled. "You're speaking with me already."

"I would have it otherwise."

"Can't muck your sandals in the steps of fools, and yet here you are."

Her beautiful lips firmed as she looked up at him from the shadows of her hood. "I've mucked my sandals with worse."

He touched his chest. "I'm hurt. Is it only *my* affections you so deny, then?"

"Your affections are fickle, like everything else about you." She responded savagely to his mocking tone, as he knew she would. Taline ul Summora rose to any challenge. Fire and spirit and endless pigheaded bashing against walls that normal people would never break through.

He knew better, at this point, to always bet against the wall.

He splayed his fingers over his heart. "Devastating. A mortal blow to my manhood."

"Your manhood always seems to survive," she said darkly.

He smiled and started a winding trek through the cloth-covered alleys, making her hurry to keep up with his pace on this haphazard path. Tying Taline in knots was one of life's true pleasures.

"Always? I hadn't known that you thought of it so often. Why, if I—"

A figure burst from the shadows behind and without flinching, Rone used the man's momentum to flip him over his back and against the wall. He stepped forward and punched the man in the spine.

The man didn't rise.

Rone straightened and worked his fingers through a series of quick motions to release the gathered power and tension there, keeping his body limber and ready for a second opponent. A standard affair after a night at the tables.

The only thing strange about the whole encounter was the way Taline was frozen in terror. Unease shifted through him.

She shook the metaphorical ice free from her limbs in a mirror of his movements and rapidly examined the shadows of the alley. She seemed to settle again and looked down at the crumpled form of the angry man from the gambling den. "Cheating at the tables again?"

"Only when bored."

She moved the man's head with her foot, so she could see his face. She sighed. "Lansson. A seal maker. He was released from his post today."

It didn't surprise him that she would know. It wouldn't surprise him if Taline ul Summora kept track of the entire population of Tehras—if only to manage her "sister."

"And now he is sleeping against one for the night."

"He was let go because the guild copied his spellwork collection. His skills are obsolete now, when the charms can simply be included in the standard set. The empire's spellmasters take, they enhance and increase, and we all benefit but for the ones specifically made obsolete. With his waning value to the empire, it will be unlikely that he will be able to secure another post. He has five children to feed." Her expression was full of sorrow.

"Aren't you specifically in the business of putting others out of theirs?"

Her hands went to her hips. "We are trying to make it so that everyone has an equal field of options to exploit and advance. Lansson currently believes himself to have no options left. He sees his life in simple terms—that his only valued skill was terminated and that there will be nothing to replace his worth in the eyes of the empire."

"A man of little vision."

"A man whose entire life was defined by a skill," she argued. "Defined by something that is now gone."

"A man who doesn't embrace change is a man who dies on his pyre in this new world."

She sighed again, her lovely chest heaving with the motion, and crouched next to the man. "A man who hasn't been given a hand to see that there are other paths. Some fail when shown, but some succeed." Anger mixed with sadness in that loaded statement.

He grimaced. "You aren't actually going to help him."

"Of course I am." At least she sounded irritated about it.

His world righted itself. He didn't know what to do with a Taline who was sad.

"He won't give her anything."

"That's not why Nin does it." She reached down, irritation bleeding into her movements, but her words were still soft. "Whatever is done won't connect to us."

"You're letting her stupidity infect you. I never thought you so foolish."

"Thank you for such extraordinary commentary, Valeran," she said tartly, sharp-tongued once more.

His shoulders eased at the return of her sharpness and he leaned back to standard lounging position as she drew a rune along the ground near Lansson's cheek. It flashed green as she drew the final line, alerting someone from a group they anonymously worked with to retrieve the man.

"How long do you think you have left of your freedom, Taline? A year? A month? Ninli will crumble as soon as people start dying, and you will fold around her," he said as she stood. The attempt at returning their dynamic to normal also caused a heightened bite of irritation in him. He pushed from the wall and started moving more directly toward his temporary lodgings, knowing she would follow. "You don't have the true ruthlessness needed for rebellion. Neither of you do."

"*Bend*—a temporary process where papyrus rests and bides its time to strike back."

"*Fold*. How many creases do you have, *Taline ul Summora*?"

The footfalls stopped behind him.

He continued walking, ignoring the unpleasant sensation curling in his gut. Guilt. Damn girls. The Summoras were the demon work of the goddess Ferra in all her maternal glory.

"Nin's in trouble," she said harshly, catching up to him quickly. "I will become a master of creases, if need be."

"She's been in trouble since birth," he said dismissively.

"This time—" Taline's voice cut off, as if she couldn't utter the words, her feet following.

He slowed his steps so her soft, slowed footfalls fell alongside his. "I owe her nothing."

"You owe her as much as I do," she hissed, then took a

deep breath. "But that is neither here nor there. She bade me *hire* you," she said with an unpleasant curl of her lips.

He almost wished he'd been a scarab beetle on the wall during that argument.

"You don't have the funds to hire me. Besides, your lot work with favors, and mine has already been used. Do you remember?" He leaned in the slightest bit, as he whispered, "I do."

She pushed at his chest and he let himself be moved. "My memory isn't the one with holes, Valeran."

He straightened his shirt and led her the rest of the way to his temporary residence, unlocking the wards and resealing them once they were inside. "What's the job?" he asked once they were secure behind his impenetrable spells.

Because he would do it. They both knew he would, even as they played this game.

Of all the people in the world, Ninli ul Summora was the most complicated and yet, the simplest. The one he could almost believe could be trusted in a higher cause.

He shook off the disturbing notion and looked at Taline, and immediately felt righted again. Her trust was in her cause, and her cause was Ninli and whatever pet projects they had mutually decided upon. She wouldn't trade that for anything. He didn't have to deduce ephemeral feelings or guess at hazy motivations with Taline.

Ninli, though... There was always that feeling crawling his spine, questioning what her endgame was. Too kind. Too helpful. Too self-sacrificing. But too streetwise all the same. Deep darkness lived in her gut, but she always overcame it.

Too lacking in a motivation he understood.

And yet, bound by it, he was. Caught in that net. Because as many times as he had paid—overpaid—hard money to even his debts with her, with *them,* he never felt as though they were even. He'd never be square with the girl who now carried the name Ninli ul Summora.

And Taline knew it and exploited it, even though Ninli never showed any expectation.

"The Scepter of Darkness," Taline said.

He paused in the act of removing his short staves. The wilder rumors on the street hadn't been wrong, then. What did that say about Taline's terror in the alley? His mind started to assemble the pieces together.

"I'm going to pour a drink," he said, continuing his motions. "Then you are going to repeat the job without the words I misheard."

"We are going after the scepter."

"You are insane," he said mildly.

"You will be paid your weight in gold."

He plucked the stopper from his Chrimoa crystal flagon. This drink needed *strength.* "No."

"Your debt will be erased. *Completely.*"

"Your *sister* doesn't even believe there to be a debt."

"But I do. And, so do you. It doesn't matter what Nin thinks about this. *I* know."

He narrowed his eyes at her, considering. "What is she going to do with the scepter?"

It was a test. A clear test that neither of them expected Taline's response to pass.

"She is going to hide it elsewhere."

He poured the amber liquid and shook his head. "Try again, narsumina."

"She is going to destroy it."

He swirled the liquid, watching the glitter of light play on golden tones. "Mmhm."

"We are going to overthrow the scholari and padifehl with it and install a new head."

He allowed his eyes to slide shut for a moment at the words that hinted at truth. So much worse than the lies. "Lovely."

"Someone found the temple and alerted Osni. We stole the totem and replaced it with a fake, but to read it, the totem has to be inside the temple."

He lifted his cup from the sideboard, unwilling interest curling sharp and dark in his gut. "You have half a map to a fabled token of power—like every other treasure hunter in the known world. Go read it. What need have you of me?"

"You know why."

Too little power in the woman standing before him who could decipher anything given time, too much power in the one whose mind was a goose-waddled mess. Knowing what Ninli was, he wasn't surprised they had gotten the totem, but from the lore, he knew they would never make it through the next chambers without his help or with the help of someone whose curse breaking skills were on par with his.

He knew of no one else in that category. And he also knew, by looking at Taline, that they would go without him, should he say no.

"You are strung tighter than a horn bow." He swirled the liquid in his cup. "Osni will never acquire the scepter without the totem, and you have it. Better to let him kill all his men in the attempts. Why the sudden haste to attain the unattainable?"

"The Hand is the target of an assassin who cannot be fought." She didn't attempt to dissemble. Taline never did. "We will be caught soon and the totem recovered for the empire. Nin has invoked an end play."

Interesting. Ninli was a dreamer, but one saddled irrevocably by the past. He had never thought he'd see the day she'd set a finish line. He lifted his cup, hoping the answer to his next question did *not* follow the clues he'd gathered from Taline in the last half hour.

"Why?"

Taline swallowed. "The assassin would have no qualms using Nin, without her consent." Using *Taline*, she didn't say. But Ninli's weak points were easily guessed and anyone with remote intelligence would know where to place pressure to get Ninli to comply. "She'd recover the scepter without recompense."

"Pentalayerist assassins would simply kill her. They don't want the scepter found." Pentalayerist zealots were always where relics were to be found—especially relics that could open gates between the five layers of the world. That there were members already guarding the scepter temple was assured, and they would have had the information before even Osni.

But the pentalayerists wouldn't be able to steal the scepter on their own or keep it from imperial hands. Rone would have already used them, if such a thing were possible.

Taline's mouth firmed. "The assassin is one who is shadow blessed."

Rone's fingers hung in the air, pausing on the way to his lips, clutched around the cup. Everything sharpened around him. "You saw him use the shadows?"

"He fought Nin with them—she barely escaped. And he would have had me."

He caught her wrist with his free hand. "Had you, how?"

She stiffened at the contact and intensity but didn't shake her wrist from his grip. "I was caught within their ice."

"How did *you* escape?"

She shook her head and he narrowed his eyes, understanding what they would never say aloud about Ninli's abilities. He cursed and let her wrist drop.

Rumors of shadows warping and burning had been whispered of for the past two days. Only one man invoked such whispers. But other than parents using scare tactics on children for good behavior, no one truly believed the Shadow Prince would be found skulking Tehrasi's alleys.

"The Shadow Prince himself saw her abilities? For which

of you the outcome will be the worst, it is hard to say," Rone said as pleasantly as he could manage, lifting the cup to his lips and draining the liquid. "Death by pentalayerist hands would be kinder. For Ninli will disappear into an imperial cage with no key, and you will be *inspected* and chained by everlasting bonds that, this time, you will not escape. Thrown to the city houses or guild."

Taline raised her chin and the enchantments she held around her face flickered. "I understand the consequences."

"I know you do," he drawled, watching the expressions of the most beautiful woman he'd ever seen move under the enchantments that purposely dulled her to simply pretty. "Which is why I'm continually perplexed by the actions you take."

"The right thing isn't always the easy thing."

"It's suicide." He let his eyes slide down her figure slowly. "Such a waste." She bristled as expected, her lovely lips parting, but he continued. "For all of the death-inducing boredom of scripture and scribes and painstaking spell creation, you excel at the skill. You could live your life as a valuable member of any number of guilds."

Her bristles started to fall.

He refilled his cup. "Or you could marry some fat merchant in Indi or Scanda. Lay in silks, bathe in milk, and have fleshy, spoiled children. Wanted and celebrated. The life you secretly desire."

Bristles...back. Perfect.

"You know nothing of what I desire."

"My mistake," he said easily. "What could it be, then? Ah, yes." He drained that drink, too, and poured another. "A shallow grave with only your tattered crusade to shield you as the jackals feast on your unidentified remains."

"If we recover the scepter, the emperor can be made to negotiate."

He rotated the cup in his hand, watching the brown liquid swirl. The totem and a map to the Scepter of Darkness... The end of a long-sought goal... The thrill curled in him, unbidden.

He lifted the cup. He needed infinitely more intoxicants in his system instead of standing before him or swirling around his head. "You overestimate all those who stand in your way."

He would bet a thousand fehlta they hadn't considered all the forces who did *not* want the scepter to be found—who would kill in order to destroy it.

"If we are killed or captured by the Shadow Prince, and Osni secures the scepter, he will key it to himself. There will be another war," Taline said.

"The emperor will kill him first."

"That would be ideal," Taline said darkly. "But the padifehl..."

Dark thoughts converged as he saw the quiet fear she tried to bank in the back of her eyes. He cut through them ruthlessly. Damn Summoras.

He dropped the cup to the table and filled it again. "I'm

not joining your rebellion. And you propose a fool's greed-filled exploit into a dragon's lair."

"But are you not a fool and filled with greed?"

If anyone else came to him with a key to the Scepter of Darkness and a promise of securing it, he would laugh in their face. He had already done so, many, many times. He had done so six full moons ago, in fact—and now that was coming back to haunt him.

The scepter was one of the lost treasures of myth—one the Carres had hidden generations ago. Their family's power resided in the scepter remaining hidden, after all.

If anyone else brought this to him... But no, of course, it would be these two.

The two women had been involved in his most fortunate—and disastrous—of schemes.

"Indeed," he said.

The exchange of barbs was all a formality, in the end. Both of them had known it from the start. But something in the air whispered that this was a true *ending*, that they wouldn't perform this song and dance again.

"I have to get back," she said stiffly. "We leave in four hours. Your answer?"

He tipped his third full cup forward. "To death at dawn." He downed it.

When his cup was empty, she was gone, as he knew she would be. He always had to change his wards after inviting Taline ul Summora into his lair. She'd have made a proper thief and an expert assassin, if she could have shed her morals.

He picked up his favorite dice from the table.

The Scepter of Darkness... He'd never let the empire have it.

"One roll to make a man rich, one roll to make a man pine, one roll to make a man marry, one roll to make a man die," he murmured and threw the cubes. As they stilled, he grimaced and poured another drink.

"To endless, repeated mistakes," he murmured and lifted the cup.

HUNTING

KAVEH

TEHRAS, TEHRASI

Kaveh wasted no time, trading rest for an acuity potion. The potion would cost him a days' worth of stamina, but there was little he missed mentally under its effects.

The more warning a fox had, the faster it went to ground. And he planned to cage this fox before it reached cover.

Any other in the thief's position would vanish to another city immediately and prolong his chase. Prolong, not end.

If she had already left, all he would have to do was wait to see the missing reports on the guild rolls, then work through allies until he found one who knew something.

But she wasn't gone. Leaving would be a move that would expose her identity fully and reveal all those who knew and assisted in her crimes.

And she'd exposed herself already to aid a conspirator.

He smiled. Weakness.

No, she hadn't left yet. The way the citizens covered for the thief, the way she had saved her friend, the way there was little to no violence in their robberies indicated that she was no fleeing rat that would leave dependents to hang behind her. She would plan an escape without leaving others to suffer. She would try to cover herself and them in some way.

The continuously updating death notices in Tehras were on a scroll in front of him. No newly entered names provoked a further look. She was still in the city. For a few hours more, at least.

Her ties would be her undoing. All he needed to do was find her. And he knew where to start.

There was a notation in the thief's file of the Hand having healed opponents, but no notation about the Hand possibly being a *healer*. Which made sense—healers had strict oaths placed upon them and the Hand did not. In addition, her evasion, trickery, and traps showed immense forward planning that usually negated true injury to opponents. When she did fight, she displayed the skillsets of two women— maybe even more than two—combining their abilities into one disguised persona and hiding any healing talents behind so many other skills.

Fighting for her life had exposed the real skillset of the most interesting woman in the Hand, however.

Arrayed in the showy, red-cloaked guise given to investigorii inquisitors across the empire, he found his street path as unimpeded as if his face were free, and as if Ifret were curled menacingly about his neck. People flattened to the edges of the street around him to avoid the torture specialist the cloak designated him as.

Weakness.

Under the concealing cloak, he searched through the Healing Guild's rolls as easily as if he'd come as himself. The highest-level healers were the most obvious. The woman had known how to incapacitate in a manner that bespoke skill. In another opponent, she would have succeeded immediately, then probably modified their memories. The conflicting memories noted in the reports spoke to the skill. She was a Level Eight, at least.

But as he looked at the roll, he dismissed the small group of eights and nines almost out of hand. The thief—thieves—were clever, and they were oathbreakers, which widened the guileful possibilities immensely. His finger slipped down the list to the much wider group of sevens.

There were three prospects in the group who fit the estimated parameters of size, age, and background.

But it was among the sixes that he smiled. Notable appointments were listed for each healer over the past few weeks.

Aros had been unknowingly useful in his diatribe in the grove, after all. A healer who would undertake such risks in *one* circumstance...

Pocketing the duplicated roll, he headed to the assembly house of the investigorii and the currently empty Office of the Investigore. The moaning from the downed guards who tried to stop Kaveh from entering without the investigore present echoed in the hall outside. He had no time or patience.

He waved away the killing wards around the office—imperial-based wards held no power over him—and pulled out the Book of Transgressions. He started his search using the spell parameters that all law-breaking codices in the empire maintained. It didn't take long—not with access to the head of law enforcement's personal files at his disposal. He cross-checked every name of interest, as well as those of the higher healers.

But there was only one name that held his attention.

He was beyond ready for the investigore to enter his own office, within a half tick of the sundial on the balcony's railing—assuredly having felt his wards breached while he was across town.

With the red cloak discarded over a chair and his face uncovered, Kaveh didn't need to glance up to see the man stiffen as he realized exactly who had infiltrated his office. The investigorii force in the hall—with their weapons raised—were desperately trying to peer over their leader's shoulders, but Kaveh had enacted a ward screen to prevent anyone but the investigore himself from seeing past the doorway.

The investigore jerked a dismissive hand at his troops and pulled the door closed behind him, reasserting the privacy wards and doing a decent job at showing none of the mental toll he was under.

"Imperator General of the Empire." The man greeted him with the lowest bow for which he was capable. It was always telling what title was used when Kaveh was addressed. The investigore, who prized law and construct, chose that of military commander instead of the more hereditary and obsequious "Highness," or the terror-induced titles of his elemental command. "It is an honor. My apologies for any trouble you may have encountered in Tehras. I offer our full—"

"Tell me about this woman."

Kaveh flipped the codex on the desk and stretched back in the investigore's own chair. A shadow slipped from his sleeve to swirl around the carefully recreated face and figure someone had drawn by spell at the right of the profile on the open page.

A complicated expression crossed the face of the head of justice in Tehrasi.

Ah. Kaveh let his lids slide half-closed, mulling his next move.

"Healer Six Summora is a delivery specialist in District Fourteen." The man's bearing was statue straight. "Level Six."

"You mentioned her power level already in her title, Investigore. A strange coincidence. A mid-level healer with little to recommend her, yet you have had cause to create a personal file on her." It was a statement that could not be denied given the evidence on the page, but Kaveh hoped he tried—he had a bit of energy to burn before he cornered his real prey.

"Healer Summora has...an integral place in the fabric of the city. She has less concern for the politics of the city and guilds. She delivers infants of the poor and rich alike without political reservation...including those on our red list. That is why she has been flagged. Hardly a cause for the empire to concern itself with."

Especially the very *top* of the empire, was left unsaid.

Kaveh smiled without warmth. His shadow tapped a section of the codex entry. "And yet, you have found traces of her at the scene of a dozen crimes."

The investigore was appointed to his position for a reason—he looked straight into Kaveh's eyes as he responded. "Healers leave traces everywhere. We would have none of their kind if we arrested each one who appeared in the web of a death or incident. They take oaths to remain above suspicion in the case of a patient's death, and those oaths extend outward. Healer Summora's oaths are of the strongest on record."

There was an absoluteness to the man's words, and an almost underlying relief in stating them—that despite any *misgivings* other evidence might indicate, Healer Summora was above reproach. After all, healing oaths were tied directly to the guild's registry and could be verified. *Kaveh* had already verified them.

"Her healing oaths—yes, they are quite strong," Kaveh said.

Kaveh lazily examined the glyphs on the band secured about his wrist that showed the status of five healing oaths. It was the one reason Kaveh was even taking the time to unwind this thread instead of grabbing the person in possession of the middle glyph straight from the birth she was currently attending. The status of four of the five people connected to the oaths were limned completely in green, meaning they were still under guild spell. The fifth had gone dark in the past hour. If he'd needed another clue, that would have been it.

In the healer's halls, he had known one of the four in green was the woman he was looking for, and that the fifth oath was likely thief number two. The investigore's files and the man's reactions solidified his first choice. The middle glyph was vibrant and steady. Ninli al Six el Healer il Tehrasi ol Gomen ul Summora was doing a fine job of carrying on as if nothing were amiss.

Either that, or she hadn't realized that all healing oaths had temporarily been set to disallow any who carried them from leaving the city. He'd missed the window to secure Taline ul Summora's oath before it went dark, but she was the secondary concern of the two.

When Ninli ul Summora severed her healing oath to leave, it would gift him the oath remover as well. There was a delay between the severance action of an oath and the actual event. And in that delay, the breaking oath would show its location in a void of magic. His shadows had infiltrated every section of the city—concentrated around Ninli ul Summora's favorite haunts.

He'd have her and whoever removed the oath in the turn of a shadow.

HUNTING

He cared little about Tehrasi's internal politics, but he wouldn't let oathbreaking go unpunished.

"She has unequivocally strong healing oaths," Kaveh confirmed, almost casually. "The true concern is Ninli ul Summora's imperial oaths."

The investigore moved stiffly in the visitor's chair of his office. "I have seen her take the oaths myself at the quarterly oath festivals. And she is registered in the book at Gomen."

That the investigore had checked so specifically meant the man had had suspicion to do so.

Kaveh had checked that registry, too, though it wasn't a living entry like the healing oaths were. Imperial oaths were just registered as being successfully administered. Being able to disentangle oaths required a very specific skillset and knowledge.

The law enforcement of the empire was able to use the oaths on others to fulfill their enforcement duties, but they were more limited in sensing—having to rely on crude tools. Imperial oath handling was something only a few in the royal family had access to for a reason.

"The thief known as the Hand holds no imperial oaths, Investigore."

The man's lips tightened. "We are aware." They would have tried to utilize the oaths the first time they'd laid a hand on the thief. "And all permitted merchants and travelers are thoroughly vetted after an incident. No oathbreakers show on the registries when we audit after an incident. Half the force believes the Hand disappears through a gate after his mission is complete."

Kaveh studied the man. He had little patience for drawn-out interrogations, preferring to get to the finale without wasting time in the narratives. A man knowing he was staring at a demon's death tended to loosen the tongue.

But this man was telling the truth—at least what he believed to be so.

"You've been saved by the Hand more than once, have you not, Investigore? Do you feel yourself...impartial?"

"I will arrest the thief when he falls beneath our spells. We are working on a way to determine a lack of oath from afar. He won't escape us once we can monitor all hours of the day."

"That won't help you, Investigore. The thief knows how to detach and reattach the oaths at will."

"Impossible."

Unlike the man's reticent statements on the woman, this one was dismissive and matter-of-fact.

Boredom started setting in, and Kaveh itched to be elsewhere. He let the shadow on the desk slither unimpeded over Ninli ul Summora's profile. It began weaving a familiar symbol. The investigore was trying not to show his attention too keenly to the shadow that was snaking an unending ouroboros symbol, while still keeping it in view, as any other reasonably smart human possessed of survival instincts would do.

"You keep a close eye on her, and I can see from your

notes that you've interrogated her more than once. You seem to trust Ninli ul Summora a great deal, Investigore, to repeatedly call her in on suspicion then let her go. Perhaps there is other enchantment at work."

The man struggled for a moment before resolving whatever turmoil had risen. "No. I've checked."

This amused Kaveh for reasons he couldn't name. "Thought yourself under a spell?"

"I'm not."

"And yet, she is hardly a simple healer, I think." Kaveh crooked his finger and the shadow became dagger thin.

"As I said," the investigore said, watching the dagger. "She is an asset to the community. One with many ties."

"You want to believe she can't be involved, and yet you've meticulously registered each of these instances and cross-referenced where Healer Six Summora was."

The investigore's lips tightened. "Investigation is part of my job. But suspicion is one thing, evidence, another. Healer Six Summora cannot have had anything to do with at least forty of the incidents on record."

"And her sister?"

A strange expression wove across the man's face. "I assume you mean Taline ul Summora?"

"Are there others?" Kaveh's brow rose. The file had only listed one. If there were known others, the census officials would need to pay Tehras an extended *visit*.

"No other Summoras have ever graced the registry. It is simply a name used on the street at times."

"Tell me of this one, then," Kaveh said, filing away the strange response.

"Taline ul Summora is a competent, unexceptional Level Four magi. Assistant to her sister in daily work, competent in simple spellbox construction. She makes a number of the base boxes for many of the guilds."

He just bet they were basic. Nothing like the exquisite work she did for the Hand. And yet, he bet there were lots of hidden elements no one ever cared to look for as her boxes proliferated the guilds.

"Her profile notes her affinity for low-level spell construction and scripture in her skill assessment, but she decided to work with her sister as a healer. Do you find that odd, Investigore?"

"Level Fives and below are given a choice in their work placement, where higher levels have little choice. I have little care as to what guild a four chooses."

"The Hand heals its victims. Even *you* a few times, according to the gossip of your underlings."

Was the investigore's reluctance simple gratitude or something more? Kaveh watched him closely.

The investigore never flinched. "The Hand has shown instances of...healing victims. But far beyond the skill level either Summora could claim—bringing someone back from the brink of death is not the same as delivering a baby."

Kaveh smiled. "And yet I found it interesting that Healer Six Summora has never lost a mother or baby, or even had a delivery last beyond six hours. Having never taken an interest in such things, and assuming you are of a similar mindset, I'll tell you that it is in her guild file that this is an exemplary statistic. Healer Six Summora has nearly single-handedly taken over deliveries in the capital city with the blessing of the guild."

"The successful birth rate has risen overall with the empire's progressively advanced spells and practices coming to Tehras," the investigore said stiffly.

"It is my understanding that babies don't normally keep to schedules." Kaveh flicked a paper toward the other man. "The delivery rate is so outstanding that it almost reeks of hubris."

The investigore stared at the notes Kaveh had taken from the healing halls. "Prodigious talents sometimes occur in lower-level magi—"

"You think that someone who can hide their oaths cannot hide their skill level?"

"You believe she is the Hand." Complicated emotions ran across the taciturn man's face. "And that she is repeatedly manipulating her skill level assessment and oaths herself, even though the Gomen Temple, which ratified her oaths, has proclaimed no interference. No oathbreaker of that caliber exists."

"And yet, you *checked* with the Gomen Temple. Despite every rational reason you can call forth, I see it in your face that you accept the accusation to have seeds of truth. Why do I not see her in chains already?"

CHAPTER TEN

The investigore said nothing for a few stretched moments. "If you speak with her, you will know."

Kaveh raised a brow and rose. "I suppose I will determine that within the hour, then." He flicked his finger and the shadow on the codex leaped to slither and tighten around the man's throat. "If I find out you have spoken with anyone about this conversation, or if you send word to anyone, you will wish for an easy death."

"I am loyal to the empire," the investigore said rigidly.

Kaveh threw the red cloak over his shoulders, and the shadow jumped into his raised sleeve. "That is the only reason you are still alive. Send men to secure Taline ul Summora immediately. I want her here by noon. Consider it a test of said loyalty. Good day, Investigore."

It was time to force Ninli ul Summora's hand.

DARK TIDINGS

RONE

TEHRAS, TEHRASI

Rone watched his death arrive. Or half of it, at least. Taline tapped one foot impatiently as dawn's shadows grew shorter, and with his enhanced vision, he saw her full lips pinch beneath the deep hood of her traveling cloak.

He watched her fume for another five dial rotations, just to be unpleasant, then dropped to the street on the other side of the building and ambled around the corner. He stretched as if he'd just woken, his own smirking features hidden under the hood of the dark gray, fitted cloak he had donned.

"You're late," she said, hands on her hips.

He waved a lazy hand at the sky. "It's dawn."

"It's after dawn."

He lifted a brow, close enough to her now so that she could see his face as he opened his disguise enchantment to her. "I don't see your erstwhile companion."

Taline frowned. "She had last-minute activities to complete. She'll be here."

"Saving one last useless half-wit?"

Taline had a hard time hiding her grimace, but she did an admirable job as she pulled to her full height and looked down her nose at him from the six inches shorter that she stood. "*You've* been that half-wit. Nin's inability to leave people in trouble is a great strength."

"One she'll assuredly be celebrated for after she is dead."

Taline bared perfect teeth and the air seemed to grow darker around them. "You wouldn't understand loyalty if it bit you on the cheek."

Rone leaned down. "Loyalty is the fastest path to a painful death." He tapped her cheek. "It's a lesson you haven't learned. Take what you can and run when you need to, narsumina."

She pushed his chest, pushing him away, cheeks lighting with angry color. "Don't call me that. And I hardly think I should take a lesson from the man with the reputation for fleeing when things start to go poorly."

He smiled lazily. "Narsum's devoted shrine protector of bounteous beauty, what else could you ever be called but a tender of the divine? You'd do well with a few lessons from me, narsumina." There was a wary feeling building within his gut, though, and he casually glanced to the olive grove between their position and the Erai gate.

A murkiness had descended that had nothing to do with Taline's anger, and it was rapidly growing thicker.

Taline opened her beautiful lips to stab him—and what a way to go—but she followed his gaze and frowned abruptly. She looked at the small wind clock strapped to her arm. "Fog is not expected this morning. What—"

Rone shoved her hard to the side and only her capability with creating spell sets in advance allowed her to catch herself in the stumble. A bolt of red landed where she'd been. She whirled toward the threat.

Rone swore as ten shapes appeared from the gloom.

A second bolt shot toward his head. He ducked and swore again. The attacker was trying to unmask him.

His cloak was specifically designed to keep his hood in place, with a spell that altered his features beneath. Although flaunting his heritage was useful at times, at others, it was decidedly not. His hair was far too distinctive.

He dodged the next blast and pulled forth his less distinct talents, wishing, not for the first time, that he could pit himself against a worthy foe—one where he would be forced to use all his abilities, including the ones he kept locked tight.

He couldn't use the specific abilities of his lousy maternal ancestors here, either. He sneered. Valerans. Distinctive, proud, and brittle to the last, like the ice in their veins. The spells would identify him immediately, and if he wanted to come out on the winning side, he needed to stay outside imperial notice.

Taline threw three spellboxes, whipping up a tornado through the street, followed by a gust of wind so strong it shoved two of the assailants into a wall.

She was annoyingly good at that.

"There are a pair of gate medallions in the alley to our left," Taline said in a breathless hiss as they deflected spells.

Stupid girls. He firmed his lips. "Does your sister *want* to be caught?"

"No, idiot. That's why we have escape medallions. Single-use only."

"And if the empire finds one?"

"They are well hidden."

He grabbed her around the waist and used his momentum to fling them both into the opening of the indicated alley. Taline came around swinging and flung out another pre-crafted spell, temporarily blinding their opponents. The containers she made, filled with Ninli's magic, were magnificent but not infinite. Taline herself did not have the power to charge those spells. Her creations spoke to her advanced crafting and meticulous planning, but she was powerless without them.

"How many of those do you have left?"

"Not enough," she huffed. "But there are the gates." She pointed at two medallions inset into the stone wall at the end of the alley.

Rone wound a spell around three of the investigorii agents. "They are going to see us go through."

"Too late, too late," she said, as five more agents dove from the skies. "Go!"

Rone grabbed her again and flung her toward the medallion on the left.

His fingers brushed the metal disk on the right as a beam of light hit the wall. The stones exploded around them—taking both gates with it but leaving another stone wall behind.

He whipped around and fired off three spells, then grabbed Taline.

He hoped Ninli was enjoying her *stroll.*

NINLI
⟫⟫⟫ ☼ ⟪⟪⟪

Nin scrubbed the last operating and embalming room while keeping an eye on the door. It was nearly sunup and she was exhausted, but she had collected nearly everything they'd need. She mentally added a third rest point to their trip itinerary as she slipped a fourth set of trauma patches into her bulging healer's bag with one hand while she used the rag in her other to wipe the surface of the embalming table.

It normally took a lot more time and stealth to steal guild supplies, but the head of the guild had been uncommonly flustered about something, making little sense as she'd looked at a guild summons and ran from the room. Nin was quickly using the opportunity to pocket extra supplies and rework the spells binding her to specific patients over the next few weeks. Trauma cloths took hours to create—hours they didn't have.

Her last birth had been as uncomplicated as expected, leaving her just enough time to "volunteer" for cleanup. She mentally promised to pay the guild back twofold when she returned.

Nin shoved the last cloth she could reasonably say wouldn't be needed in case of guild emergency into her bag as footsteps echoed on the hall stones.

"I thought you had cleanup duty last week." Larit strode into the room, making Nin sag with relief. "Where is Taline?"

"She went home sick," Nin said lightly. "First traces of croupa showed up in her health scan. She took a potion two hours ago, so she'll be fine by the full moon."

Croupa was one of the only things that had no magical cure and yet was not alarming in the long term. It took two weeks to run its course and was highly contagious when open wounds were involved. It was the one ailment that kept healers from work, and even better, kept them out of public view totally.

Larit raised a brow at Nin's innocent smile. "And you?"

"You know how these things go. I'm already on pre-leave. Household companions often catch it, so I got a deep scan. Precursors show it'll move through my system in"—she checked the time—"four hours and make me contagious."

Larit snorted. "Qara left for an emergency council appointment an hour ago and I haven't seen her since, but she left a package that *mysteriously* disappeared from the hall table while I was in the other room. What are you two planning?"

That meant Taline had gotten the gate passes and magic distortion tags. Nin blew out a breath she hadn't realized she'd been holding. She still had to go back to their home, pick up their last bag, and set the "sick" wards—but then they'd be set.

"It's common for croupa to crop up a few times a year, Larit, you know that. Even the best in the guild can't avoid it. Hence the procedures."

Nin and Taline were strict about using croupa excuses only for emergencies, though, so that they never overused it.

Larit's eyes sharpened. "Ninli."

Nin looked through the window to the sundial in the guild courtyard again, where the shadows were just starting to turn sunwise in the growing brightness. They were going to cut this ruse close to the sandpronga teeth.

Just enough time to get out of the city without raising suspicion, and if they were lucky, leave identities in place when they returned.

"It will be fine, Larit. I'll see you after our convalescence. Hopefully this bout will last no more than five days," she said with emphasis.

Healing oaths were temporarily disabled upon a forced convalescence—otherwise, a sick healer could be forced to attend an emergency. Croupa flagged the guild spell, and Nin knew how to simulate the conditions of the sickness so that the oath went dormant. Taline's healing oath had gone inactive two hours ago. It hadn't been hard to undo a few *extraneous* things in the oath as well.

She'd hook everything back together when they returned.

And when they returned, she'd—

Larit shrieked and Nin turned sharply toward her, hands already out to heal whatever had happened.

Larit's eyes went unbelievably wide, hands rising to her forehead, then she was pushed from the room in a wave of darkness—as if a tsunamic wave of black sand had risen and thrust her from existence.

Nin shot protective magic toward the dwindling feel of the other healer and let out a breath of relief when she felt Larit deposited into the street alive. The rest of the guild were there as well—small oath-ridden pinpricks of confused light.

Everyone who'd been in the building had been deposited into the street, except for her.

She grabbed for her magic, but wisps of darkness swirled around the edges of the room, pushing her power inward.

She pulled her hand against her chest to form a traveling vortex. But her magic bumped firmly against an overwhelming ward set she'd never before encountered—but one whose underpinnings were terribly familiar. She'd seen the edges of such a cage only five hours before.

Darkness pulled from the corners of the room inward, like a wisp spider pulling in his seductive web.

Overwhelming dread gave way to resolve.

Her magic whirled out to find the holes as the web of furious shadow constricted around her. There were always holes. This web didn't have any of the ones she'd exploited hours ago—he had fixed all those—but that meant she'd just have to find new ones.

Concentrate.

Outside panic struck her sharply and suddenly, breaking her concentration. Her awareness of the outside world was fading fast inside the hardening cage, but she felt the spiked, splintering echo of two of her gate medallions in the city. Destroyed, not used.

Taline. Rone.

A coordinated attack.

She needed to get to them. Panicking, she hit the warding wall hard, burning her skin on the shadows pulling toward her. She shoved the panic in a deep hole and fell into a ready stance—anger thrumming through to cover her fear.

She felt the dark oppression of him before she saw him—the shadows growing, swirling, and coalescing into a large, sleek, unmasked form.

There were always vendors and merchants eager to sell likenesses of the emperor, princes, majexes, and consorts, and of the high-level generals and officials. Nin had made certain to know each by sight.

She knew exactly what Kaveh ul Fehl, Shadow Prince of the Empire, looked like—usually immortalized in portraits surrounded by wailing death. The portrait makers were also overly fond of wraiths and demons bursting from his ever-present black cloak to bring destruction to all those on the edges of the scenes.

Oh, she knew Kaveh ul Fehl's face and form.

And he stood before her in the Healing Guild's embalming room, darkness swirling around his feet. She hadn't seen his face when they'd fought, but the sheer *feel* of the man before her—dark, deadly, and overwhelming—left no doubt that this was the same man she'd fought in the alley.

It had been a *gross mistake* not to leave the city the moment after surviving his attack. Five hours after was far too late.

She tamped the instinctive urge to flee. He had constructed additional wards, knowing she could travel. If she fled, she'd hit the warding cage again and be disabled.

She swallowed. Sehk-Ra be damned. *Kaveh ul Fehl* knew she could make ripgates.

Her seeking tendrils were overloading her with worse and worse information. He had attached all of his restrictions not just to the room, but to her healing oaths, which were strongest inside the guild's halls.

"I had the guildmaster add a few things," he said casually, reading her expression. His eyes slid half-shut. "Didn't expect that, did you?"

She shifted to the balls of her feet, and a shadow curved around her, hovering, ready to strike.

"Don't disappoint me now, Ninli ul Summora."

She would have bet against the ability of her insides to twist in panic further. But just hearing her name on his lips did it.

He smiled. "Let's discuss what you've been up to."

~*~

KAVEH

Kaveh watched her steady herself, weight shifting, magic at a highly controlled point that was too pinpricked to be anything other than a funnel for a great well.

His thief. No doubt about it—not that he'd had any doubts when he'd initiated this little game.

He let a slip of magic tell him what he already knew—imperial oaths were laden over her. *Nothing to see here,* they said; *just another citizen of the empire.*

But they were too fresh. Imperial oaths in a population ten years conquered should be worn and used—the edges smoothed, not sharp. It was nothing that would strike anyone else's notice, not even the investigore as an oath handler, but being an oath owner of the empire gave Kaveh a far greater eye for precision.

He didn't need that precision to know what her next move would be.

"I've built this lovely little cage with you in mind. I wouldn't mind testing it a bit, though." He let his fingers trail along the shadows, sparking darkness as they went.

She very carefully stayed away from the shadows nipping at her from all sides, holding stiffly beneath the one hovering just above the soft meat of her neck. "What do you want, Your Imperial Highness?"

"I want to know what you stole."

"Crelu ul Osni is the one to ask about the temple you seek."

He appreciated that she didn't try to dissemble completely—that she recognized part of that game was well past.

"Osni holds no knowledge I desire, Ninli ul Summora. What did you *steal* from the temple?"

He watched the bob of her throat, the leap of her pulse as he circled her.

"I hold not the scepter, Your Imperial Highness." Truth. "You will find the temple chambers as intact as ever, bar the bodies of the dead the scholari will amass in his quest."

"You seem very certain the scholari's men will fail."

"They will discover the same thing all who seek the scepter find. Death."

Something haunted flitted through her gaze—a fiery desire, then grim certainty. An odd combination that did nothing to tamp the burn of his curiosity.

"Death can mean many things. I find it interesting that *you* are quite alive. I know you went to the temple," he whispered in her ear.

"I didn't go past the first chamber."

"Lie," he responded casually.

"You credit me with skills that I do not possess. You will find the temple untouched, unless the scholari has succeeded."

"No. We both know the scholari will fail."

He watched her throat bob, and some quickly lost

emotion burned hazel eyes flashing between brown and...something else. "For now. The scholari will sacrifice greater men until, eventually, one of them will succeed."

"Is that why you stole what was inside? To stop him from succeeding?"

Other than that vague hint of other in her hazel eyes, there was nothing outstanding about her features.

But there was something *compelling* about her. About her steady gaze, about whatever was going on in her mind. How she held herself—subservient, as propriety demanded in the face of royalty, yet with quiet confidence.

This was a woman who understood her strengths and weaknesses, who knew herself, and quietly believed in something greater.

"I went to the temple to ascertain information, nothing else, Your Imperial Highness."

"Another lie."

"You choose to believe what you will, Imperator General."

He was used to the overt confidence of the women at court who knew how to use their bodies and minds as weapons. And he applauded the use of any weapon at one's disposal, but he found it easy to sidestep palace advances and schemes, as most of them continued to endlessly play the same games on the same game board, and those games had ceased to be intriguing by the time he was eight and on the battlefront, bathed in blood.

This woman would be swallowed to nothing at court in

games of beauty, but she was far more interesting. A watcher, a strategist, but also a *doer*. One who instinctively drew others—even rigid law abiding men like the investigore—to them through sheer force of will.

He examined her, and all the little human tells that made the difference between life and death. "You have it already."

"I do not have the scepter."

Truth, by itself.

"Not the scepter, no." He prowled around her. "You found something else. A map or key." His gaze slid over her throat and the tick of her pulse.

"Perhaps a lamp of power?" she asked lightly.

"If you had found that, you would have already used it." He leaned in. "Things aren't going so well for you, though, are they?"

"This is not how I planned to spend this hour, no."

"Such confidence."

"I've been told that in me that quality is a mere hairsbreadth from being defined as stupidity. Can I offer you another expectation?"

He tilted his head. "My normal expectation would be stabbing at a gibbering, pitiful mass before summary execution. You are a bit out of the ordinary in that respect. I'm torn between wanting to tear the information from you quickly, so I can be finished with this task, and wanting to play some more. It's seldom that I find anyone interesting. I've not had to construct a new piece of magic in a long, long time."

"How boring."

"Exceedingly. So, I propose this—you tell me what I want to know, and I'll let your sister, who is currently being held by the investigorii, live. And you, as well." He let a shadow twist around his wrist.

Her lips curved in a short smile. "But not freely."

"No. The option to live freely no longer exists for you, gatemaker. However"—he turned his hand in an enticing motion—"the option of death at my hand will be much, much worse. What will you choose, little thief?"

"Living in a cage or dying on a sword?"

"A cage can be a sword all its own."

"And a sword can be a cage. What would you know of such choices?" she asked bitterly.

His fingers tightened on Ifret. Gilded cages and deadened eyes...

"I choose to die by the sword every day." He touched a shadow to her neck. "Let us see about your cage, Ninli ul Summora, with a reputation for good works. And the light of the people in your eyes."

Dangerous, that light. He'd seen it many times on the battlefront. Those with that look were always the ones who thought they had nothing of themselves to lose and everything for their people to gain. The self-sacrificial lamb with a sword in her hands and belief clenched in her teeth. The calm gaze accepting death.

She held herself firmly in his grip. He admired strength, and she had plenty on display.

Careful, hold, wait, floated in the carefully constructed breeze of her thoughts.

He smiled. "You've had practice with mind reading."

"Practice guarding against invasive skills," she said.

"You are a thief," he whispered along her ear as he circled her once more, fingers still sliding along her neck. "What is a theft of thoughts to someone like you?"

Something flashed in her gaze.

"You will tell me what you took and where it is." He inserted the demand into the shadow now wrapping her neck.

Calm, wind, ride the breeze, hold. "There is nothing to tell."

Strength in spades. She was an asset he would cultivate. "Perhaps your sister has whatever you stole? Should I be interrogating her instead?"

Her eyes flashed. *Taline, danger, never, escape, puzzle, revenge, Ro—*

The thought cut off as a strong mental breeze shot through.

He grabbed for the trailing current of the last thought, trying to gain the feel of it so he could grab it when it appeared again. "Truth. Now we begin."

An ugly sound ripped through her. "You will never—"

A sudden light cut through the cage, pushing him back. The light knit quickly around her form, as if cutting a diagram from a page.

Swearing, he pulled the cage tighter, but the light simply sliced through it. How—?

He caught the thief's look of surprise, then her panic, a split second before she was cut from the fabric of the room.

DARK SUMMONING

NINLI
THE PALACE OF TEHRAS

Nin was unceremoniously dumped on a stone floor not softened at all by the large, luxurious carpets spread out across the space. She quickly scrambled to her feet. Only three people in Tehras could have pulled her through space using enough capital magic to override a trap as powerful as Kaveh ul Fehl's—and two of them weren't in the city.

It had been a long, *long* time since she'd experienced the call of a scepter.

Etelian ul Fehl stood before her, fingers gripping the golden staff of the lit scepter tied directly to him.

A conceit of the Carres—to be able to call anyone to heel in their capital city with the flick of a scepter.

The padifehl hadn't chosen to do so from just any den in the palace, either. He had called her to the center of the palace—the circular chamber at its heart. The one where the stones beneath the carpets were stained black with ancient blood. Her gaze caught on the evenly spaced scepters that mirrored those around the acropolis. Other than the one Etelian held, the eleven others were dark. Her gaze caught on one scepter in particular. Her heart lurched as it always did at its unlit state.

The padifehl stared in disgust at the scepter in his hand. "Sehk-Ra-be-damned-Osni feeds falsehoods again. That *barely* worked."

It was a particular circumstance of living in the capital. The royal scepters could take a person and pull them through space distinctly, cutting around their figure and anything attached. The spell could be set as thin as a two-finger-wide radius—cutting loose anything that was outside that reach. Clothes that were too loose would be cut or shed entirely. Weapons would be expelled, unless they were tight to the skin.

She scrambled backward, physically feeling the back of her intact bag, while she inventoried the wards around her to determine whether her spells still camouflaged her eyes.

Her bag would never have survived, had the wielder of the scepter known how to properly use what he held.

"The last fifty people you used it on brought no such trouble," a voice behind her said.

She scrambled sideways to see Aros ul Fehl lounging across a chaise in the middle of the large chamber.

Sehk, Sehk, *Sehk*. She stumbled backward until she hit the

northern curve of the chamber, careful not to touch either scepter to her sides while keeping them both in view.

"Sehk-be-damned scepters," Etelian hissed, looking as unhinged as ever when something wasn't going his way. "Sehk-be-damned Osni and his worthless promises. I should kill him and save Father the trouble."

Nin took stock of the room, adjusting plans quickly, while the padifehl raged. He hadn't raised any extra wards, but all the usual ones were in place—all the wards that had been present when she'd been here days before. She was both in a far better position, and one far worse. The confinement wards that Kaveh ul Fehl had created around her were gone, but the call of the scepter bound her to the chamber for two minutes. Two minutes that she, as a citizen of Tehrasi whose oaths were *currently* connected, could *not* override. Not even her personal attachment to the city could override a command from the scepters that ruled it.

But she had two minutes without *Kaveh ul Fehl.* Her eyes strayed to the four arched doors that led to different areas of the palace, checking for the Shadow Prince. There was no way this had been part of his plan. He had *had* her. No, more than likely he was flying through the streets uncloaked right now, searching for her, leaving devastation in his wake.

He'd be here soon. She just needed that moment to be eighty seconds from now, because the padifehl had very helpfully raged for the first forty seconds of his two-minute hold on her.

She carefully shrugged, working a specific spell paper

down her sleeve and into her palm, then connected it to the spell Taline had painstakingly unlocked. As soon as Etelian's time expired, she would activate it.

"Seeing as the emperor expressly forbid the scholari's death until other issues are resolved," Aros responded disinterestedly, "I highly doubt you would find him amenable to your rage's end, little brother."

Nin touched the curved wall behind her, pretending to steady herself. She pressed paper to stone.

Etelian shook the scepter. Nin stared blankly, losing track of the spell for a moment, as the idiot *shook* the Second Scepter of Tehras a second time. "It's going to stop working, just like all the damn gates."

"Perhaps you are blaming the wrong thing," Aros said, lazily. "Curious, don't you think, that the spell took so long to attach to this girl specifically?"

"Maybe I'll let you satisfy your *curiosity* before she dies," Etelian sneered, finally turning toward her.

Her life was in the hands of time and the working spell beneath her fingers now.

"The healer and plague *warden*. Your time alive—and that of your compatriot—has been ticking down since you inserted yourselves into my affairs."

What?

Defying the grave circumstance she was in, her heart squeezed ridiculously with relief. She was here because of the girls? She looked quickly to each door in the room for the

Shadow Prince again, then at the padifehl—a petulant child throwing a fit over a toy.

Relief nearly buried her. The padifehl had no idea what he'd interrupted.

Sehk-Ra, she had *never* felt any positive emotion toward Etelian ul Fehl, but right now, fervent relief and gratitude at him being a petty man jarred against habitual hate. She shuddered. Thank Sehk, thank *Sehk*, that she had undone Taline's oaths earlier. The monster couldn't pull her sister in without the oaths being active.

She darted her gaze from Etelian to Aros ul Fehl. The eldest prince was splayed across the largest lounge—one that the Carres had always used for such purposes of casual interrogation. A man whose features might have well been cut by the gods in a masculine copy of his mother's celebrated beauty—she'd think him bored, but for his sharp, *familiar* eyes.

Two guards stood at each of the four entrances to the room.

Osni was nowhere to be seen but being in the orbit of three princes of the empire in the span of a quarter turn of time was far more dangerous than a visit to the man she hated above all others.

She released her magic in tiny tendrils along the wall behind her, feeling for additional traps or chains, and finding none.

Being brought to Osni's regard would be dangerous, but Etelian ul Fehl would forget her as soon as she passed through his view. She'd not be able to resume work under her current name, not after this, but that could be fixed. She'd done it before. The padifehl would rage about the healer who slipped past him, but he'd never remember her face. There was nothing physically outstanding about her and she had made very sure that she knew how to stay unremarkable.

Be opposite of Lorsali in every way. The strategy hadn't failed her yet.

Lorsali had been interested in both men before her, the three of them near in courtly age. So long ago, it seemed another lifetime. Nin couldn't help but think the eldest princess had found a better fate in death than to have been shackled to either.

Of the two, she kept Aros in central focus. She knew she was biased—that she held his "rumored" paternity against him. But she would never be able to see him as anything but the central threat.

She had to appear nonthreatening, but still normal. Someone trying to appear unremarkable—even a simple civilian—was more likely to catch Aros's attention than someone shouting in the streets or showcasing their wares. Dealing with Etelian would take an entirely different skillset than dealing with Aros.

She called upon every bit of childhood training she could recall on how to handle powerful men. It wasn't as if she'd had to practice much on the streets or in the shadows.

"Your Imperial Highnesses," she said, heart in her throat, and gaze turned to the floor. She stood motionless, not letting herself double-check the spells laden over her, no matter how desperate she was to do so.

"Why are you still alive?" Etelian demanded. "I thought I had you executed. But then Aros taunted me with the death rolls and I saw not your name."

"I...uh...." No training had taught her how to respond to a demand of "you should have been executed already."

"You lost me my favorite of the week, as well as the others in my court."

She kept to her bow, gaze tracking the corners of the room, the distance to each wall, and the ward layout as the spell paper worked, imperceptibly eating away at one set in particular. "Perhaps your execution order is awaiting me at home. My apologies, Padifehl. I did what I could to save your household."

She watched the spell while keeping the padifehl's lower half in view and counting down in her head. Thirty-five, thirty-four, thirty-three—

"*Liar.* You've lost me *fifteen* girls over the past two years." Water glistened in the palm at his hip. Thirty more seconds. Just hold off for thirty more. "I had someone check the logs."

The water in his palm grew in volume. Twenty-eight seconds. Too much time remained. Nin's gaze narrowed on the forming spell. She would have to use a fire spell at two degrees, wind at four, disable all his pressure points, and throw at least one sha—

"Now, now, none of that," Aros said, temporarily defusing the situation. The water in Etelian's palm steamed, vaporizing with a hiss, and she was suddenly lifted, forced from her bow.

Flames flickered on the edges of Aros's fingers as he lowered them. Aros's gaze, though, was narrowed in on *her* hands. She mentally gathered the alternates to his favorite spells as well, marking the defenses for immediate use.

His gaze rose to hers, something interested sparking in familiar amber eyes. Unease rose in her. Twenty seconds.

"You dare?" Etelian whirled and bared his teeth at his elder brother. "You do not rule h—"

Aros pinned him with a gaze so black that Etelian froze and sank back, furious terror forming in his eyes.

When the eldest prince turned back to her, it was with a calm smile. She shivered. Unlike the overwhelming hell of his shadowed brother or the uncontrollable vice of his second, Aros was a steel tine that killed while his opponent was focused elsewhere.

"Brother *dear*," Aros addressed Etelian without looking away from her, head tilted in the manner of a predator trying to suss out the exact nature of the prey shaking in the bushes. "She stopped the spread of plague in your household. Surely that is a deed worthy of praise, not death. Such foresight should be rewarded, wouldn't you think, girl?"

"Your Imperial Highness." She bowed her head, eyes tracking their body movements, ready. Ten seconds.

She could feel the scepter's influence unraveling around her as the spell's time ticked to conclusion. And she could feel Kaveh ul Fehl growing closer with every tick. She shuddered at the *feel*—his shadow connection against her skin had been cut by the scepter's power, but the edges of it remained. He would be here any moment.

"She will be *executed*."

Aros shrugged. "You have always been inordinately stupid. Do as you will, Etelian."

But Aros's sharp eyes watched her with slightly interested disregard—as if she might pass a test, or she might die—and he would only care if it was the former.

"Are you questioning—"

Seven, six, five...

She concentrated on Aros instead of the padifehl, who was raging at them both. Aros was as dangerous to her as the Shadow Prince, just in far different ways.

The son of Jisarek Carre stood before her, no matter what the empire professed about Aros's birth, and Jisarek was as twisted as all those bearing the Carre bloodline.

Her gaze caught on the set of unlit scepters across the chamber.

She brushed the wall behind her, as if steadying herself, careful not to touch the set of scepters held on the same section of wall. The last knot began unraveling, faster and faster as spell after spell dropped. Three ticks. Three ticks more...

Eruptions shook the palace's foundation and silt rained from the ceiling. Shadows swarmed into the room from every crack, furiously resolving into a tall, dark, familiar shape forming in the center of the mass. A maelstrom of destruction followed a moment behind—one hall tearing apart in his path as if the devastation couldn't keep pace with the magi himself.

Both Aros and Etelian stiffened and turned fully to address the advancing figure whose fingers flashed in motions too fast for the eye to read. But she could guess what they were forming.

Three, two, one—

For all of the classical handsomeness the elder princes possessed—the emperor bred his children well—the thirteenth blessed prince in his natural state looked as though he had been cut from a beauty so overwhelmingly savage it was hard to gaze upon. The culmination of a god himself—terrible and beautiful to view, a glorious sight before the darkest of deaths.

The Shadow Prince was *livid*. Imperial chains flew from his fingers.

She was already in motion, though, dodging restraints while the two other princes were busy trying to anticipate the actions of their furious brother. She dropped her healing oaths, and with them the last restrictions on her, dodged the whipping chains and threw herself over the diving shadow and into the path she *ripped* between stone and space.

"Kaveh, how *dare*—" Etelian moved forward in her peripheral view.

Kaveh ul Fehl didn't hesitate: he threw out a hand, pinning Etelian to the floor with a shadow around his throat, then dove for her.

CHAPTER TWELVE

She felt the wisps of his fingertip shadows as the vortex of her ripgate swirled over her, then she was spit into the street. She hit sandstone and piercing sunlight then scrambled forward, immediately healing her internal bruising.

Find Taline and Rone, get out of the city, leave everything else. Kaveh ul Fehl *knew* her. Their house wasn't safe. Nowhere was safe.

She hadn't just revealed her powers to Kaveh ul Fehl. She'd revealed them to Aros and Etelian, too.

Nowhere was safe. And she had no time for miscalculation.

Early risers stared at her as she scrambled forward wildly, healing and scrubbing herself for shadows, frantically checking the oaths in the street and the oath lights in the distance.

The Shadow Prince had said Taline was being held by the investigorii, but he had said nothing about Rone. If Taline was being held, Nin had five minutes to free her. If she wasn't, going to the penitentiary would result in another meeting with Kaveh ul Fehl.

Nin had no time for being wrong.

Trust in Rone. Trust in Taline.

She dove forward, splitting open another ripgate, and prayed.

KAVEH

Darkness. *Rage.*

"I will kill you for this." Kaveh shot the assembled cage in Etelian's direction.

The fool didn't dodge, and that was his first mistake. He tried to flick away the magic, tried to cast his stripping magic against the offending force like he did everything—evading consequence through long-standing, overwhelming privilege. But the cage had been assembled *specifically* to hold a Level Nine gatemaker. It was almost strong enough to hold the *emperor.* And with the shadow secured around his throat already, Etelian was immediately ensnared.

It was a cage designed to capture Ninli ul Summora. And he'd *had* her, until his idiot half-brother had interfered.

Hunt. Find. Ifret leaped from his throat and launched from the room in a dark blur.

He squeezed tighter as Etelian vainly tried to neutralize the magic around him—flickering and pulsing with light. Kaveh relished the fear in his eyes when he failed.

The neutralizing, stripping magic Etelian used against those already weakened by guards and circumstance was *nothing* to Kaveh, who dealt with death and war every day.

Ifret rose in his mind, snaking forward to capture and destroy. He watched through shadowed eyes as the girl opened a ripgate, then...

Gone.

Kaveh gripped the shadows around his brother's ankles and heard one crunch, then two. Etelian screamed. Kaveh moved to Etelian's knees and broke those.

"Now, Kaveh, you know the emperor would be displeased with Etelian's death." Aros was examining his fingernails in seeming boredom, but Kaveh could see his excitement as his intensely focused gaze was rapidly switching from examining the cage that held Etelian to the spot where Ninli ul Summora had just disappeared. Kaveh could see the edges of the dark, exultant smile Aros was unable to contain.

"I don't know." Kaveh squeezed harder and Etelian went unnaturally purple as he clawed at his throat. "He might *encourage* it in this case."

Aros's mouth turned up in satisfaction. And that action, in the end, was what made Kaveh release the Padifehl of Tehrasi, who fell ungracefully to the floor.

"Too bad," Aros said lightly, as he looked dismissively at his younger brother hacking on the floor, broken legs unnaturally splayed.

"I will have your head for this." Etelian coughed, fingers scrabbling at his throat, then clicked through a spell that would bring someone to heal him. "No one will stand for this. Mother, Father—"

"You have no idea what you interrupted with your little games," Kaveh said coldly.

"Games? That girl was mine to kill. You entered *my* palace, tore up *my home*, and strangled me? Broke my legs?" Etelian rubbed his throat. "Father will *hear* about this."

"Of course he will, brother dear," Aros said to Etelian, though his gaze stayed on Kaveh. "Every last detail."

Etelian went pale.

"The girl is connected to the Hand then?" Aros asked idly.

Kaveh reached through the shadows of the city instead of answering. He knew she was nowhere within the city limits anymore, though. His hands tightened into fists.

"Her?" Etelian scoffed. "A two-fehltan healer? I wouldn't even pay two fehlta for her," he sneered.

"The Hand is something of a folk hero, or so they say in the winds of your districts." Aros hummed. "It would make sense for the thief to have followers of all kinds. Ones with unique skillsets..."

"Petty gambits," Etelian sneered, then jerked to look at the scepter he had dropped, as if remembering that it could heal him with its "petty gambits," tied as he was to its power. Etelian reached out to lift the scepter. "I'll get that stupid girl back. Then I'll torture her until she begs for death. She will pay for *all* of this."

"Your scepter trick won't work again," Kaveh said coldly. "And even if it did, she would tell you nothing."

"Everyone tells," Etelian said, darkness in his gaze as he touched the scepter to his chest and gritted his teeth as light infused him. "Everyone spills their secrets eventually. Scrawnier and plainer than my tastes, but I'll get past it."

Kaveh looked scathingly at the other man. It was something Etelian would never understand, never having had true passion for a cause. Those like the girl, with that look in their eye... The ones with violently shaking hands, who had the ability to stand in front of enemies and meet their gaze, nevertheless. She'd tell only false information. And then she'd die. With the real names and locations clutched in her dead heart.

"You are a fool," Kaveh said.

"I am a king, a *god*." He gazed condescendingly at Kaveh, but very carefully kept his shields raised to their fullest levels—it could be seen in the thin blue haze around him— ready to neutralize anything Kaveh threw as he rose on healed legs, scepter in hand. "I think you have a fool's notion of what it means to be a fool."

He held the scepter in front of him as a weapon. Kaveh eyed it with disdain. If a Carre stood before him with a scepter, he'd be wary. But Etelian was a child playing with a ceremonial pole.

Etelian loved his opulent position in Tehrasi with a grip that would only bend by force. And Etelian's strength was nothing compared to Kaveh's power, or to Aros's cunning. But like any child of the emperor, he was never one on whom to turn a back.

Etelian was a snake in the grass, a coward, who would attack from behind. Aros, too, was a snake, but he, like Kaveh, was more the black snake of death who slithered toward you outright with venom coating his fangs and vengeance in his gaze. Etelian was the asp who fled and hid, then bit when an unknowing hand drew close.

"You will die a fool—with a woman's dagger slipped between your ribs," Kaveh said.

It wasn't a secret that Etelian, who shared the good looks that every Fehl child was gifted—even further enhanced by physical gifts from his beautiful mother—was a bedmate who even the staunchest of courtesans treated with wariness.

The emperor, for all his ways of spreading his empire through vast amounts of blood and seed, treated the thousands of women he bedded with disinterest at worst, pleasant feelings of continuing his legacy at best. Though the emperor only seemed to possess lingering feelings toward two of his many bed partners, he usually compensated any who produced children with some form of financial legacy.

Etelian simply left pain in his wake. His existence was a net negative on the world. Kaveh would treat his passing with a celebratory drink.

Kaveh knew that their father deliberately kept them separated, for Kaveh would kill Etelian given any extended time spent in his company. And Etelian and Aros were the eldest sons of his first and favorite wife. Nera would be...displeased by the snuffing of her sons. And the emperor, even at his greatest, made stupid decisions when it came to Nera's designs.

Aros would have been shuffled to a faraway kingdom long ago, otherwise.

Aros, who was looking *far* too intrigued.

"The girl bothers you," Aros said.

She bothered him a lot. Like a missing piece that was trying to connect in his mind.

He capped further thoughts. Giving Aros any cause to speculate was destructive.

"She has information."

"You tried to capture her, not kill her," Aros said, almost contemplatively, though there was no denying his dark amusement. "She is useful to you in some way. You are *intrigued. Magnificent.*"

Kaveh turned to Etelian, unwilling to play Aros's games. "If she leaves the country, it will be on your head," Kaveh said coldly. "And I will happily collect."

"The greatest warrior in the empire. A general the emperor proclaims the greatest in history. I'm certain you will find this girl," Aros said casually. "This cavity in heretofore water-tight emotional wards."

"Toss your dice elsewhere, Aros," Kaveh said tightly, searching through shadows, listening as ones far away connected to others, then formed a line back to him.

Aros smiled. "Always your mistake, Kaveh. A ruler should never underestimate the game of wit and politics. It is a game that warriors always lose."

South. Gate of Kiet. Three, the shadows whispered.

"Then you will have your day here while mine is far from yours, brother." He pulled the shadows around him and disappeared in a swirl of darkness.

She wouldn't get far.

Mythic Undertakings

Rone

Tehras, Tehrasi

"Mistress Summora. We need you to come quietly."

With the crumbling stone wall of the alley at their back and no other escape route, Rone shifted closer to Taline as the investigore approached. The wall had been targeted. Someone had guessed where they were heading, and what the medallions might be used for.

They had *known* that they could be illegal gates.

That meant Ninli's secrets—at least some of them—had been discovered.

At his side, Taline erected the last of her premade shields. They would last maybe two minutes more. Unfortunately, more investigorii were pouring into the alley, perching on the rooftops above, and hemming them in.

The investigore walked slowly toward them, attempting to peer under Taline's headdress and through her covered form. "Mistress Summora. We know it is you, though you seem to have misplaced your oaths." There was a strange tenor on the last word.

Rone released the latches inside his sleeves.

"Your sister has been apprehended," the investigore said. "You are wanted for questioning on an imperial matter alongside her."

The Shadow Prince had captured her then.

Rone had dealt with the investigore many times on matters where he'd been accused of something he'd definitely done, yet couldn't be punished for. And though the man hated him, he seemed to have a soft spot for Ninli. Unfortunately, that soft spot would not be able to be utilized—there would be no freedom for the girls now that the Shadow Prince knew about Ninli's abilities.

Taline shifted but said nothing.

"Come quietly and I will do all I can for you and your companion."

Rone let the edges of his smile show beneath his hood. "I think not." He pulled two long folding knives from the sheaths in his sleeves and flicked the blades out. He curved the blades through the air into starting position behind the weakening shield.

The investigore matched the movements with care— marking the death form Rone had chosen.

The investigore drew the final glyph that would activate his strongest incarceration spell, keeping them both carefully in view lest they slip the shield for a final attack. Behind him, dozens of his minions drew the same, motions nearly hypnotic in their synchronization.

"You cannot escape. Surrender and live."

The investigorii spells were all tied together, and they were, all of them, tied to the investigore. Breaking the investigore would shatter the others—forcing a backlash that Rone and Taline might be able to use to escape.

Rone gripped his right knife and let power seep through his middle finger pressed against the blade.

Three, two, one...

A dark, shadowed maw rose up behind the investigore and dove toward them. Rone's heart clenched in unwanted fear.

Sehk-Ra.

He scrambled. Battling the investigore was one thing; facing off against the Shadow Prince's pants-wetting familiar—a shadow that ate the hearts and souls of his enemies—was something else entirely. There was only one thing Rone could do in the face of such forces—but it would reveal far more then he wanted known. A last resort.

He took a synchronous step backward with Taline and grabbed the dormant ability deep in his chest—

A crack sounded, then small arms wrapped him and Taline, pressing him against Taline in a far too pleasant bundle.

He yanked his power back with a smirk of relief and, with the residual power still in his finger, he flicked a vulgar hand gesture at the investigore, who lunged toward them far too late, then shifted the gesture's aim toward the shadow whose eyes were windows to its master's soul.

The shadow roared.

The landscape shifted, swirled, and resolved into rock, wind, sand, and whipping magic. Immediately, the arms around him retreated and Ninli ul Summora—looking far worse than when he'd last seen her—scrambled to her feet, raising shields around them. He looked down at Taline, pressed in his arms. She shoved away from him, as though she had suddenly found herself holding the plague, cheeks bright.

He smirked at her response, then surveyed the landscape Ninli had brought them to—a desolate wasteland strip of uncompromising storms and unsettled magic. They were in one of the continual storms that pulled in twisted magic and churned out new, ready streams in order to keep a city stable.

The storms were extremely dangerous to traverse.

"Well, this is a lovely spot," he said dryly, pushing back his hood to check his enchantments. "Not that your timing isn't impeccable."

"Rone," Ninli said fiercely over her shoulder, acknowledging him as fondly as she could under the circumstances. Her attention quickly returned to tracking shadows and holding shields. "Sixty ticks to expel any unwanted *parasites*, then we can leave."

"Got yourself trapped in a sandstorm, little scarab?" He flicked the back of her ear and let it seem as if he cared that she was happy to see him.

He had an inconceivable number of enemies who would

use any tie against him, and yet he couldn't deny the weakness of allowing Ninli ul Summora to think he had fondness for her.

He would never let himself believe that he did.

"You're late," Taline said to Ninli, brushing herself down and checking her satchel to make certain it was intact and free of unwanted additions.

"I had a little trouble with a few princes," Ninli said dryly. "*Legitimate* ones."

"Princes?" Taline's question was sharp.

"Those are hurtful words, Ninli." Rone put a hand to his chest.

"Don't worry, you are still the prettiest." He could see the edge of Ninli's smile. He could also see how it fell as she girded herself to answer Taline. "Kaveh ul Fehl grabbed me. Etelian called me in by scepter to answer for the plague. Aros was there. It was...a mess."

After giving the landscape one last visual search, Ninli turned to Rone, seemingly satisfied that they hadn't been followed. "The empire is chasing us."

"So it would seem. Your sister had implied such in her ramblings."

Taline hissed at that, restarting her search through Ninli's bag.

"Kaveh ul Fehl knows about Taline, but not you," Ninli said seriously. "Your identity enchantments remained unbroken. They are still fully in place. You can get out of this still. The thirteenth prince is furious right now, and I don't know what he'd do to you if you are caught with us. We are in the continual storm strip that is a half-day's ride south from Tehras. There is an oasis to the east, about an hour's walk." She pointed. "You can hitch a ride to the city or go elsewhere until you can wind your way back."

"As if I care about an idiot whose famed ability is that he can speak to imaginary creatures." He flicked grains of sand from his sleeve at Taline's rude, disbelieving gaze.

That automatic backward step when Kaveh ul Fehl's familiar had appeared in the alley had been good combat sense.

"He will follow," Ninli said. "He won't stop. Taline and I are lost to Tehras now." She looked away.

"We will get the scepter," Taline said fiercely. "Make our deal for Tehrasi, then disappear. Start fresh elsewhere. It doesn't matter what Valeran does."

Rone lifted a brow. "I'm going to find the scepter before you two imbeciles."

Ninli smiled, shoulders loosening.

It was dangerous enough to play this much of the game. His well-controlled emotions never seemed to get past the unpaid debt to a ten-year-old slip of a dumb, overpowered orphan who had put her life on the line to save him from having his hands and magic removed *twice*: first while he had hung uselessly over a chopping block—his burgeoning but blocked powers making him nauseous and ineffectual—and a second time when she'd prevented him from using those powers in his cell to stop the census takers from cataloging and revealing him.

There had been no avoiding the census in the empire, though, and he'd followed her to Tehrasi, where she'd assured him she could hide his abilities and limit his oaths with help from her dark past.

The census had been a boon. Ninli and Rone had gotten new starts. With Rone's maternal family's well-known looks, he had gotten a last name he hadn't wanted, but it had been better than taking Fehl. He'd gained a "poor, but passing grade" on the imperial test given to every citizen who might have imperial blood and gained "protections" from the paternal and maternal families he despised, but it had meant there would be no third anonymous escape.

Ninli had been able to change a few things in his census file, but there was nothing she could do about his lineage marker, which had been automatically recorded to the imperial capital so that agents could be sent to assess him for official recognition purposes.

He had severely underperformed his recognition test with Ninli's help, then he had gotten smarter at not getting caught, while Ninli had continued being the naive girl who never expected anything in return.

On the other hand, Taline, the far smarter of the two, made sure to grab Ninli's debts and use them to their advantage.

There were many debts that had been gathered.

His eyes couldn't help shifting to Taline. Her beautiful

eyes were watching closely, protectively. Waiting to slip a dagger between his ribs, if he spoke against her beloved "sister."

Someday she'd do it, because someday, he would sell out Ninli ul Summora—fulfilling his promise to cut the last tie to his humanity—and also sell out her too-beautiful sister who stirred in him far more dangerous things. Taline had read the threat of it in him well enough to be wary.

But then, Taline had always been sharp. Far sharper than her adopted sister when it came to offensive action. Taline was a ledger, whose columns all balanced, save for the one she'd made for Ninli, which would forever be in the other girl's favor. Although Ninli would never call in the staggering numbers of debts that cluttered her broken head, Taline had no problem doing so on her behalf.

"The Shadow Prince *will* kill us," Ninli said, still serious.

"It is one of his skills," he said blandly.

"Do you know him?" she asked curiously.

"No."

Rone made certain to stay as far away from his half-siblings as was possible. There were hundreds of the emperor's progeny, scattered far and wide, so sometimes it wasn't easy. But he made certain to stay far away from the "blessed" ones at the top of the chain—the children the emperor had recognized through ceremony. Rone wanted nothing to do with the empire.

The emperor kept loose tabs on his bastards once they reached a certain age. But his scouts were easily located, and

Rone made certain that he always showed his clearest and dumbest hand when one was near. Hiding would mean he had something to hide. So he made certain to "hide" only semi-illegal, foolish activities.

A two-fehltan gambler with a too-handsome face who could "acquire" stolen properties, but never seem to keep them. It was stupidly easy to show what he wanted them to see, especially with the legacy of his mother's family.

Valerans were vain and flighty, given to shiny things and easily distracted. Everyone knew that.

He smiled. "Now tell me your idiotic plan."

Her eyes lit.

Ninli was only a year younger than Taline—two years younger than him—and she'd had an equally brutal life, so it never ceased to amaze him how fiercely optimistic she was. So determined to think the empire could give this forsaken country something the Carres had never been able to.

Determined, even more so when the shadows of darkness that she vainly tried to suppress lit the back of her spelled eyes.

Those shadows were always gone quickly, converted into a resoluteness that could do great things, if given the opportunity.

An old soul with fresh eyes.

Rone did his part in burning the world around him in subtle ways as he casually strode through it. No use caring too much about it, but also no use wasting opportunities to cause destruction and chaos.

Covering the past by adopting a new outlook was something they both had done successfully, as opposed to Taline, who wore her cynicism like a cloak of maturity.

Maybe the type of trauma mattered.

"The only idiot here is the one you would view in a mirror," Taline said darkly.

"Why would I wish to look in a mirror when you stand before me? You are looking especially mussed at the moment. Quite the sight." He leered.

"Don't talk to me of vanity with that 'windswept' hair spell laced over your head."

"Well, I don't want to give anyone the impression that I'm *tame*. No, if I talked of vanity between us, it would be to see you without all those spells you plaster on. A truly divine affair."

She bared her teeth. "I'll remember to grant it as your last request before I carve my blade through your chest."

It was enormously tragic that he couldn't unwrap the package of Taline ul Summora. He had no doubt it would be both extraordinary and completely damning.

Meanwhile, Ninli had carefully unwrapped the bundle in her hand, ignoring them. His gaze—his entire world—narrowed in on the totem cradled in the softly creased linen draped over her hand.

"You got past the traps," he murmured, fingers itching to reach out. Only long-standing control kept them still. "You got through the first chamber."

"You've been to the temple." Ninli didn't sound

surprised, even though a normal person would be astounded. The temple was secret, after all. *Mythically* secret.

"And never laid hands on that totem," Taline said grouchily. "Why exactly is he needed?"

"No one outside the old palace knows scepter lore like Rone." Ninli cocked her head. "But you've never tried for it."

He looked at her from hooded eyes. "Hand-sized emeralds and medallions of power are easy to hunt and easier still to part with for payment. I know what would happen if the scepter were in my hands."

Calm understanding flooded Ninli's gaze.

Taline, however, frowned deeply. "If it were in your hands, you'd sell it. You are a profiteer."

"That I am, narsumina." He flashed her a smile and leered again. "And you have hired the very best."

She set her jaw and he couldn't resist a wink. She growled, slung Ninli's bag over her shoulder, and stomped over to the edges of Ninli's protected plateau, setting enchanted pieces she dug from the bag to the cardinal directions around them.

He turned to Ninli, who was looking at Rone with a far too knowing gaze.

"Someday she will spit me upon a spear," he said lightly. "And you will be down an ally."

Ninli didn't say anything for a moment, then murmured too low for her sister to hear above the raging storm outside, "I trust you to get her out. When...when things go wrong."

Rone shifted uncomfortably. "How unwise of you."

"You can tell her I paid you for it." She looked at the

other girl as she continued to irritably orient the pieces to their correct directions. "Just...please. I don't need you to promise anything else. No balm to any other betrayal you might decide upon. I just need to know you will get her out when things go wrong. That she will be safe." She looked at him.

He searched the deep conflict in her eyes. "You are certain about doing this?"

"Yes. Even if we flee, Kaveh ul Fehl will find us. His reputation precedes him. He'll never stop. He'll take the totem and Osni will eventually decode it. Osni is the definitive scepter scholar for a reason. He has the entire palace library at his disposal and all the finest—bar the two of us—scepter scholars and minds in Tehrasi. All of them can be bought for the chance to see it found."

"Osni's standing has decreased. Rumor has it that the emperor will see him dead."

"He's a muck beetle. Rotten. Too narrowly focused and driven. But he'll survive on pure malice and drive until there is nothing left of the world around him," she said bitterly. "He made certain the Carres were executed, and yet he still lived. He hasn't solved the real problem with the scepters for ten years, and I destroyed his stolen patchwork of blood and spells, and yet he still lives. Never count out the rat."

TALINE

As Nin and Valeran whispered in tones too low to hear behind her, Taline dug through her sack until she found the last lodestone. She didn't like having Valeran around, period. She hated the turmoil he provoked in her—emotions she would *never* examine. But she liked even less that he had some influence over Nin.

She had no good feelings about any of this. It felt like the end was coming. A dark end she couldn't see.

Nothing good came from princes.

She could feel the shadows gaining ground in the distance. Their largest problem.

She trudged back over as Nin's gaze switched to the distance—feeling the same thing Taline had. "The Shadow Prince has found us. We have to decide what to do."

Valeran grimaced. "We use Ninli's lovely ability to create distances between us once more."

Taline crossed her arms. "Nin isn't an inexhaustible power source, Valeran. She will pass out eventually, especially when transporting the two of us along with her. And moving in less familiar places requires more processing, more brain mapping, which means expending more energy. And the more she uses, the longer it takes to recover. She can't keep moving us. And she can't transport us blindly without consequence. The image of you falling into a volcano is almost enough for me to allow it, but I'd rather keep *my* skin attached."

"And such lovely skin it is. But we will not stay hidden for long. Long stretches of desert or tundra are one thing, but we have to go through towns for the supplies that were left behind." He lifted his hands at her bristling to indicate he wasn't casting fault. "And we will need to traverse the forest eventually—and there, no corner will be safe. Rather than wasting energy, Kaveh ul Fehl could simply wait for us at the temple. I would."

Nin shook her head. "He'll come after us directly. He can't count on us going to the temple. We could wait weeks to go. We could change our minds. No, he won't simply wait for us outside. He'll come after us and we have to anticipate fighting him."

"We will, eventually, have to go to the temple, unless you change your plan," Valeran pointed out.

"There's a hidden entrance." Nin looked up at him. "It's why we didn't disturb the wards established by the raiders who sold the location."

"There are three chambers in scepter lore," Valeran said. "The key chamber. The lock chamber. And the antechamber. Your secret entrance leads to the key chamber? What of the others?"

"The secrets of the key chamber were the only ones gifted to those in the palace who might traverse them. Information on the other chambers was zealously guarded by the king, queen, and crown prince."

"An antechamber means that there is a bigger chamber beyond," Taline said. "So, there is a fourth chamber."

Nin and Rone exchanged looks. "The scepter, by lore, does not reside in the temple. It is accessed elsewise."

"By gate."

"Yes."

"But there is a chamber, somewhere, that holds it."

"Somewhere. Yes."

"What if it's in the heart of beasts? The worlds beyond? What if we find something worse? Something that will come after us, too?" Taline asked, heart sinking.

"The Shadow Prince is already after us. What's another beast?" But Valeran's forced joviality only increased her guilt. She saw him stiffen strangely at whatever expression crossed her face.

Taline picked at her sleeve. "We need to go to the shops in Urshna then."

Nin winced. "You don't have your scope?"

Taline gripped her hands together. "I lost a bag when we were fighting. If I hadn't—"

"I didn't have time to grab the last satchel from the house either," Nin pointed out, touching her hand. "It had our other scope inside. If you are guilty, so am I."

"Was there anything left in those bags that will lead them to us?" Valeran was concentrating on the shadows growing nearer.

Nin hesitated. "No, but the items left behind will reinforce that we are going to the temple."

"Maybe Kaveh ul Fehl will go there directly after we leave this Sehk-forsaken rock. Osni has to be at the temple already."

CHAPTER THIRTEEN

"We can purchase the glass in Urshna," Nin said.

"Of course we can. Only the dreadful get caught," Valeran said.

"You've been caught how many times, Valeran?"

"Do I look to be in a prison cell, narsumina?"

"No, your tongue is too silvered and your palm too gilded for that."

"What I hear you saying is that I'm clever and rich."

"More like slippery and oathless."

"What is that ward I see shining on you right now?" He peered at her, then gasped, one gold lock dramatically overlapping a red one as he reared his head back. "Is that a hypocrisy ward?"

The sound she made was more of a growl than a hiss. "Three Fehl princes know Nin might be a gatemaker. The entire empire will be on the lookout for her."

They couldn't go back to Tehras. That bothered her less than it would bother Nin. As long as they were together, Taline was happy to start fresh. But starting fresh was going to be a lot harder now.

"By now, I have to assume Etelian or Aros ul Fehl have gone through my identity and flagged it—there is nothing in there about gate affinities. Lying on a census roll is punishable by death, and if that was the extent of the infraction, I'd take it. But we all know what happens to gatemakers. And Aros..." She shook her head. "Unlike Etelian, who relies on his handlers, Aros is clever. I assume he knows that I, at least, am the Hand. We have to assume that both pieces of information have been shared with the investigore by now."

She could never go back. Not as Ninli ul Summora, and not as a healer. Not as...anyone.

"We'll become something new." Taline nodded sharply, switching from castigating Valeran to comforting Nin. "I've always fancied the name Lilin. From Bahra, maybe. And Areda is so common, we could make it work. Lilin ul Areda. We can go to Indi. Attend the masked ball. Experience a cassirie."

Nin smiled and squeezed her hand. "Yes."

Nin's gaze slid to Valeran. "Thank you for helping," she said to him.

Taline grimaced and Valeran's expression pinched. "You are paying me. I do expect my reward. But 'dark and vicious' comes, so we should be going." He waved toward the overwhelming knot of darkness flying over the barren landscape.

"Thank you for helping," she repeated, even more seriously.

He looked skyward for a count of ten beats, then dropped his gaze, first to Taline, then to Nin. "Fine. Yes. Ready?" He pulled his hood back into place.

They jumped.

GLASS SURPRISES

NINLI

URSHNA, TEHRASI

It took them two days of careful jumps to reach Urshna. Every distorted shadow caused a skipped beat of the heart. Every whisper of darkness preceded a missed breath.

But they were still in Tehrasi, and Nin held some advantage on the lands of her ancestors—lands bound tightly by blood and servitude.

They had visited twelve towns and one oasis and secured all but one of the critical items that Taline needed, while spreading rumors and sightings as they went. The glass was the key component in the scope, though, and it was only available in Urshna—a medium-sized village of glassblowers and workers.

If they were going to be ambushed before they reached

the temple, Urshna was where it would likely happen. Both lost bags had contained a scope. A clever tracker would note the contents and consider the possibilities.

They had debated going to Urshna first but had decided that it was too obvious and that waiting might imbue impatience in their follower.

Tensions ran high as they carefully surveilled the town and glass shops. They hadn't seen a wisp of shadow out of place, but it didn't mean one wasn't lurking.

"I should be the one to buy it," Taline said. "I know which lens we need."

"No." Nin was implacable. "I know the glass we need, as well. And if things go wrong, I can get out."

"Right. Like you were able to get out at the guild," Taline said pointedly.

"I still had oaths upon me. Besides, he'll go for you." She didn't look at Taline as she said it. "To use against me."

"Nin—"

"And, I know the feel of his shadows now. Each time he uses them, they become more familiar."

She had the feeling very few people had escaped after having one attached. And although shadow attachment was said to give away the thoughts of the one trapped, she had glimpsed some of the prince's thoughts in return.

"I can anticipate him," she insisted.

Taline looked unimpressed.

"You are both amusing," Rone said, shifting a throwing knife rapidly between fingers. "The solution is quite obvious."

"If you say that we should go in posing as a married couple, I will kill you," Taline said.

"Sehk, no. Married to you? Horrible. *I* will be going in alone." He plucked up the scarab pin that allowed shared spell owners to see the view when worn.

"I should go," Nin insisted, trying to grab it back from him. "I stand a better chance at getting out."

"I am fully capable of removing myself from danger."

Taline snorted.

"You can't go in fully covered, though," Nin said, still trying to reach the pin from her far smaller height. "It will be too suspicious. And uncovered, you'll be exposed."

"You worry too much, Ninli. I'm wounded, frankly."

He bounded over the edge of the building and Taline swore.

Nin sighed. "Well, here we go."

Nin and Taline crouched beneath a line of billowing bedsheets set out to dry on a rooftop with a direct line of sight to the glassmaker's shop. Taline tracked Rone's route through the scarab pin as Nin canvassed the area around the town. The town was small, but there was still a lot of area for one person to cover.

The itchy feeling of darkness started to beat under her skin.

"He's here." Nin scanned the area where the feeling was emanating. "South quadrant of town, but moving in your direction. Hurry, Rone." She pushed the preset spell on

Taline's communication box that fed to the black scarab on his scarf.

From the street, he waved a negligent hand as if to say, "Understood. Don't rush me."

He strolled into the open-air glass shop as if he were simply browsing. Rone's scarf was pulled over his distinctive hair, but his face was covered only by the barest of face-changing spells.

Nin didn't like it. She didn't like it at all.

Picking up a few things here and there from the shelves, Rone flicked his wrist in signal, and Taline used the spell that would allow her to see through the scarab pin. The view wavered with the glass, but it was enough for her to analyze the samples.

"That one," Taline murmured aloud, clicking a series of commands into the scarab. Rone correctly lifted the glass sample indicated.

He paid for it, along with five other random items, then strolled from the shop. Taline breathed a sigh of relief, but Nin felt none of it. Something was coming. She grabbed for the controller.

RONE

Rone could see the girls in their cramped hiding spot on the rooftop, Taline looking reluctantly relieved as he approached from below.

The last pulse he'd gotten from the scarab had indicated that the Shadow Prince was now meticulously making his way from the south through the west quadrant of town.

So when the shadows formed into spikes in front of him and the eyes of the girls blew wide in panic, he...sighed.

The scarab lit his nerves with the warning of danger five seconds too late. *Thank you, Ninli.* He sighed again and slowly shifted to allow his fingers easier access to his short swords.

"You aren't at all who I thought I'd find in the skin of the third traitor," a dark voice said behind him. "I almost passed you by, but for that odd piece of jewelry clasped to your chest."

Rone slowly turned to survey the man who had appeared from the shadows. He touched his headscarf, checking the spells that subtly changed his features.

"I am but a weary traveler, my lord, who is in need of funds and looking to sell this lovely piece you have so admired."

"Play not, Rone, born of the Valerans. Your death is not ideal, but will be served nevertheless, should you hinder me."

A litany of curse words chained through his mind. "Who? I think you have made a mistake, kind sir."

Kaveh ul Fehl looked distinctly unamused. "You think you have not been marked? You are a son of the emperor, no matter the last name you were given upon registry."

Rone gritted his teeth. Marked? He'd made damn sure never to be on the empire's scope. He'd passed dozens of half-siblings with zero recognition. Staying far from the elite ones had possibly been a mistake—he would have noticed them casting their gaze his way.

The Summoras had gotten him into a world of red-slicked necks again.

Rone had always been a *little* in trouble with the empire. His position as an unblessed prince had shielded him from some of the more grievous trouble he'd gotten into after being registered, but he'd pushed the boundaries in both directions, against both sides of his lineage.

Still, fighting against the darling of the emperor was a certain way to gain a death glyph. It sucked doubly that the darling was the most physically capable of their lot.

He pasted on his most vacuous smile. "Your Imperial Highness! I didn't recognize you there in the creepy darkness. What a joy! Whatever are you doing in Urshna in the middle of nowhere?" He subtly moved right, and the Shadow Prince mirrored him.

Unlike the majority of Rone's foes, the prince was not someone who would make combat mistakes. "Where is Ninli ul Summora?"

In his periphery, he saw the girls duck from view. Rone shrugged, and the action loosened his short swords completely, each falling to the bases of his sleeves. "I can't say I know. I would look for her in Tehras."

"You don't deny knowing her, though. Interesting."

"Knowing Ninli ul Summora? Everyone who has lived in Tehras knows her, at least by reputation. Hard not to with all the women yammering after her like she's divinity."

"She is wanted by the empire."

"I didn't know you were expecting! Congratulations!" He shrugged forward in feigned anticipation, leather handles falling into his palms. "Who is the lucky lady giving birth to the future shadow princeling?"

The tic in his half-brother's jaw grew more prominent. "You are a son of the emperor. You are honor bound to serve the empire. But I will enter your name in the death rolls, if you prove difficult. Where is Ninli ul Summora?"

Where indeed—the scarab was shocking his chest with all sorts of panicked messages and directions.

Rone wrapped each short sword's leather hilt with his fingers, hiding the ends within his thumb grips, and pressed the blades flat against his forearms. He cocked his head, looking to the distance, then pointed with the single left finger that wasn't wrapped around the hilt. "She's on that roof over there. Strange. How did you know she was here?"

Rone was already in motion before the end of the last word, but then, too, so was Fehl. Rone's cloak swung out and his scarf snapped to grab the pointed shadow flying at his throat before throwing it to the side. Another shadow hit him, but his blade sliced the outside of the Shadow Prince's left arm.

Wreathed in shadow, darkness surged over the wound, then fled, leaving golden skin unmarked. "You think to stop me with blades, Valeran?"

Kaveh ul Fehl was one of the brethren he'd never had a single desire to meet across a battlefield.

Rone sighed. "Yes."

Rone wasn't a soldier on the battlefront, and he would never beat the man across from him on one, but in back alley brawls? He knew how to slip a knife between ribs. He held tight to that thought.

"You are still only a man," Rone said.

The Shadow Prince smiled, then disappeared.

"Three-quarters of a man," Rone corrected, wanting to sigh again—damn the Summoras—but he had no time, already striking the first shadow as the second wrapped around his throat. He stuck the blade that Ninli had enchanted on the first night of this damnable quest into the first shadow. He twisted the blade, watching the shadow burst.

He pierced the second at the same time a poison-laced dagger slipped between his ribs. Not good. Rone pivoted, withdrawing the burning blade from his body with a hiss and throwing it in an arc toward its owner while freezing the wound to temporarily seal the poison with his other hand. Ninli could heal anything. He just had to survive this encounter.

Rone struck to the right and was hit on the left side. He guessed better in the next strike, and found his target.

Kaveh ul Fehl swiped savagely at the blood running down his arm and flicked it to the ground. Three shadows grew from the drops and swarmed up to fix the slice.

Damn Summoras.

Rone wasn't accustomed to losing. But he knew within those three hits that he wouldn't win this fight.

KAVEH

Valeran's arms rose and his teeth gritted against the pain as Kaveh sent an infected shadow into his latest wound.

Boring, but irritating.

Another sibling. One of the hundreds who lived outside the palace's protections. Most of them were worth little thought or concern. Other than as an addition to the gilded roll the emperor kept that contained the names, talents, connections, and gifts of his many children, most unrecognized children of the emperor would be lost to history and knowledge.

Children of the emperor had a *chance* at a strong bloodline, but those who weren't scooped up for their manifested power contained no real threat or reason for the rest of them to care.

Kaveh knew this one by reputation. He supposedly had their father's charm and the emperor's skill at getting what he wanted.

He was listed as an independent player with little care for either house of his birth, but his notorious parental heritage allowed him some freedom in the worlds that lived in the shadows. His reputation painted him a charmer, adventurer, gambler, and no more.

Charming, clever, and uninterested—the perfect cover for a person with enough wits to keep secrets.

Kaveh stabbed him again, twisting the shadowblade and infecting the wound with a third poison.

Valeran knew how to fight, and he championed trickery in his movements—a tactic which would stand him in good stead in most fights. But it took more than that to escape once Kaveh focused his power. People simply didn't know how to fight him and win.

The Valerans were masters of elemental magic. Reportedly, little of the Valerans' talents had manifested in the bastard they scorned, but there was a chance that the man in front of him had hidden his abilities well.

He carved a brutal slice up Valeran's side, wondering whether Valeran had any talent with ice at all. He'd be doing better if he did.

Another hit, another injection of poison. The man was stumbling now.

It seemed so odd that he didn't display more ability. Bastard son to the third granddaughter of the family head—a *powerful* line by all reports.

It was how their father worked, after all. He saw someone with interesting abilities or a strong family line, and he sought the combination with his own. Bastard children were spread throughout every conquered land—and those beyond, like the Valerans in their icy northern estates. Connected only by three gates to the vast, ocean-bound lands of the desert, rainforests, and sea-gilded shore folk, the Valerans guarded their lands well.

There were as many peoples as there were climates in the

Medit and Ersine ocean-bound lands, and the emperor was keen to collect them all under one banner, before setting off across the waters to the distant lands.

With the Scepter of Darkness, they wouldn't have to build a single boat.

Losing an underperforming and unacknowledged prince in the duty of gaining the scepter would be an acceptable loss.

"Will you kill me, Your Imperial Highness?" It was said casually, but Valeran's weight remained on the balls of his feet. Valeran's gaze remained impassive, but magic had steadily been thickening the air.

Kaveh's eyes narrowed, pulling on his knowledge of the man before him.

The Valeran heiress had been kicked out of her family for not terminating the child, then somehow clawed her way back into the family years later, abandoning her son to the streets. It had only been the census registration rolls that had revealed that story and the child—and by then Rone ul Valeran had shown as merely midrange in ability and completely disinterested in contributing to the empire.

Kaveh sent a blow just short of mortal. Valeran took the hit, but the magic around them thickened again.

Kaveh's eyes narrowed and he pulled Valeran's registered name from the invisible marking on his magic that every child of the emperor was scored with.

Rone al Seven el Interpreter il Copen ol Gomen ul Valeran floated into the air in smoky lines.

Gomen. The same oath temple as the Summoras. And this wasn't Level Seven power thickening the air.

"Royalty are not exempt from oathbreaking and treachery." Kaveh flicked away the smoke. Maybe this fight would be a little more interesting here at the end of Rone ul Valeran's life.

"We are all only human, after all," Valeran said with a sharp red-splattered smile and death in his eyes.

"You have no true line. No loyalty." Kaveh lifted his hand.

"And yours is nothing but blindness. I'd say I'm the smart one."

Losing an underperforming princeling would hardly cause a stir. Kaveh raised Ifret in the air.

NINLI

Anxiety curled within Nin, along with grim acceptance as the Shadow Prince lifted his familiar against Rone. Blue eyes shot with brown and blond hair shot with red, Rone was a man whose entire existence was a battle between two sides—neither that he wanted.

"He won't stop," Nin murmured.

Taline's fingers moved rapidly over a gold spellbox, grim lines carving her face as she set power anchors. "Haven't we already identified that?"

"No. You misunderstand. Kaveh ul Fehl won't stop chasing us, and Rone won't stop defending us. And Rone is about to lose." She watched him dodge one last time and felt magic flood the air. Tactics and enemy vows ran like lightning through her mind. She'd lost her ability to read, but the ability to strategize had been left as intact as her guilt when she'd awakened after her five-story fall. "Our game changes. Now."

"Defending us? Valeran—"

"Is about to lose," Nin said grimly as the Shadow Prince's familiar opened its jaws. "We can't let him lose."

"He just needs to hold out for another minute," Taline argued, though Nin could see Taline's strain as she, too, recognized that Rone was likely about to die. "I'm almost finished. We throw this, then you can get us all out of here."

Magic thickened suddenly, overwhelmingly.

"He doesn't have another minute."

"Nin, *no*—"

But Nin understood something about Rone that Taline hopefully never would. A secret that Nin had promised never to tell.

She grabbed Taline about the waist and dove from the roof; Taline's screams echoed in her ears.

Both men looked up.

Nin set multiple maneuvers to quick succession. She pointed her free palm at Kaveh ul Fehl, who smartly dodged the blast, and threw her sister at Rone with the other hand while opening a ripgate beneath them. Taline and Rone dropped into the oasis that had been their backup plan, if things went poorly.

Nin sliced the ripgate closed before a shadow could slip inside. Gold burst in a wave, shooting outward from the closed ripgate.

She flipped in the air and used a slip of wind to slow her momentum as she landed, crouched on the stones in front of the Shadow Prince and his deadly familiar.

She rose to meet his wrath.

CONTRACTS WITH DEMONS

NINLI

URSHNA, TEHRASI

Slicing through space and throwing Rone and Taline had depleted her energy fiercely. She had to be smart. She had conserved just enough energy to get herself out, too, but there were...opportunities here. Opportunities that might mean the difference between Rone and Taline staying alive, and their plans reaching fruition.

Final moves took shape in her mind, as death incarnate swirled around her—incarnate shadow given life.

Kaveh ul Fehl couldn't fully wrap her in shadows and hold her like he had in the alley or at the guild. He had neither the thick night shadows nor an oath trap in place to do so. But he could kill her.

He was too fast, now that he knew what she was capable of. Only the element of surprise had given her the precious moments it took for her to open space from one place to another, dive through, then close it again. The more people she took, and the more unfamiliar the territory, the larger the time it took to open and close a successful ripgate.

If she had gone with Rone and Taline instead of defending, Kaveh ul Fehl would have hitched a ride with them.

She carefully watched his shadows and the way the wind unnaturally fluctuated around her shoulders, anticipating the placement of the cage he held. She might not make it out intact, but she *would* leave—intact or with missing pieces— before he got *that* on her.

He seemed to understand, because he held the cage instead of throwing it, his sharp gaze carefully watching her in the same way she watched him—looking for opportunity.

She had been raised to see opportunities and to crush and take advantage of them, the same as the man before her. And though she'd tried putting her training to better use, she couldn't deny an advantage when it fluttered before her.

His dark eyes were intensely focused. "You could serve the empire in ways that could hardly be imagined."

"Imagination is not new to the empire, Kaveh ul Fehl. The Carres knew how to use gatemakers," she said, without bothering to hide her venom at the memories. "You would not be singularly clever by thinking up ways to use rare skills on a battlefield."

"And yet the Carres died powerless."

She gripped the knife in her hand.

He was watching her as if trying to delve within her soul, looking for a hook, the same as she was. "Once more, your oaths are gone, as if they never existed. You are too young to have been an oathmaster under the Carres, yet you express anger on their behalf, which points to a palace appointment."

"The scholari has been quite lax about what he allows to be *stolen* from his capital. I need not have known how to do *anything* before he took power, or have any emotion concerning rulers who existed before I was old enough to care."

"You expect me to believe that you know how to manipulate royal oaths and yet were not of the palace elite?"

"I don't care what you believe." But that wasn't entirely true. And if she were going to try this gambit, she needed to offer something. Interest. Bait. "But yes, my parents died in the palace purge."

"Carre supporters?"

She laughed without humor. "Through and through."

"And your position?"

"None."

"Lie."

She thought of Lorsali and her sadistic instructions. "I was in training for one."

"So you are a Carre supporter. Trying to mete out revenge on Crelu ul Osni and the empire for their deaths?"

"Tehrasi is better without the Carres. But though I welcome many of the empire's aims, you are not without failure. Especially the failure to appoint the right leaders."

"An oathbreaker complaining about appointments. Amusing."

"I have no oath to your people, only a personal one to support the populace and fight tyranny."

"Tyranny—yet you say you welcome the empire."

"Many of its aims. Blind support is failure, however. The scholari, for instance, does nothing to increase benefit for Tehrasi, or indeed the empire as a whole. And the current padifehl wants only that which will benefit himself. The elite are a problem on their own, but with a change in leadership—"

"Etelian ul Fehl will rule Tehrasi until his death," he said, voice flat.

And here was the gamble.

Kaveh ul Fehl was singularly loyal. Of all the princes, he was one of the few she held in regard. His loyalty and honor were without question. She wouldn't have thought him swayable a week ago. Would have said there was nothing to bind their views.

But she had seen him pin Etelian ul Fehl.

As she'd ported from the palace, she'd *seen* him wrap a shadow around the padifehl's neck, pinning him in place. Like *no* assassin had been able to.

And she could see that he *disdained* the man in the way he formed the syllables of his name and the flat look on his face.

Common ground. *Opportunity.*

"They say you are unaffected by emotion." She pivoted

slowly, keeping him in view as he stalked a slow circle around her. "That you are loyal, above all else, to the emperor."

Death incarnate didn't pause his predatory steps.

"What would an oathbreaker know of loyalty?"

She didn't respond to the deliberate taunt. "They say that you are as powerful as a worldbreaker, but that you ruin with rational intent."

He stalked. She pivoted. A dance.

"They say that you are full of a simmering, insatiable bloodlust, but that you can be reasoned with."

A terrible smile turned his lips. "No one says the latter."

She kept peripheral watch on his hands and shadows, while never disconnecting her gaze from his, variables and strategies whipping through her mind.

Etelian ul Fehl was Tehrasi's bane, but he might also be a far weaker link in the empire than she'd thought. Etelian had part of the emperor's gift. It was a weakened, diluted version, but enough of the gift at all that she had thought the emperor would never remove him. The emperor sought the manifestation of his own gifts—and in Etelian there was a chance for future generations.

But the other children of the emperor had no such constraint... And rumors stated that there was little love lost between those of Nera's lineage and those of other strong maternal lines. Battling for regard and legacy at the highest levels left little room for filial emotion. The Carres had been no different. Only the youngest members had sought connections—and that undoubtedly would have been bled from them as well.

The emperor's legions of children were vast, so some of them surely held regard for others. But at least between Nera's spawn and Irsula's, there seemed to be little.

Opportunity.

This was how Nin and Taline could *win.*

"I will give the Scepter of Darkness to you."

He laughed. "Try again, little warp sparrow."

"I swear it."

Death incarnate stared back at her, eyes measuring, darkness spiking. "The word of an oathbreaker means nothing."

"Not if I tie myself to the oath with the power I use to break them." They were still on Tehras soil, drenched with hundreds of years of blood. "And if I make the oath unbreakable with that power." It was the only true way to hold someone in Tehrasi who could manipulate oath.

The darkness around him spiked again, this time with interest.

"The scepter will be yours, free to use," she said. "Free to reset the entirety of the Carre scepters, under two conditions."

He tilted his head, the incarnate shadow draping his neck like a seductive lining of a too expensive cloak.

"The current Padifehl of Tehrasi and Scholari of Tehrasi must be dethroned," she said.

He watched her for a long moment, gaze dissecting. "The emperor makes such decisions."

"Not if his favorite is tied to the oath involved."

"Your death will solve that problem." He casually threaded the handle edge of a throwing knife through his fingers.

"You need what I stole from the temple. You know I stole something. You can't acquire the scepter on your own." She pivoted and kept him in careful view as he circled her again. "If Osni lays hands on the scepter, he will key it immediately. He makes a play for the last of his revenge."

"He will die in such a play."

"At what cost?"

"Scepters in hand, the Carres still lost."

"Yes." She smiled grimly. "But they did not wield the Scepter of Darkness in that fight. And without Osni's engineering and betrayal, the result might have been far different for your side. You see a weak, spineless man, but you aren't looking for the fire asp beneath."

"So you want to give me the scepter instead. Foolish of you."

"I wish no one to have the scepter," she said. "But it *will* be held soon, so I will put faith in the empire because the alternative, to me, is worse."

"And how is it that *you* are able to provide such an unparalleled relic of power?" His movements changed from casual prowling to intensely predatory.

"I know the Carres' tricks. You've said so yourself."

"Detaching royal oaths are not the same as dismantling royal traps."

"And yet they were done by the same hand. You need me to get the scepter."

"Then I will use you to get it."

"You need me *willing.*"

All of a sudden, he was a hairsbreadth away, the hair on her neck lifting beneath his breath as his fingers brushed the skin. "Doubtful. I only have need of your sister's windpipe beneath my curled fingers."

She laughed without humor, then slipped through his fingers and *pushed* herself to the other side of the street. Moving herself within the same relative space—she could do *that* forever. "Death comes for both of us without a deal. I learned more than *tricks* from the Carres." She bared her teeth and let an endless vortex spin in her palm. She could take the entire street out. She would not be spared, but neither would he. "I learned instrumental lessons on vengeance and pure intractability."

"You are mistaken if you think I leave enemies alive for vengeance to form."

"Crelu ul Osni and Etelian ul Fehl are your enemies. They are both enemies to the vision of your emperor. But I will be your enemy, if I must."

KAVEH

Kaveh watched the purple light swirl. He could consume her completely in shadows, disintegrating her entirely, before it fully formed. She was doubtlessly aware.

But she *interested* him. And there were opportunities here to exploit.

He cared what happened in Tehrasi only in so much as the gates remained active. The jewel of Tehrasi lay in its gates and scepters and their abilities to connect places far away that could be conquered and united under the banner of the empire.

Being swayed by weaker emotions had never been a problem, but the hard benefits of her negotiating points were solid. The gates were all that mattered, and if the current stewards couldn't keep them going, then another solution was needed.

Osni was disposable, and Kaveh had seen Etelian's end in Aros's eyes. He would be cannibalized by Aros on the day Aros chose.

Kaveh had never much cared for scepter lore. There were plenty of others obsessed with it—there had never been any need for him to be—but something told him that this girl spoke truth. Her words weren't false. She believed that she could retrieve the Scepter of Darkness.

And he was *interested*. There were secrets here. Questions

that spoke of something larger than finding a gatemaker with massive power.

"You give me the scepter; Etelian and Osni are deposed." No timeline there. "Those are your terms?"

"Yes."

They'd get the scepter no matter what—either through Osni or this girl.

He shrugged. "Done."

"I'll want an oath on those terms plus ones protecting my friends."

Kaveh's mouth curved unpleasantly. "An oathbreaker demanding troth?"

"Yes."

"And yours in return?"

Her lips firmed. "Yes."

Kaveh laughed, rusty and hard. "You are ill if you think naivete one of my failings."

"You will get neither scepter nor renewal without me. Your agreement is one of negative consequence."

"I gain only if I play?" He leaned forward into her space. "I could find the temple through Osni. I have only to strip the key from you. You think the threat in your hand will stay mine, but I could break you right here."

"You would have already tried it, had you thought there nothing else to gain."

He narrowed his eyes at her assurance.

"A binding oath," she said. "A direct tie to the end. Life-force bound."

His eyes sharpened. Life-force bound? For the first time in this discussion, she actually had his attention for negotiation. The Carres had been famous for their life-force bonds—irrevocably tying all servants and staff to the lives of the king and queen.

None of the palace staff had survived the death of their rulers, and this girl claimed to know how to put such a bond in place.

Questions within secrets, and a gatemaker besides. Instinct said tying this girl to him would give far greater rewards than the scepter alone. He tapped a finger against the living shadow around his neck and began. "A custodial bond. Proximity based."

She gritted her teeth, but he saw her eyes light with the understanding that this was a negotiation now. "A promissory oath."

"Custodial and life-force on your end, if you don't deliver," he said. "I kill Crelu ul Osni—in any manner you choose—if the scepter is in my possession by the start of the next dark moon."

"The Fehl of our choice on the throne."

"Etelian will be dealt with...eventually."

"Eventually?"

"Your life and that of your sister. A fortnight's running start."

She firmed her lips.

He leaned in. "I can kill you now," he murmured.

"Osni deposed within a month. Etelian within three

years. You will protect the three of us and vice versa while finding the scepter. You will claim Rone helped *you,* not us. Three imperial travel cards, cloaks, and you let us go with a month's head start as soon as the scepter is in your hand."

He smiled. "My protection is not often sought."

"Your company likely isn't either. And yet, we will be traveling with you for at least the next two days. I don't want to find Rone one morning with his head casting a separate shadow from his body."

"*You* have put him in danger."

He watched her face crease. She cared about her companions. A true weakness. He had seen servants in the palace who cared—dying upon their own sword for some paltry intrigue of the person they served, forgotten the next week. He wondered which Carre she had served, and how she had survived.

"I have," she said. "I will find a way to make that right."

"Nothing will make it right. The empire will hunt Rone ul Valeran down."

"You will claim him as your partner, not ours."

"Do not look through bad glass, little sparrow. Make your deal and live with the consequences. Show me your vows."

She closed her eyes and held out both hands, palms up. Light shifted and formed whorls above her hands, then the coils pushed themselves into the terms of the oath—each piece separated by space and intent. The intentions of a life-force oath were important. Intentions could be seen and felt.

Honesty. Desperation. Intense drive. All of the things he had learned about her through written and oral reports, through seeing her actions and resolve, were laid before him in clear, stark lines.

Life-force oaths were unbreakable. Most people thought imperial oaths were unbreakable, but there were ways—keys held secretly by oathmasters. But life-force oaths could only be broken by death.

He watched her intentions weave.

He had seen this type of Carre oath once before. He would have accepted nothing less to bind the woman before him, but he had also wanted to see whether she could *do* it.

He looked at her, other possibilities taking shape in his mind. *Interesting.*

He tried to remember the faces of those slain en masse— the palace staff alongside the royal family—going through each until he arrived at the one he wanted.

"Now you," she said.

He slowly extended his palms and she took his hands in hers. Smoke rose from his fingers and blended together with her rose clouds, nudging at her oath images to form ones blended with his own. Most of the clouds were in alignment, needing only small pinches. Some were radically different and had to be sharply negotiated in the intention-driven space.

Etelian's fate was a wedge. Kaveh's intention to "let" something happen to the second-oldest prince wasn't enough to satisfy the enormously intense desire of the woman whose skin was pressed to his to see him unseated. Her fierceness for deposing Osni was so easily explained as to be absurd in the face of her working for the Carres. Etelian was a harder desire to unmask. Etelian hadn't recognized her in the palace. Had spoken of her as beneath his notice.

If she had tried to attract his notice and failed, the emotion would be far different, tinged by envy or spite. This was an emotion born of pure hate. A hatred just as strong as the one she held for Osni. Stronger, maybe, for the fact that it shone with something more gripping. Whereas Osni's was tempered by time—an old hatred that would never die, more resolve than burning rage now—Etelian's was a hate far fresher. Or maybe not fresher, but a hatred that was continuously stoked.

Interesting.

He let his intentions waver, examining extended possibilities—watching as different intentions mixed with her rose colored ones while others formed a wall between. Ninli ul Summora watched him and watched the shifts, no doubt feeling the mixtures as they shifted, and her own intentions shifted around and within his to match or oppose.

The strongest of the possibilities clicked together in the shifting intentions, the oath urging compromise.

Three years. If Etelian was still breathing in three years and the scepters were under Fehl control, Kaveh would take care of him. Nera could groom her grandchildren for revenge.

Aros would make his move long before then, anyway.

He didn't know the thoughts behind her compromises, as

those weren't things that could be read, but he could *feel* her resolve in the oath set that now stood before them. Her emotions painted a deep picture.

He narrowed his eyes. "This oath I take."

She took a deep breath. "This oath I take."

Long, sensuous ribbons wrapped around their wrists—a promise in the ancient traditions—securing their vows in rich, gold-and-white silk bands.

His mindspace shifted the smallest amount, letting a small piece of her settle within.

Try to get away now, warp sparrow.

Don't forget your vows, Kaveh ul Fehl.

The bond settled.

"Let's not keep your traitor friends waiting."

Companions and Foes

Taline

Tehrasi

"You did *what*?" Taline's entire arsenal of spellboxes hadn't shifted aim from the Shadow Prince's face since he'd arrived together with Nin in her ripgate. It had taken a solid tick of the sun to even get to this position of cease-fire, and Taline was *hoping* Valeran would make a problem disappear for once.

Nin held her free hand out while she healed Valeran's remaining injuries with the other. "We made a—"

"With a *what* restriction?"

"A life-force oath. With a distance limiter, if one party desires it at any time. It's not required, though. Plenty of—"

"*A distance limiter?*" Taline's finger twitched on the spelltrigger.

Valeran eyed her hand and shifted, a shield forming in his palm.

"If you kill him, I die too," Nin said with a sigh, not even looking up this time.

"*Nin.*" But Taline's fingers snapped back from where they'd been hovering over the spell ignition.

Nin held both hands out in supplication, and Valeran stretched, steel gleaming at the tips of his sleeves. "No one from the empire can kill me either! Or the two of you! Protection! We can basically walk through the temple's front door! Covered in shadows! Think of the possibilities!"

"I am. He's going to take the scepter, then kill us!"

"No, we get a month! And passes! And Osni and Etelian gone!"

Taline exchanged a look with Valeran and was furious for having to agree with him on anything.

"Ninli, think this through," Valeran said.

The utter *horror* standing blithely behind Nin took that opportunity to interject, "It's too late for that. It can't be removed. Even an oathbreaker will die when breaking a life-force oath."

A smile stretched slowly across his mouth. A horrifyingly dark smile beneath cheekbones that could slice a demon's throat.

Taline looked at their doom in that smile.

"Sehk-Ra, Nin." She let her spellboxes drop and rubbed her fingers across her forehead.

"I know you are uncomfortable with this, Tali. Everyone

is uncomfortable with this. Even he is uncomfortable"—she thumbed at the bane of every army—"though you can't see it."

But Nin could see it because their connection was so strong? That made *nothing better*.

"What can't be undone can't be lamented," Nin said. "Onward we travel."

"I don't think you understand what the word lament *means*."

But it was Nin's default setting—to roll with the punches, to continue on with whatever new hindrance crossed her path. She put up a good front, too. Made it seem as though it didn't bother her.

But you could see it every time Tehrasi was brought to play. She made herself let go each day, but she never moved *on*. Her trauma was as fresh as it had been ten years ago, just hidden beneath layers and layers of others' problems she made her own.

Taline gripped her spellboxes. Like *Taline's* problems. Nin had lifted them from her almost completely, freeing Taline from their harshest grip. Unfair. Unequal.

She had no idea how people left Nin. A part of her hated each one who did.

She looked at Valeran, who stood negligently, a hand in his pocket. An outsider might see him and think him casually watching the proceedings. She couldn't read the Shadow Prince at all, but he, too, looked as if there were no threat to be had.

Maybe for him there wasn't.

But she'd never bet against Valeran. He had lived far too long for the type of schemes he pulled. And she'd never bet against Nin.

"We need to make one more stop before going to the temple." Nin pulled the purchased glass from Valeran's pocket, then handed it to Taline.

Taline blinked and took it from her. In the craziness, they hadn't even checked it. She examined the facets, mind starting to shift the components of the scope into place. She gave a nod that she knew Nin would register.

"Why?" the Shadow Prince asked.

"The scepter is in the non-magic lands, and we'll need something to combat that," Nin said calmly.

"The non-magic lands?"

"One of the key reasons the scepter has remained a secret," she said. "Never put your power in a room with your enemies." The grim little smile curving her mouth made Taline certain it was a quote.

"And you know it is in the non-magic layer, how?" the prince asked, twisting a shadow through his knuckles.

"It was on the inscription we...found with the totem."

"And where is the inscription?"

"It's in my head." Nin looked dead straight at him. "I read it, then destroyed the tablet."

He smiled. "Of course."

He said it as if he knew Nin couldn't read.

Doomed. Taline shuddered.

"I know where the items you left behind are—should that be the reason we need to make another stop. Simple enough to retrieve them from Tehras with your skills." The prince's smile grew, and Taline shuddered again.

"Pass," Taline said. He could lead them anywhere in the city. Etelian's scepter would be a factor in Tehras, and he could have already committed any manner of trickery to their things. She didn't like that their things were in the hands of the empire, but lamenting it was unhelpful. Forward was their only move.

Nin nodded in agreement. "It will be quicker our way."

Nin opened a vortex and motioned them through. Taline shuddered again at the look in the Shadow Prince's eyes as he watched it form. The empire, like any regime, coveted the skills Nin possessed.

"Your sister goes first, then I go, then Valeran, then you," the Shadow Prince ordered in his pit-deep voice.

Doomed.

Taline stepped through the ripgate, then quickly stepped to the side—arming herself to make certain Valeran didn't get extinguished by his half-sibling before Nin made it through to stop him. Sehk-Ra, what was the world coming to that she cared that *Valeran* stayed alive?

Both imperial spawns came through, both with sharp eyes—blue shot with brown, and brown shot with black—similarly taking in everything. The parallels didn't comfort her, even as they held each other in obvious distrust and distaste.

Nin closed the ripgate cleanly behind her and they all looked out to see a town that Taline was familiar with.

"Kaveh and Rone will get what we need while Taline finishes assembling the mechanism that we acquired the glass for."

Doomed.

RONE

No one missed Ninli's first-name use for the Shadow Prince. Ninli had done that on purpose. Addressing him as an actual person and now a part of their group.

Rone shifted his gaze, resting it for a moment on Taline, who looked both angrily resigned and furiously on edge. When they'd been dropped in the oasis, she'd panicked. Then she'd gotten angry.

At him.

But as soon as Kaveh ul Fehl had appeared, attached to Ninli—literally, as it were, if those bands had anything to say about it—Taline had shifted immediately to his side. Better the enemy she knew, he supposed.

His gaze switched back to Ninli, who looked steadily back. Moisture rolled down one of her temples, then the other. He tilted his head slowly—a question that only she would understand. She made the sign of no return with her banded wrist. Then the one giving him leave to flee. There was no judgment in her gaze.

"I know what the item is and where to find it," Rone said. "The death prince and I will get it as long as neither party in this death oath activates the distance limiter."

Taline opened her mouth to argue—an inherent gesture of hers when it came to him—then abruptly shut her lips and nodded. "Good idea."

The world was ending. Escape at the first opportunity, indeed.

Kaveh ul Fehl stared at Ninli through dark, narrowed eyes. "I wouldn't recommend testing the boundaries of your oath."

She stared back at him, unflinching, and Rone felt a surge of pride he tried vainly to pretend he didn't feel. "I made that oath with clear intentions," she said.

The Shadow Prince looked at her for another moment, then shrugged the corporeal shadow from his shoulders. It dove and wrapped around her ankle.

Ninli froze. Taline uttered a sound somewhere between a gag and choke. Kaveh ul Fehl turned to Rone, then started walking. "Let's go."

Rone pivoted without looking at Ninli and Taline—he had to trust that they would survive—instead taking in all the details of the half-sibling he had never hoped to encounter. Knowledge was all, and any tics he could use needed to be noted.

The town wasn't far. Even so, it felt forever in the

distance when traveling with an enemy as dangerous as the one before him. Working from the shadows was a far different game when you played with someone who could *control* them. Another game was needed here.

"You walk a crumbling path," Kaveh ul Fehl said. "The emperor's allowance only goes so far."

"I need not his allowance."

The thirteenth prince smiled, a small and deadly thing. "No? You have not used it before? The ability to turn officials and officers? To evade while they arrest all those around you, but never arrest *you*?"

Rone's lids fell to cover only half of his eyes as he smiled just as falsely. "My charm does that all on its own."

"You are without honor, so that is not a surprise."

"Honor requires cost. Honor requires privilege."

"You have the emperor's privilege. And that of the north."

Rone's smile wasn't settling into the lines he wanted. He forced his mouth to smooth into casual lines. "That has served me well, indeed."

The entrance to the town had a large fountain with fish statues shooting clear water arcs into the center.

Rone's eyes trailed over the water settling in the basin, reflecting his wavering image back. He could leave the girls. Escape now and get a massive head start on the empire.

The empire might not even come after him.

The emperor might never learn how to use the scepter.

He might never figure out everything the scepters could do, if used by a competent and knowledgeable hand.

Ninli might even fail to obtain the Scepter of Darkness without Rone to help.

"Which shop, Valeran?"

Rone looked at the gentle waves for an extended moment. "The second one to the left. Come."

NINLI
꙰꙰꙰ ✿ ꙰꙰꙰

Nin stared at the deadly shadow wrapped around her ankle as Taline dragged a privacy bubble around their upper halves, enveloping them without including the nightmare below.

The shadow didn't like being shut out, and Nin couldn't withhold a cringe as it sharpened against her skin.

Taline pulled her face close, as if that would help. "Can that thing hear us?"

"No. As long as I don't try to leave this area, I don't think it can do anything to me." She'd caught the emotion around Kaveh's order, but not the language itself. "It—she's?—under orders."

"This is going to end in disaster," Taline said bluntly, staring at the shadow as if it were a flesh-eating asp.

"We'll be fine," Nin assured her, trying to assure herself

as well. She tugged at the band around her wrist. "Kaveh ul Fehl is under the binding oath the same as I."

"He will take the scepter, then take you."

"The oath states we get a month's head start."

"I don't believe him."

"He believes in the oaths he takes. He's like the investigore—he honors the commitments he makes. I don't just say that. I, er, know it. The spell tells...erm, a lot about the other person emotionally." She tried to insert that information as quickly and painlessly as she could.

"*Nin.*" Taline looked at her as though she'd just admitted she had embalmed her own brain, stuck it in a jar, and left it behind.

"He believes in them, is all," she added hastily. It wasn't as if Nin's emotional spots hadn't been obvious already. It was more surprising that Kaveh ul Fehl exhibited depths extending far below the stone floor of his duty and devotion.

"Whether he believes in them or not, there are always ways around oaths. You, of all people, know this."

Fury, pain, and loss crashed through her.

"There is one way around this type of oath," she acknowledged. She pushed the memories aside with practiced motion, just like she did the happier memories of being in the servants' quarters—of Farrah ul Osni's bright smile as she patiently helped Nin with her glyphs. "But the Shadow Prince would never use it, and neither will I."

Never.

"Nin, the Shadow Prince—"

"He won't." This, she was certain of. One thing Kaveh ul Fehl was not, was Crelu ul Osni. Osni would die for what he'd done ten years before.

"Nin—"

"He *will* honor the terms, Tali. He will give the month," Nin said, certain of it. "Because he believes he'll be able to find us at the end of it anyway."

It was a truth he hadn't even attempted to hide. She had adequately expressed her own intentions about the matter as well.

"*Nin.*"

"There are plenty of places for us to go, Tali. You've always wanted to travel. We'll just move up the timeline."

"Move up the timeline while a mass murderer chases us!" Taline looked angrily down at the shadow hissing around Nin's ankle.

"We're alive!"

"*Nin.*"

"We're going to get this done, Tali." She grabbed Taline's shoulder, the silk binding fluttering. "Then we are going to go travel the world. You hear me?"

Taline's expression softened. "But Tehrasi—"

"Will be forever closed to me," Nin murmured. The pain of that was fresh, but she'd have to deal with it later. "There is nothing I can change about that now. We must go forward on the plans that are active, not on the ones we wished for."

"But we can—"

"No. It's time to let Tehrasi go." Nin looked to the

distance and tried to let her guilt die. "With Osni and Etelian gone, my work will be as well. Let new heads, strong heads prevail. Tehrasi is strong. Her people are strong. I'm a relic of the past. The past folds beneath the future's hands."

"You can be part of that future."

"Maybe..." Nin forced a smile. "Maybe. Let's travel a bit and find out. We'll have a month. What do you say?"

Taline examined her, eyes searching hers. "You mean it."

"Yes." Nin squeezed her shoulder. "Hold steady. The Shadow Prince isn't the only one with plans."

Taline carefully squeezed her arm in return. "I'd like to go to a cassirie." With *you*, was unsaid.

How many times had Taline tried, not to get her to stray from her path, but to take side trips for pure enjoyment?

How many times had she encouraged Taline to go on her own? How many times had she assumed Taline would leave like all the others?

She squeezed her hands. "Then we shall."

Get the scepter. Complete the plan.

EMBERS IN THE NIGHT

NINLI

TEHRASI

If Nin thought obtaining the last supplies and hammering out who wasn't going to kill whom had been tense, deciding to make camp for the night after four more jumps and an additional stop was an even tenser affair.

"We aren't sleeping, Nin." Taline stacked another kindling stick. She'd been on edge for hours, and Nin couldn't deny that Kaveh had deliberately riled their emotions with his pointed comments on every law-breaking move they made. Combined with detailed descriptions of what happened to citizens found guilty of each crime, it had made for hours of unnecessary fear.

His dark amusement and the satisfaction she could feel from him over his desired results, made it all the more apparent. Nin could believe he and Rone were related at this point, though Rone had been unnaturally silent for the past hour, looking off into the distance as they traveled.

It would have been far better if he'd been the one needling Taline.

"We have to sleep," Nin said, exhausted. "The totem only works at sun peak in the midday sky, which is a long time from now, and we *must* be alert once inside." Taline knew this. She'd *been* to the temple. She knew what would happen if Nin made a mistake because she hadn't slept.

Taline stubbornly pointed at Kaveh. "With him around, we don't sleep."

Nin had stopped using anything other than his first name, even in her own thoughts. Once they were unbound, all bets were off, but it was hard to separate emotionally from someone whose emotions—however dark—were lurking in the back of her mind at all times.

"I'm tied to the sparrow," Kaveh said casually. "I can hardly kill you all in the night."

The spell Nin was using to start the fire stuttered as his desire to do just that—kill them all—spiked. Nin looked sharply at her bondmate. He looked back, unrepentant.

"I trust nothing about this binding on your side, Fehl," Taline spit at him.

He looked at her with distaste. "You are a pawn who has bound herself to a queen. You are a gnat. An inconvenience. Killing you would be useless at this point." Killing intent rose, in opposition to his words.

"Tali, he's trying to rile you up again," Nin said quickly.

"You are saying he doesn't want to kill us?" Taline demanded. "That he isn't deliberately projecting *honest* intent right now?"

"He's trying to rile you."

"What does he *feel*, Nin?" Taline had been getting more aggressive over matters of the bond as Kaveh had continually poked.

Nin winced and stoked the fire. "It doesn't matter. He can't do it."

A dark curl of amusement wound through her—a feeling that was not her own. Kaveh was watching them from beneath half-closed lids, his gaze intense even so. He looked bored but she could *feel* his satisfaction.

Taline's hand cut through the air. "Perfect. Let's sleep and die."

"He wants us to be upset," Nin said stiffly. "I won't let you die. He took an oath promising that he won't let you die either."

"Remember your promise to *me*. Your promise can't be fulfilled if *you* die, Nin."

"She won't die," Kaveh said. "I'll make certain her cage keeps her quite alive."

Taline threw her sticks down and strode to the other side of the fire and furiously gathered her scope supplies.

Nin felt Kaveh's satisfaction curve with his amusement. He stood and strode to the edge of the small open hill site they'd chosen. All attention shifted to him as they watched him pace a careful circle around their campsite. The shadow at his throat stared pointedly downward as he walked, as if in conversation with the swarm snapping hungrily at his feet.

Taline shuddered at the sight, then angrily rifled through her pack.

"She isn't wrong about not sleeping," Nin murmured to Rone.

Rone looked casually at the woman in question. "Yes, but she also knows that we need to sleep. You grew sluggish hours ago. Even the Shadow Prince looks worn after chasing us for two days, plus another night before. Her anger will fade quickly. Especially toward you. But she has better instincts than you do when it comes to trusting people."

Nin looked at him with a raised brow. "She trusts no one."

"As I said—better instincts than you." He raised his own brow and cast a pointed glance at Kaveh's back, then took the spellbox Nin handed him.

"That's not trust, Rone. That's a contract."

"As a fellow oathbreaker, Ninli, I think I must protest this strange opinion you seem to be in current possession of that people follow their word."

"I know, Rone." She took a deep breath and watched Taline grimly piece together a new scope on the other side of the fire, gaze rising every few moments to watch Kaveh set traps. Kaveh paused at the completion of his circle. He lifted his hands and shadows fled into the night. Both were too far to hear their whispers.

"You didn't run," she said.

"No," Rone murmured. "That doesn't mean you can trust that I won't when Crelu ul Osni tries to kill us all, your new bodyguard included. And while I am thankful for your save, you should know we no longer have the same goal with your new oath in place."

Nin watched Taline angrily put together the delicate instrument. "I know. When you go, take her."

Rone carefully weighed Nin's expression, but when he spoke, his words were airy. "Would you really do that to me, Ninli? She will hate me. I'll never win her heart."

"If you are running because you have to run... If you are running to keep everyone else with rare abilities free—" The band tightened around her wrist. She took a deep breath and thought repeatedly of her own commitment to the oath. The band loosened again. "I'd rather her be angry and alive than dead. Will you do it?"

He tilted his head at the golden band. "Betray one of you or the other? Yes."

She nodded. He had worded that deliberately so that she didn't have to dwell on the implication. "Thank you."

"You will die," Rone said. Darkness, as if the moon had suddenly been covered, descended behind them.

"I promised to survive," Nin said.

"Betrayer."

She smiled tightly. "It's in my blood."

"Fascinating to know," a dark voice said over her shoulder. "I'll take the first watch."

Nin looked behind them to see Kaveh leaning against a tree, looking darkly pleased about something.

"Sehk, no." The curt response from Rone were the first words he had spoken to his half-sibling in hours. "Pairs. You and I will—"

"No," Taline said shortly, joining them once more. She seemed to be fighting internally, her mouth twisting into a grimace. "Pairs, yes, but not you two together, not for this. Nin and Fehl will take first watch. You and I will be second. I don't care if the Fehl sleeps or not. We will sleep"—she indicated herself and Rone—"and Nin will."

Rone put his hand to his heart. "Narsumina, you do care."

"Stop *calling* me that."

Kaveh's eyes narrowed on them, gaze cold, but satisfaction overwhelmed his emotions. Over further dissension among them, maybe.

Nin wasn't surprised by the pairings. They would make the most sense, especially from Taline's perspective, who didn't trust Nin's ability to suss out Rone's nefariousness, and didn't trust the men together at all. More importantly, Nin had shown at least the barest ability to counter Kaveh ul Fehl.

Taline exchanged a look heavy with warning with Nin—and a bit of apology—then promptly dropped into their traveling blanket, already halfway to sleep now that she had accepted the rationale and put her mind to the task. They had significant practice with watches and three-hour chunks of stringed sleep. Criminal activities lent themselves to taking watch and grabbing sleep whenever it was available.

And Taline trusted Nin to guard her back. Even in a situation with one of the most dangerous men in the empire, Taline trusted her.

Of the four of them, it wasn't the man who had three enemies and no human allies available who had the most dangerous watch.

Nin sighed.

Rone winked and took his pack over near Taline. He, too, was out quickly, easily sleeping the light sleep of the damned—the deepest sleep available to those who couldn't afford to go deeper.

By the time a turn of her clock had passed, shadows had slunk out around Nin in every direction. She took careful notice of each instead of looking beyond them. She doubted anyone was going to be able to sneak past Kaveh's protections unless he allowed it.

But then, the purpose of her "watch" was not to look for outside assailants.

Still leaning against the gossat tree he had claimed, Kaveh's dark eyes took her in. Something almost amused curved his mouth, as if he knew exactly what she was thinking. He probably *could* deduce her thoughts from the precise emotions she was feeling. Lovely.

"Don't take your eyes away," he said languidly. "I might strangle all of you in your sleep."

"You won't." She fingered the band around her wrist.

"Besides, all of us are needed to get through the temple. There's a reason we conscripted Rone. And you vowed to keep him physically safe for the next five days."

"Killing another child of the emperor is discouraged." He pushed away from the gossat tree and prowled forward to sprawl next to her. The shadows sunk around them, three deep, shifting and curling like eels—or like palace cats, seeking the best spot. "But I would have done it anyway."

"You'd be punished?"

He shrugged and the right side of his lips lifted. "It's occurred."

"The right hand of the emperor? Imperator General of the Empire? He Who Has Never Failed? I doubt it."

"I'm flattered."

"You lie," she said simply, feeling the truth of it.

"Flattery is a useless waste of air, and I despise those who use it. Valeran is well versed in its art."

But Rone used it tactically, always with an eye for its best reward. Not like Lorsali, for whom flattery was as necessary as breathing. The most essential use of air for the high princess of the realm.

"You care nothing for any of us," Nin said. "I am under no assumptions. But you are known for reading situations with accuracy. It is part of what makes you an unparalleled commander. That we are not dead or broken already speaks volumes for your intent."

"Perhaps I find you amusing."

"You don't."

His lips parted to show his teeth. "Oh, I think that is false, little oathbreaker."

She chose not to read his emotions at that, studiously ignoring him and poking at the fire instead.

"I suppose it should not be a surprise that an oathbreaker knows the secrets of the temple," he said, his tone putting her on guard again. "*How* is the question that I'm curious to find an answer to."

"A palace servant told me."

"Lie." He shifted, shadows drifting with the movement. "Perhaps, though...*you* were the servant. Companion to one of the princesses?"

Her heart cantered into a gallop.

He looked at her through heavy lids, continuing without her input. "The Carres chained all high magi directly to them. Anyone showing promise of Level Nine skill would have been swallowed into Carre service—*especially* one showing the ability to gatemake. A high-level servant with a child... The Carres would never leave someone unchained who had the ability to influence the gates. A skilled enough girl who wheedled her way into the good graces of one of the princesses... Such a girl might prove skilled enough to learn to break her own vows."

Her throat moved heavily in a forced swallow.

"A girl who knew enough about the palace to escape? Who made friends with the other servants, maybe? I wonder if I look at the record of servants and companions and those who died... I wonder if there would be a young girl missing?"

She met his gaze with hers. "There wouldn't, because your story is just that—a tale."

"*Truth.* Interesting." Her heartbeat increased to a flat-out sprint. This wasn't like an interrogation with the Investigore of Tehras, who couldn't read through her careful words. "The daughter of a high official, then, perhaps. Someone of the elite, someone killed by Osni afterward."

"All you need to know is that I can access the inner sanctum of the scepter with help from my companions."

"Truth. But I don't think that is all I need to know." A shadow prowled around her, even as he stayed motionless, resting back on his hands. "Besides, you can believe you know how to access the scepter and be wrong."

"I'm not."

"A girl who can travel... There was a rumor that one of the scepters was keyed to identify those who could wield them. Is that how they found you?"

She clenched her fingers into fists. "The Carres stole children who carried the ability to make gates from kingdoms far and wide. And they dealt severely with those who tried to slip their grasp."

It was something Etelian's scepter—the Queen's scepter—was specifically capable of. But Osni had believed it was in *his* scepter—the Crown Prince's scepter. He had keyed them immediately, *mistakenly*.

Because Osni had already killed the one person who could have prevented his mistake.

Killing intent rushed through her and she forced it back

down. Calm. Osni had never figured out how to find others like her, because telling Etelian what his scepter could do would have laid waste to Osni's usefulness.

A clever person might have found those secrets on their own eventually, but Etelian had always been too spoiled to be clever.

The Scepter of Darkness, however, *could* reveal the secrets of the others. If the emperor trusted others to examine the scepters, or if he was capable of that examination himself, they could be revealed.

That capability was the crux of it it all—anyone who lifted the scepter would need to stave off the madness that would set in immediately as soon as they gripped the shaft. Learning the secrets of the other scepters would be a secondary concern.

Of course, if a person already *knew* the secrets... But activating the search mechanism was a secret Nin would take to her grave. She looked at Rone. That promise was for all of those with rare abilities.

She closed her eyes. If she had the strength to do it, she would destroy the scepter. But she knew as soon as she laid her hand upon it, it would infect her. She would want to *use* it.

Once the empire had the scepter, she wouldn't be able to return to Tehrasi, even if she was free to do so. She would need to stay far away.

"What were their given names again?"

She jolted. "What?"

"The names of the Carres. Every citizen of Tehrasi knew

the names of their rulers and shuddered in terror to cross their paths."

She stiffened. "You must have respected their rule a great deal to follow so closely in their terror path."

He tilted his head. "The Carres were relics who fell beneath progress. Fear is an essential component for animals to stay alive. Rising above that fear—not letting it lead you—is what defines true warriors."

"Speak to me not of fear, *Shadow Prince*."

He smiled. "Names breed fear. And fear breeds docility."

"You disdain docility."

"I do." He leaned forward. "Tell me their names, then."

"Is this a test? Of my citizenship?"

"Let's call it a curiosity for your oaths."

She tapped her fingers against the branch in her lap. Fine, then. What difference did it make? "Giran and Salare—king and queen of all—Savvan, firstborn and crown prince of the world. Lorsali, fairest in the lands." She swallowed. "Fein, general elite. Allit, of the mathematicians. Memni, of the clerics. Jolan, of the sword. And Zehra."

"The beetle princess, smallest of all," he added. "But you forget Jisarek, brother of the king."

She looked at him, willing her heart to steady. "Jisarek. And others, if you go off the main line. Anyone who could claim the magic of the Carres was called to the palace by the light of the First Scepter during the last stand to combine their family magics. They were defeated. All assembled—even the children—were purged."

"But Jisarek was the first slain. The catalyst used to kill the rest."

"For crimes against the emperor." She said it carefully. "For kidnapping the emperor's first wife decades before. Vengeance so old."

"So little forethought on what would happen." He tilted his head. "The emperor had started to show his might. Jisarek thought to make a statement. For those for whom might is all, it takes little to interpret a declaration of war. His statement was the end of the Carres."

"The Carres had ever been prideful and full of wrath." She took a breath. "It was little surprise when the empire grew larger than the Carres could handle that they were all slain."

"Oh, I think their mass slaying was a bit of a surprise."

She tried to keep her emotions together. "You were there, when they were killed."

He watched her through half-slit eyes, firelight shifting with shadows over his face. "Yes. I watched them fall."

She couldn't stop her lips from peeling back from her teeth.

A shadow wrapped around her shoulders, then slipped up around her chin, stroking along her cheek. "Do you want to kill me for it, little sparrow?" His voice was dark and seductive, like death. "Was one of them your charge? Did you witness their last moments? How did you avoid their fate?"

She thought of Lorsali's face—how it could change from disgust to beautiful radiance in an instant. How the eldest princess was master of her own expressions. Osni's locket, containing the memory of that night, always focused on the elder Carres when he played it to soothe himself after a troubling day. She didn't know what face Lorsali had worn at her end.

"I was not there." Unwillingly stuffed into a kitchen chute, thrown to the streets—a survivor of nightmares. "It was a tale long told, however. Until it was sculpted anew by the empire. Most still remember the two tales."

He cocked his head. "Generations will forget. Moving forward, it will be the empire's tale alone. And Crelu ul Osni will be painted anew with it. Is that not what you desire?"

She stared at him. "Osni is a plague to Tehrasi. He must go."

"But that isn't the *true* reason you want him gone. He's a traitor—a traitor to the household you served."

Farrah ul Osni's gentle, encouraging smile bloomed in her mind—eyes warm with life and skin soft with care. The image quickly juxtaposed empty eyes and the memory of her bone-cold body as Nin sobbed and tried to heal her from the type of death that had no cure.

"He is a traitor," she said coldly. "And it seems the empire has little use for those once their merit runs out. I could likely do *nothing* and still see Osni fall."

He smiled slowly. "You aren't willing to let that happen, though. You want to see him fall."

She looked at the fire and said nothing. She didn't need to. Her swirling memories would be providing him with enough emotional fodder to fill a state banquet.

He cocked his head. "He was a traitor to Tehrasi, but an ally to the empire. There is no proof that he laid the spell, but it is truth that had the Carres lived, he would have died by their voice. The Carres would have *negotiated*. Osni would have been obliterated if they wove a spell of cooperation with the emperor after their defeat. The Carres had lost their throne, but they hadn't lost their ability to live or rule in a limited way. To plot forward. The emperor was going to punish them, to kill Jisarek, but the Carre family still held *ability* he wanted. And the emperor isn't blind to power and use. He would have risen above his vengeance long enough to work out a deal. A deal far in his favor, but one that would have kept the Carres and gates alive. Osni couldn't let that happen. And he must have thought he had the gates figured out. But even if he didn't, he couldn't let them live. They would have ordered his termination as part of their deal. Osni only had one option. He lost his left hand as a result. But better a hand than his life. He would have lost that instead."

A good motivation, if not a true one.

"Osni wanted revenge," she said lowly. "Even before power, though power drives him to madness now. Do not mistake his reasoning. You have no idea what was happening in the palace before the empire came. Osni wanted Tehrasi to pay for the death of his son. Killing everyone in the palace was more than just him covering his path to rule. But killing the servants was unnecessary, cruel, and beyond any redemption."

His eyes narrowed. She jerked her gaze away.

"But not killing the royal family? I remember the princes and princesses at their ends," he said casually.

"I'm certain it is a tale you long to tell—their horror and indignity at death," she said bitterly.

"Some of them. But there were those among them who handled themselves well." He moved a shadow around his fingers. "After Jisarek fell, the chain spell commenced. The king knew immediately. He uttered his final words, then fell, dying in silent agony. The queen sneered and said nothing as foam burst from her mouth. The crown prince screamed invectives until he could no longer draw breath. And all those connected to them fell around them. And after the queen, as the crown prince was taken by the spell, you could see it register on the rest of their faces—could see their fate, their fear, their response."

She could no longer feel the fire. Ice. She was made of ice.

"What a lovely show for you," she said.

He played with the shadow. "The spell was initiated without our knowledge. Osni claimed—and still claims—it was a Carre death pact. But the shock in their faces, in the faces of the servants as they watched their charges fall, said otherwise. That the servants all followed them in death was not a surprise, however."

Indulgent faces in the kitchen, secretive allowances in the library by the stewards, handmaidens who... She took a shuddering breath.

Kaveh watched her closely, continuing to speak. "It was

the reason the emperor had not thought Osni capable of such an act—he thought Osni was also connected by life-force directly to the king."

She said nothing for long moments, staring at the flames that no longer held warmth. Then, in the lowest tone she was capable: "He ripped his life-force oath apart during the palace siege. And he will die for all of his actions therein."

"Osni said he didn't have a life-force oath. The empire believed him," he said, voice still casual, as if they were discussing a failed cassirie.

"Everyone with a *permanent* position at the palace had one," she said savagely.

"Did they?" His voice was dark and cold, suddenly, all of the casualness gone in the ripped mask it had been. "So you know how to get yourself out of this oath?"

"*Yes*. A sacrifice more reprehensible than any other." Her fingernails bit into her palms. "*Never*."

In the sudden inferno of the bond space, his cold fury evaporated, replaced with something stronger.

He leaned back on his hands, observing her in firelight and shadows once more. "I *believe* you. How *interesting*." Dark pleasure rode the bands of the oath. "I may truly keep you."

"I will hold to the rules of the oath, and so will you, Kaveh ul Fehl. You get the scepter. I get a month."

"You can run."

"You can *follow*."

He leaned toward her—the cracking flames a backdrop

to the sudden, overwhelming silence of the forest. "I look forward to it."

~*~

"Will I be able to wield your scepter?"

"Stupid girl, you will be lucky to wield a knife into your own foot. You will never *take it from me."*

The scene shifted.

"You could *wield* any *scepter, if something were to happen to...certain people in the palace...."*

Oily words from a familiar voice.

The gem glittered a red as bright as two spots on her image in the looking glass. She touched the glyph in prayer, then reached forward.

"Stupid girl. Don't touch *my scepter."*

Lightning arced and a rough hand jerked her.

Nin jolted awake, her hand reaching for the shoulder Lorsali had paralyzed in her rage. The old ache disappeared, along with the tendrils of the memory. Along with the unclean feel of Osni's carefully crafted words.

Too many memories dredged up by conversations in the night.

She pulled shaking fingers over her face. Another hand joined hers, smoothing down her cheeks.

"Shhh," Taline murmured softly. Rone looked studiously in another direction, lounging back against a rock in the predawn gloom.

"The guild cook forgot to add salt to the stew pot," Nin said.

"That is a nightmare for sure." Taline just continued stroking, not negating the obvious lie of her words.

Rone looked at her briefly, before looking to the other side of the fire again. "Go back to sleep, Ninli. The narsumina and I are watching your newest attachment."

She felt a spike of emotion and looked over to see dark, narrowed eyes watching her from where Kaveh was pretending to sleep.

"Go back to sleep." Taline tucked the thin traveling blanket under her chin. "Valeran and I are finishing the last of the spell seals for you to power. All will be better when you wake."

They both knew that was a lie.

TEMPLE OF THE SCEPTER

TALINE

KHURSEN, TEHRASI

The lush, lowland forests of Khursen stretched and intertwined within the arms of the Telb Mountains, leaving the desert at its back and the sea over its shoulders to create some of the most breathtaking landscapes in Tehrasi—green and blue to one side, brown to the other. With the Telb Mountains stretching fingers through both sides, the landscape became one of patchworked wonder.

Khursen had always been considered an especially mystical area of Tehrasi.

Strange creatures were said to live in the woods. Creatures of lands far removed from theirs—creatures split off in the breaking between magic and non-magic—left stranded in the lands of humans instead of in the world created for beings and beasts like them.

In the fringes of the forest, strange things happened to travelers caught unaware. Worse things happened to those who sought the dark depths beyond.

It was to the heart of the forest that they traveled. And if there was an upside to traveling with the Shadow Prince—and Taline was loath to find any—it was that the darker denizens could be felt, watching, but didn't show themselves. They were too apprehensive of the larger predator marching through their forest.

That the Shadow Prince was only *mostly* human became more apparent with every step deeper into the woodland.

Even Nin, recognized by her power at a base level by the creatures of the land, had needed to negotiate passage when they'd come before—giving away mythic tokens and riddles as though they were honey rocks to children during the Festival of Light.

They had few tokens left, and fewer golden riddles, so they had grimly planned to use vast amounts of trickery between the three of them. Having the Shadow Prince basically carve a path was...easier.

Having him as an ally would be useful only up to the point that he became an enemy again, though. And watching chimeras and sphinxes stare from the forest shadows without making a move toward them was terrifying all on its own.

Following the river of Eire, they emerged from the forest into a protected grove that abutted a medium-sized waterfall cascading from the rocky land above.

There were other waterfalls in the forest that were more

beautiful, but this one was remarkable for the sharp rocks that jutted out from its sides—rocks not smoothed by the water flow, enchanted rocks that protected the entrance to the temple from being accessed by a wanderer stumbling upon the grove.

The sounds of construction reached them before they reached the grove, and the reason became clear as they stepped forward. At least fifty workmen moved through the space, some repairing a previously constructed bridge and hammering fallen stone, while others guarded and stabbed pikes into the bushes while swearing profusely—pointing to obvious past troubles.

Taline's gaze was drawn to the bodies stacked in five piles at the side of the river. Osni's minions were moving two fresh bodies to the large stacks—those who had had no more luck in their attempts either to gain entrance to the temple, to navigate the totem maze, or to get to this spot in the first place.

Taline wondered how many men Osni had lost forging through the forest. She wondered how he had gotten through at all.

She covertly looked at Nin and saw her grip her pack strap hard under the edges of the deep cowl she, too, wore.

Taline looked back at the men working. This was Taline's possibly least favorite part of this new plan.

The Shadow Prince strode into the encampment, shadows flaring far and wide. "You are all dismissed," he said coldly, not even waiting for his appearance to be registered before he was pulling at the air of the grove.

The plan *had* been to use the secret entrance and quietly maneuver around Osni's minions once inside. But the infernal Shadow Prince, for all his powers of stealth, didn't *sneak* when he could simply walk into battle, weapons swirling around his limbs.

Eyes blew wide and breath grew harsh as the workers stumbled over themselves, backing away from the demon before them.

Taline wanted to run, too, but she stood stiffly with Nin and Valeran.

"Sir...Your...Your *Imperial Highness*...we are tasked with—"

"And now you are dismissed." Killing intent blanketed the grove and he raised a hand wreathed in writhing black.

The workers fled into the woods en masse—woods they had previously been guarding *against*.

Valeran's eyes narrowed in on the last two workers, at the back of the scurrying pack. They glanced over their shoulders—their expressions a mix of terror and resolve. Valeran's sudden sharp smile unnerved her.

But before she could ask, Valeran walked over and toed the corpse the workers had dropped to the dirt in their haste to flee. "Ah. Good help is so hard to keep," Valeran said, freeing the man's farhani with his boot and flicking it upward along with a gust of wind to catch in his hand. "Especially when all your companions keep dying."

He stuffed the farhani into his pocket, then walked over to toe the next corpse. Taline dredged up enough outrage to stifle her terror for a moment.

She never got to berate him.

"Your Imperial Highness." Crelu ul Osni strode into the sunlight, appearing from whatever dank pit he normally occupied when he wasn't in her view. Coming from the same direction as the fleeing workers, it was likely one of them had clued him in. "I hadn't expected you. Welcome."

Taline immediately stepped back and pushed her shoulder against Nin's. Crelu ul Osni stood within an arm's length of both of them—without guard.

The Shadow Prince barely glanced Osni's way. "You are dismissed."

Emotions flitted rapidly across Osni's face, then settled into lines of polite confusion. "Dismissed? I think there's been a mistake. You see—"

"You are no longer in charge of this site."

Taline held her breath, a curl of hope rising. It was distinctly possible that if Osni argued, Kaveh ul Fehl would strike him down.

She didn't seem to be the only one who realized this. Osni bowed deeply and took a submissive step back.

"Of course, Your Imperial Highness. I didn't realize that the emperor was sending his most accomplished warrior to the temple. I am at your service."

"We have no need of your aid."

Paused in his bow, Osni's expression was hidden from

Taline, but he swiftly lifted to an upright position, genial smile painting his mouth. "I am the foremost scholar on the scepters. I am a priceless assistant," he said, almost gently.

Taline leaned back instinctively. Nin had gone stiff at her side, but Taline didn't need a bond with the Shadow Prince to know how unwise those words were.

"And yet the bodies of your men say otherwise," the Shadow Prince said. His tone was casually disdainful, but everything in her hind brain told her to *run*.

"The totem maze has been...unexpectedly corrupted." Osni's eyes slid from the Shadow Prince to the rest of them. "I wonder, who are your compan—?"

Osni's face turned crimson and his eyes bulged unnaturally as he was lifted from his feet by a shadow that hadn't been wrapped around his neck a mere moment before.

"Do you wish death, Scholari?" The Shadow Prince's tone was almost bored, but his eyes were dark and malicious. "I believe I will be forgiven for yours."

A part of Taline—the bloodthirsty part—hoped he would finish his squeeze. The rational part of her knew Osni would leave here alive.

Osni, for all that Taline wished him in the grave already, was not an idiot. His bulging eyes were focused solely on the prince—and his own survival. He shook his head within the grasp.

The Shadow Prince dropped him to the ground.

Taline had exhaustively harassed Nin on the oath's components while they'd walked the forest. Killing Osni before the scepter was retrieved would put the Shadow Prince in a weaker position to the oath's end—a position that an oathbreaker might take advantage of.

Osni took long moments to collect himself. If Taline tried to slip a dagger between Osni's ribs to finish the deed herself, she bet the watching shadows would intercept her before she got within a foot.

No, the scholari would remain alive until the scepter was in the empire's grasp.

Osni rose with care. "My apologies, Your Imperial Highness. I wish you caution all the same." He cast a feigned glance at the pile of bodies, while running fingers along his neck. "It would be a tragedy if anything should occur."

"Leave."

"May Sehk-Ra smile upon you today."

It wasn't until the scholari was in motion that Taline realized that he was headed toward them. That he was planning to walk *past* them.

Nin would need to let Crelu ul Osni walk past her. *Brush* past her.

Taline stepped forward and put herself in Osni's direct path instead, uncaring what the action might give away. Valeran knew more than was good for him already, the Shadow Prince had a straight pin right into Nin's emotions at present, and Osni was a dead man walking.

Hidden in their deep cowls, neither of them could be seen, but as Osni passed, his eyes narrowed and he stopped walking. He turned on his heel and his gaze swerved to Nin

with pinpointed accuracy—ignoring the rest of them—
something complicated working its way over his face.

"Who—?"

Taline hated the Shadow Prince, but as Kaveh ul Fehl
strode forward and forced the scholari back three steps,
hiding Nin from sight with his body, Taline found herself
fiercely grateful. The barest edge of a grimace touched Kaveh
ul Fehl's mouth, and she wondered whether he had
instinctively stepped between them.

She wondered what he had felt through the bond to be
called to make such a motion.

Osni looked at the Shadow Prince with a sharp smile and
his gaze dropped to the prince's covered wrist. The band
couldn't be seen under the concealments they had put in
place, but that Osni *looked* set Taline's teeth on edge. "Fairest
luck, Your Imperial Highness. And to your companions as
well."

His eyes drifted to where Valeran was still searching
bodies, head covered and identity hidden, seemingly oblivious
to the rest of them. Osni smiled, turned, and disappeared
quickly into the trees.

"I don't like it," Taline said tightly. Taline didn't like any
of it.

"I don't care." The stupid, terrifying prince motioned to
the cave entrance writhing with carved monsters. "Go."

Valeran rose and strode in, as if he'd been awaiting the
signal, but Taline took a long moment to search the horizon.
She didn't like this at all.

She turned sharply and followed behind Nin, letting the Shadow Prince guard the rear. After traversing a long, ominous hall lit only by torches and half-filled with bodies, the first chamber looked much as it had when they'd been here previously—bar the fresh, dark stains splattering the walls and floor and small pieces left behind from the bodies dragged outside.

"Lovely." Valeran paused at the doorway and pushed back his hood to stare at the fake totem with its rictus grin. His own enigmatic smile curved. "Nice touch on the counterfeit, ladies."

Taline had worked hard at getting everything right except for a few subtle insults that only those who knew the real thing might see.

It bothered her a great deal that Valeran had examined the real totem well enough to note the differences.

He turned to them. "We are inside and only a vindictive man and his legion of minions stand between us and freedom. Our chances for death stand at even once more."

"They will not return," the Shadow Prince said dismissively, eyes tracking the space—and them.

Nin quickly stepped forward, hand dipping into her bag to bring the real totem out. "We need not linger here either. Our work begins in the second chamber. Better to be away from those who might try to follow. Follow me exactly. The trail will only last a few minutes."

She charmed her slippers to leave a light trail and led them through an invisible maze field only she, as the totem possessor, could see. Valeran stared at the trail, a strange look on his face that was quickly wiped away as he followed. They bypassed the fake totem in the center of the room that was surrounded by blood splatter so thick it must have been equal to the full capacity of five humans.

There was no avoiding the dried blood pools in other parts of the room where foolish men had tried to get through or around the invisible maze.

"Very nice, Ninli." Valeran looked back at the trail of disappearing footprints. "Hopefully we won't find ourselves running back through here later, screaming at what chases us, only to find our insides on the out."

"Osni will do nothing and his minions are scattered to the forest," Kaveh ul Fehl said. Shadows seeped from him, but instead of flinging to all sides, as she'd seen him do in battle recreation globes, his shadows tentatively slithered along the edges of his cloak as if tasting the air of the invisible maze and finding it too dangerous to explore. "With you along, getting through the temple should be *easy*, should it not, Valeran?" There was a threat in the words.

"Well, let it not be said that hubris ever destroyed a man." Valeran strode negligently behind Nin, as if they were taking a stroll through the bazaar. "Our most valiant prince has said not to worry."

As they gathered at the end of the invisible maze, Nin outlined a tight perimeter of green in front of the door where they could safely stand. "There's just enough room for the four of us. But don't step out of position."

"Or do, if you want." Valeran knelt as Nin softly pointed at the knots of enchantments around three keyholes that, correctly deconstructed, would allow the totem to be placed and turned, leading them to the next chamber. "Would save us some trouble, if the thirteenth prince did himself away now."

"I will make certain to throw you on the first spell that hits, Valeran."

"Excellent. It will save me from your company." He turned his head the slightest bit, gaze focused on the spell knots. "What do you have for me, Ninli?"

Identifying the right enchantments and turning the totem within its correct slot would open the door. Choosing incorrectly would mean death.

Magic flashed in Nin's palm. "Twelve sets of glyphs. It's one of these at its opening." Nin's voice was apologetic. Guilty. As if she were responsible for being tossed headfirst down a chute and left with the ability to write anything she had learned before but not the ability to read.

Taline studied the Shadow Prince from the corner of her eye, hoping he wasn't putting two and two together to figure out that Nin couldn't have read the totem inscription as she'd professed. Perhaps he would just think Taline had read it to her.

"I have it," Valeran murmured, eyes shifting rapidly, then narrowing in on one in particular. "What a diabolical little set. Perhaps the key magic will take the prince as payment."

The Shadow Prince looked around the chamber behind them with narrowed eyes, watching the shifts in darkness.

"Your thief dies if I die by your hand—or by your machinations—during the period of the oath."

"The problem with such a thought is that you credit me with caring what happens to her." Valeran narrowed his eyes in concentration, then twitched his fingers around a blue line.

"The base will be something to do with pride or arrogance," Nin said, thoroughly ignoring them, as she opened her palm to display another set of glyphs. Valeran stared at the magic in her hand, then poked three of them. Nin changed the set again. They engaged in a silent back-and-forth, exchanging knowledge of some kind. He nodded and hummed, fingers moving at the lock once more.

The Shadow Prince's expression pinched as he looked between them, and Taline hated being in accord with him about anything.

"She is the only thing staying your execution," Kaveh ul Fehl said to Valeran. "If you think my knowledge dead after I breathe my last breath, you should reevaluate the decisions you've made on that premise."

The living shadow around his neck slithered in agreement, as if to say that it would be carrying said knowledge directly to someone who would act on it.

"Well, I'm not certain my shaking hands will be able to undo these enchantments now, princeling. How crass of you." Valeran's steady fingers moved through the knots of the first spell. "I might need to rest for a bit after such a threat. It's just such a wonder that I manage to draw breath under such dire warnings."

"With that mouth," Kaveh ul Fehl said, "it is a wonder you've survived this long."

"You underestimate the glory that is my sleight of tongue." Two spells bloomed under the knots in his hand—spells he had put into place while directing attention elsewhere. He rose and they all drew closer as Nin carefully slotted the totem into place above his hands.

"Nice work," Nin said, releasing a breath.

"Well, I might as well pass on my tricks, now that my death is assured." His smile was all teeth.

Valeran and Nin worked together as well as Nin and Taline did—they always had. It caused a pit in Taline's stomach every time she saw their connection. Valeran was untrustworthy, but invaluable. She hated it.

"You aren't going to die, Rone," Nin said, in the casual, unconcerned way she always did whenever he made irritating quips.

"Blessed by Gripna as you are, Ninli, well, now I can truly rest easy."

Taline reached out and pinched his arm hard. "*Quiet.*"

Valeran rubbed his arm, a ridiculously satisfied expression riding one side of his mouth as he looked at her. "I told you, narsumina, you don't have to resort to violence in order to touch me."

"Last set," Nin said, only pausing for the briefest moment to give them both a *look*.

Taline bristled. Valeran could say whatever awful things he wanted about Nin without reprisal, but once Taline and

Rone started picking on each other, Nin was suddenly all wounded looks and sighs.

Valeran reached forward once more and a grid of complicated spells appeared with a twist of his wrist—encapsulating the decades-old set that was hardened in place around the totem lock. Even the Shadow Prince's eyes narrowed at the skill that was needed for such a web.

Valeran rotated the grid in his palm, then pointed to one spell thread. "Ninli, be a dear and sever this one."

Nin gamely did as Valeran commanded. Their two heads—deep brown and mixed gold and red— bent together as they unraveled the rest while Taline and the Shadow Prince watched.

It took another agonizing hour to complete. An agonizing hour of standing in the same cramped perimeter of space. An agonizing hour full of Valeran's needling remarks.

Nin was too used to Valeran to have any reaction to his quips—unless they were overly rude to Taline. But Kaveh ul Fehl was *not*. By the end, Taline had to mull whether she could beat Kaveh ul Fehl to killing Valeran first.

She was working up enough motivation to fight the head of the imperial forces for the pleasure.

Valeran looked up from his work to stare directly at her, and for a blank moment, she wondered whether she'd said that part aloud. He turned back to Nin.

"You did this on the totem with only the narsumina and survived, Ninli? I'm astounded."

"Taline is excellent at warding," Nin chided.

"True. She wards that cold heart of hers better than most."

"Rone."

"Ninli."

That the Shadow Prince looked just as annoyed as Taline felt lifted her mood the tiniest bit.

The chamber door groaned as it opened. Decades-old dust blew into the air. An hour beyond ready for the moment, Taline opened her palm, and in it, she opened the box she had built to pull the dust and spores inside. She tossed it forward and as it spun in the air, the elements were sucked within.

Valeran looked at the dwindling cloud. "Dust means there is another way out. Good news, narsumina. You might survive another empty-hearted night. One trap down, and only..." He peered carefully into the other room. "A dozen more to go?"

A plinth lay in the center of the room, similar to the totem chamber, but like the door, this one had a specifically shaped keyhole.

"Totem in the center."

"Totem in the center," Nin agreed. "But we can't remove it from the door. Unlocking the plinth pulls it into place automatically."

"So no easy totem path." Valeran was eyeing the space already, though, clever, sharp gaze plotting.

The Shadow Prince's eyes glittered as Nin and Valeran spoke, but his gaze focused solely on Nin with a raptor's predatory stare.

Taline shifted uneasily.

Nin pointed to Taline's belt. "Hence the scope. Specially formatted spell jewel. We could have used it in this chamber, too, to reveal the path, but the totem was just as easy. Activate the plinth, turn the totem, instructions appear. Then, *okun*, scepter." Her hand punched vaguely with the okun exclamation. They all knew it wasn't going to be that easy.

Valeran said something in that vein, but Taline couldn't take her eyes from the sudden dark bloom in the Shadow Prince's eyes as he looked at Nin. Something overwhelmingly dark and satisfied—some verified revelation—had just occurred.

Apprehensive and uneasy, Taline took a step toward Nin—but her earlier shift had put her closer to the wall. Her elbow hit a stone outside the perimeter. The door in front of them slammed shut.

"Sehk-Ra's *goats*. Which utter *idiot*—"

Any further condemnation from Valeran was lost in darkness and shrieking madness, as chaos reigned—the first defensive movement from one of them triggering a second trap, then that triggering a third. They'd planned for traps. Every temple that held something worthwhile contained snares of death and insanity.

Taline couldn't even apologize for springing the first trap, since each of them was setting them off now. Nin was shot from her feet and thrown against the wall, back first. Wails of soul-deep agony rose, along with three overwhelming clouds of horrible magic, and a burst of traps were immediately engaged along the wall. Horror took Taline as she realized what had just broken in Nin's bag—please let it just be *one* jar—but she couldn't dwell upon it as she defended the rending blast that split the stone in two where she'd just been standing.

With nowhere to go—as the second chamber was once more closed—the prince's shadows flared in response, and three more snare shots activated. Valeran had somehow triggered one from the ceiling that shot spell darts, and they were falling everywhere. The Shadow Prince's pets ate the spell darts, and Valeran obliterated the snares. Nin and Taline worked back-to-back, hitting one oncoming spell into another, then sending them into the shadowy maws opening everywhere around them.

Nin hooked their backs together and whirled them in small slices of air—evading one barbed spell, then another— letting Taline's magic fly in her wake as they whirled to maximize their combined damage. Magic flew in two arcs around them. Rone was fluidly ducking around them and freezing stray spells in place, and Kaveh ul Fehl...

Shadows were now everywhere, swarming and eating anything they shot toward them, or anything that dared come close.

Taline would like to think they hadn't needed Kaveh ul Fehl—and she wouldn't have activated that first trap if she wasn't so Sehk-damned *tense* about having him death bound to her sister—but she couldn't deny that the infernal prince was excellent at defense. His shadows gained strength until the entire room was blanketed in darkness.

By the time they got the situation under control, they were all tense and guarded.

The blanketing darkness receded while pushing them back into their original positions near the second chamber's door.

The...closed door. Taline pulled a shaking hand down her face. They were going to have to open the damn door again.

Five of seven spellboxes were gone from Taline's provisions. Taline breathed heavily and carefully collected the used spellboxes at her feet. Two of them were intended for getting out of here. She grimaced and set her mind on an alternate path. If she used the sandbox and the airbox, she could combine them to replace the sandstorm box. If she used the waterbox and the lightning box, she could—

"Your sister is going to get us all killed," the Shadow Prince said to Nin. "We had already *cleared* this room before her fumbling made us fight it. Now we have to open the damned door again."

Nin was looking into her bag with an unreadable expression, but she looked up fiercely as his words registered, slinging her bag strap back over her shoulder and hip. Taline hoped it contained at least *one* unbroken container.

"We should be able to open it faster this time. And her scope is going to get us to the plinth in the next room without triggering a spellfest in that chamber—spells which are increasingly worse—so I'd take care with your words," Nin replied succinctly.

Taline froze and slowly looked down to see whether the scope had survived. Relief made her wilt. Valeran's fingers smoothly relieved it from her sash, brushing her hips.

"I'll hold this, yes?"

"Yes," she agreed. Even she knew when to toss aside pride.

Traps were resetting themselves around the room. Still temporarily under the aftereffect of a burner spell she'd had in one of her boxes, she could see flashes of the magic connecting to all the spells that hadn't been triggered. Spelltraps were *everywhere*. Damn the Carres.

She shut her eyes and tried to will the unhelpful tracers of light to cease—it was not a friendly spell, or useful, since seeing the magic didn't mean she could pinpoint it, as the tracers moved in all directions away from their spells.

Taline stayed penitently quiet as Nin and Valeran worked the door open again. It was quicker this time, now that they were certain of the spells, but still took thirty-some minutes.

"Do not fret," Nin whispered to her. "We will make worse mistakes before the day's end."

"Not reassuring, Nin."

Nin squeezed her shoulder and carefully stepped into the next chamber after Valeran, who had her handmade scope pressed to his right eye.

"I'd ask how you made this, Summora, but I will save my curiosity for another day."

"Your curiosity can stay unsatisfied, Valeran."

Nin gave them both a chiding look as she manually wrapped her wounds and slowly followed Valeran as he negotiated the second chamber's plinth spell maze.

Taline had created the first scope with a broken glass jewel and half-ripped diagram that Nin had solemnly given her. Taline had had plenty of practice to perfect and fill in the design, aiding them in their endeavors and allowing them to target foes.

Taline had never asked Nin from where she'd gotten the original jewel and half-finished design. But then, Nin had been doing her work long before Taline had joined her—Nin, like Taline, had scars on her body that even a Level Nine healer couldn't fix.

They made it to the plinth without trouble, and Valeran inserted the totem into its slot. Taline refused to credit him with the ease with which they'd navigated. The whine of disengaged traps groaned in the air, thank *Sehk*, and an incomprehensible map bloomed around them.

No one spoke for long minutes. Taline took the opportunity to push the remnants of the burner spell away. Valeran would either figure out the riddle or ask for help. She disliked him, but when she was honest with herself, his expertise in this area had never been in question.

Valeran ran his fingers carefully along one set of points. "By design, a sacrifice of requisite strength is required."

Kaveh ul Fehl motioned for Valeran to be that sacrifice. Taline bristled, and Valeran raised a brow at the prince.

"Lovely, truly. But you need me to hold the wards when the scepter appears. Luckily for *you*, we have..." At his pause and the swift tightening of his features, Taline followed his gaze to Nin, who was wincing. "Ninli? That guilty expression is my absolute least favorite of yours."

Nin dipped her bag forward. Broken, shattered glass clinked and groaned as she shifted it. Taline sharply inhaled, worst fears confirmed.

Before they'd stolen the totem, they had very *carefully* stolen three sacrifice jars from a secret set of royal catacombs. Nin had been uncertain which temple chamber would require a sacrifice, and they'd been beyond relieved when they had discovered it wasn't the totem chamber.

Sacrifices had been a barbaric activity the Carres had routinely practiced—draining a person's life-force and magic and trapping it for later use, leaving only a husk of a body behind. The more powerful the person, the greater the sacrifice. Most of the palace jars had been destroyed when the palace catacombs had been razed in order to undo the palace's central spell network during the last battle of the Carres.

But Nin had known where the special reserves had been kept—the sacrifices from those deemed ultra-powerful.

Nin had been sure the jars would satisfy any sacrifice that would be required, considering the Carres would never sacrifice themselves.

"Broken during the fight?" Three wails of agony. She'd hoped it had been an echo.

"Yes," Nin said softly. "The released magic is what activated ten traps alone."

Valeran closed his eyes. "Yes. Well, I want you all to know, I will not be taking any of you on my next adventure."

"Maybe we don't need you in the scepter room," the Shadow Prince said.

"You do, but I'm half-tempted to be the sacrifice just so I can lay here and watch you die, too," Valeran said calmly, fingers trailing over the glyphs.

Nin fidgeted at his side, waiting to hear what the glyphs she couldn't read said. Valeran's recitation was nearly indistinguishable, but the cost was obvious.

"I'll do it," Nin murmured.

"And that would be effortlessly foolish, even by your standards." Valeran's fingers trailed a specific set of glyphs again, pausing. "You are needed more than I am, and I know you won't sacrifice Her Excellency, not that it would work anyway. And there is a zero percent chance of the princeling giving up his ghost willingly."

Valeran tapped the glyphs, then sighed. "Sacrifice of a whole. And we aren't a pack of day laborers. We probably have enough to get away with a split four ways—half of each of the four of us. This type of spell would demand an inequality in splits, so by design, we'd have to give more than a whole in total. And none of us is at one hundred percent after going through that last chamber, so this ought to make the scepter chamber really fun."

"No," the Shadow Prince said, voice hard.

"Excellent." Valeran clapped his hands together and rose. "Shall we all go home then?"

"You three can split your magic and life-force."

"That won't work," Valeran said with a tight smile. "It won't be enough."

Taline stood stiffly. As opposed to the powerhouse abilities of the other three, she was decidedly average. Her prime asset was her mind. Planning. Constructing everything they'd ever need in advance.

That, and having Nin's overwhelming reserves to fill whatever she constructed. At root, Nin was always the power that Taline held in her hand.

"We will all be drained of some of our powers temporarily." Nin was speaking directly to the Shadow Prince. "But we will all be on the same footing with each other that we are now. No one will have an advantage over you."

"Just far beneath any magi we might meet outside," murmured Taline. If Osni was still around...

"I should have enough to move us to the other side of the forest," Nin said calmly. "I marked a spot near where we entered. We can recover for a night, then separate according to the oath."

And even if she couldn't move them, the scepter would be in play when they emerged from its chamber. Taline could see everyone shift around the unspoken thought. The scepter would be either in Nin's hand or in Kaveh ul Fehl's hand.

"Hold up your end, princeling, and you don't need to worry about anyone or anything else," Valeran mocked.

Nin shut her eyes. "You are not helping, Rone." A pulse of her magic pulled at theirs, indicating where to stand if they were going to do this. "Please."

"I will aid you less in this than I wish," Taline admitted, carefully getting into position.

Nin looked at her. "You provide a heart that is always needed. Never underestimate the human characteristics that cannot be replicated by power."

The Shadow Prince's eyes narrowed, and Nin looked directly at him. Expression displeased, whatever was communicated between the two of them caused him to step into the place Nin's power pulled him.

"Rone?"

Valeran glanced down strangely, and suspicion rose in Taline—always eager to have an outlet in Valeran.

He shrugged something from his sleeve—a small silver ball. He twisted it and placed it back in his sleeve. Then his magic joined theirs.

Nin solidified the field of joined magic, then passed it to Valeran.

It was immediately apparent, however, that the enchantment wasn't happy with their version of a "sacrifice." Seeing Nin and Valeran struggle with directing an enchantment was a strange and unwanted image. That they had the aid of the Shadow Prince and were *still* having trouble was sort of mind-boggling. The Carres had *really* not wanted the scepter found.

"Sehk-be-damned, Valeran," the prince said.

"You are barely keeping *your* thread active, Your Imperial Darkness."

The prince narrowed his eyes on Taline. "If the weak one can't hold up her end, we need to deplete her totally."

"You will *not*." Nin bared her teeth and pushed more of her own power toward Taline.

Taline tightened her lips together. Wasn't this always the case? She couldn't defend herself against those who bought her. She couldn't defend herself when she'd been used and beaten beyond recognition. She couldn't defend herself when the Shadow Prince had pinned her down, causing Nin to expose her powers to save her.

"Weak links are weak links," he said. "Useless."

Never good enough. She'd only been able to defend herself in this world once *Nin* had freed her. Once she'd been given the tools and access to knowledge. And still, she was the weakest. But Sehk-be-damned if she wasn't going to repay what had been given to her until she was drained of her organs and wrapped beneath stone.

"Taline built that scope as well as countless items we've used to get this far. You can take your condemnation and light a pyre beneath it with you on top," Nin said. "And you have no idea the *use* she has. Taline is full of a power you can scarcely understand."

"Enlighten me."

She didn't do it verbally, but whatever she did through the link—pulsing it under the spell they were all trying to hold—caused the prince to narrow his eyes.

"Weakness," he repeated.

"And that's why you will *never* understand that power."

"A beautiful discussion," Valeran said, eyes narrowed on the plinth. "Love is so splendid. And determination, so keen. Back to the Temple of Death spell now, please."

"Aren't you supposed to be the scholar? Isn't that why you are still alive?" the Shadow Prince said.

"Yes. Intellectual superiority is why I'm still alive. I'm proud of you, princeling."

Not that she didn't want to tell Kaveh ul Fehl to shove himself into a pit, but Valeran was going to get himself turned to dust with his derogatory diminutives. Princeling? If the two weren't roughly the same age, Taline would eat her cowl. Everyone knew the ages of the blessed spawn of the emperor. The thirteenth blessed prince had seen twenty-two springs. What she knew of Valeran put him somewhere in that range. Older than her twenty autumns, and Nin's nineteen summers.

"You don't need certain parts of your body in order to still serve your use." The Shadow Prince wasn't looking at him, dismissive, but the threat seemed real.

"How very *incisive*, since the spell is seeking to do just th—"

Purple flared.

Nin threw an arm in front of Valeran, then crooked her wrist and batted the offensive spell with some of her own. The spell skidded along the floor then dispersed in a blast of purple.

Valeran sighed as the threat to him retreated—taking with it some of Nin's own dwindling reserves. "I hate it when you do that."

Nin rotated her shoulders while still holding the spell and pulling all the threads back together, even with the hit to her power. "I know."

"Ninli—"

"No," she said softly, gaze on the interconnecting threads of magic. "We can do this."

And this was Nin's strength, her ultimate power—her ability to believe.

"Again," Nin commanded softly, pulling from them.

Taline closed her eyes and let that ability flow through her—Nin's ability to believe. And suddenly, she felt it. As she opened her eyes, she could feel it from all of them.

From the Shadow Prince, whose expression was as incomprehensible to Taline as his very being, but whose own power was absolutely zeroed in on Nin, allowing her to use it. From Valeran, who looked and felt overwhelmingly resigned, who willingly gave up his own power to the force of nature who was asking for it.

And for a single, blinding moment, the four of them worked in perfect synergy—four pillars surrounding the plinth—and it moved. One part broke to become four, then the pedestal turned in on itself, four parts falling forward in synergy. The pieces continued to move, faster and faster until a boom and shaft of light burst from the center, and the whole thing began to shift and transform together.

The shaft of light pulsed, and the air began to shimmer. A wave of horrible loss washed over her as the inverted plinth converted downward one step after another into a curving stone staircase. Another burst of loss pulsed upward, and it felt as if she'd been suddenly stripped of a limb.

They'd prepared for this. Still...

"The null zone is spreading outward." Kaveh ul Fehl's eyes were grim. He had already shrugged off his cloak, leaving only a covering of black bands around his chest and shoulders, arm muscles rippling freely as he started stripping items from his cloak. Shadows dispersed from him in large clutches, blending into the darkness of the antechamber as whatever enchantment was used to hold them was released. "Do your legends speak of a bleed between worlds?"

"It should be fine," Valeran said, but he had dropped his casual facade for the razor-edged attention he seldomly revealed. The plinth enlarged, forcing them all to back away as the staircase expanded as it descended. "If we move quickly."

The steeply curved stone steps ended their descent in a flash of bright light, and a large cavern opened up below. A floating island hung, suspended below the steps, high above the cavern's floor. On the island was a glittering black-and-gold scepter embedded in a stone.

Taline stared at it, uncomprehending. Despite being thirty feet away, retrieving the Scepter of Darkness was a thought Taline could barely grasp. Giving it to the empire...

Taline could only handle one problem at a time.

And believing in Nin had never led her wrong.

Taline flexed the pitiful amount of magic that remained in her. Giving up half her magic to activate the layer gate, after fighting the second chamber that had already drained much of it, had left her with little. Still, she was used to having to rely on cleverness.

Having the Shadow Prince and Valeran more than half depleted? Not bad.

Having Nin depleted far beyond that due to her actions in wrangling them together and defending them? Not great.

They still had a numbers advantage against the Shadow Prince, though, and the oath remained in place.

The world continued to bleed and morph around them as two layers fused together. The floor crumbled and fell in front of them, stones falling into the cavern underneath. A short bridge connected to the steps, but they were the only thing of substance leading to the island floating below.

A cavern stretched below and all around them, flickering wildly as it resolved into place. They could see both worlds— like a sunspot that had caused the eyes to see two things in the same location. They were near the ceiling of the vast cavern of the other world, standing on a cliff, and yet the stone of the temple was strong beneath their feet.

The Shadow Prince's last shadows swarmed his ankles, as if wanting to create a disc on which to carry him should the stone floor disappear into the ether of the other, like the area around the steps had already done. Then they, too, felt the absence of his magic as the null field continued to spread, and they dispersed into the darkness of the temple beyond.

The combined world crystallized in a breath-stealing loss of magic.

A world layer of non-magic laid over theirs, nullifying their own powers. The disconnect between the antechamber and the cavern beyond was stark. The Temple of Darkness was in an enclosed building, while the other plinth was located on a floating island in the middle of a cavern.

And there were *people* in the other layer. Hundreds of people in strange, rough-hewn dress, flooded into the cavern through all the archways to drop to their knees. They bowed, pressing their foreheads to the ground while chanting crazed words that gained in speed and volume.

Hundreds of people steeped in sweat and zeal.

Taline looked down at the floating island. "How does it stay suspended?"

"It is using power from our world layer. Separated power. Magic can be held in pockets—purposeful cavities of great power," Kaveh ul Fehl said, dark eyes searching the cavern. "We are in their layer—a world lacking magic that yet has a specific spot where magic exists. They gather to worship this unknown power that is seldom seen in an event that was likely prophesied for having happened in a previous retrieval of the scepter. In this activation, they cross to our world as well, sealing us in a null-filled void. The two worlds layered atop each other, now fusing together for this moment in time. A specific magic event."

Valeran side-eyed him. "How astute of you, princeling."

"Get the scepter, Ninli ul Summora."

"Don't you want to give them a legend worth such worship?" Valeran tilted his head at the chanting crowd. "We could really sell this moment for future generations."

"Get the scepter," the Shadow Prince said to Nin, "before I kill your extra."

Valeran didn't pause in his appraisal of the crowd below. "So touchy without your magic."

"I don't need magic to kill you." The prince's fingers danced through the air in an assassin's caress—an elegant, patterned strike of each digit.

"I think you will find killing me much harder without your powers." There was something cold and clear in Valeran's eyes as he finally looked up. "I wouldn't test such a thing, Your Imperial Highness."

"I'm going," Nin said softly, moving to the first step.

"Not alone," Taline said, unnatural panic running through her.

"You stay. So does Valeran," the prince ordered, gaze on Taline.

"It's fine, Tali."

Valeran laughed—an unamused sound. "Is it, Ninli? And when the scepter fuses to you, then what?"

"I know what to do," Nin said quietly. "I...know the gifting magic. I will gift the scepter to him. I've promised."

Taline's panic intensified into a painful throb. Something

about the throb said this was an *end*. That she wouldn't see Nin again, if she pulled the scepter from the stone.

"I'm not letting you go alone."

"You stay, or your sister dies at the end of her broken oath," the Shadow Prince said. "There is no other entrance. No other exit."

"One way in and out except to go through the non-magic world with no hope of return. Not concerning at all," Valeran said languidly, hand resting on his belt.

Nin put a hand—one that was only a quarter-powered, at most—on Taline's arm.

"Can you even pull the scepter in this state?" Taline asked, harsh breaths straining her lungs.

NINLI

"I'll get it," Nin said quietly, staring at the scepter. "Power isn't the key." Nin shrugged her bag from her shoulder and handed it to Taline, trying to communicate that everything would be well. "But take this, just in case."

Rone looked at her askance. "I'll keep watch, shall I?"

Taline's lips thinned—sensing a secret message—but Nin tilted her head, faintly relieved at the coded words that he'd strike her down. Better to have someone like Rone who could make decisions that were in other interests, for Taline's would only be what she deemed best for Nin.

Kaveh's narrowed eyes looked hard at Rone, then turned to study her fiercely. She turned from his piercing gaze and took a step downward.

The chanting grew louder, the smell stronger, and the zeal more rapturous.

Eiser panee watre sakri ousa pater

Her throat tightened and her chest constricted. Foreheads bowed so low that she could see the dust and dirt painting their foreheads as they rose and fell. She took one more step.

The crowds gathering twenty deep in the back weaved back and forth, hands lifted to the sky.

Eiser panee watre sakri ousa pater

Her last connection to the world was yanked away. Her chin dropped and she gripped her chest. Power that she'd relied on since she'd fully awakened fled from her veins. The increased power that had festered in her after the palace slaughter—nine years old, overpowered, orphaned, and alone—slipped from her grip.

It had taken years, but she'd learned to rely on it, to see some good in a bad start. And now...

She closed her eyes and took a deep breath, then continued forward. To the worshipers below, she must look a sight—a person appearing from the thin air above, descending a stairway from the heavens to grab a weapon embedded in stone.

She wondered whether Queen Salare had ever come to bask in the adoration as the king checked the scepter protections. Lorsali would have loved such a thing, but she had not been in line to wield such power in Tehrasi. Lorsali had been a tool to be used against other kingdoms—a glorious tool—who had sneered at Nin being too small, too dull, too *useless*. Had ridiculed her every time Nin had looked hungrily at Lorsali's glowing scepter, or at the unlit scepter in position nine.

Try to lift the ninth. Go on. I bet you lift it and it does nothing—that all that they say you will be able to do is false. The tinkling of cruel laughter. *Useless.*

Nin froze Lorsali's poisoned words of memory from leaking further. It didn't matter. She was here, and Lorsali was not. Lorsali was a footnote in history, and Nin was trying to change the future—Nin would fade in the shadows of history under a cowled guise and a different name, but she would make Tehrasi *better*. She curled her fingers into her palms and slowly stepped onto the island.

The scepter glowed in its stone sheath.

Oppressive air, lacking magic in any measure, coated the entire space. The chanting voices rippled around the cavern and something pulsed against her throat. Carefully, she pulled off her farhani necklace, which contained her base eye color-changing spell, and placed it on the ground, never looking away from the scepter stone.

Bringing magic into a non-magic field could do nothing—or it could very much bring about destruction. Best to listen to the warning ripples.

She carefully stepped to the stone.

Wards were wrapped around the base, and glyphs were carved into the stone. She could read none of them. But she didn't have to read them to know the dire warnings for anyone trying to retrieve the scepter.

Nin closed her eyes and dipped her hand into her knife pocket. She had put a plain, unenchanted blade in there for this exact purpose. She dragged her palm across the edge, feeling the skin part.

Keeping her back to the others, with only the frenzied mob in view, she placed her bloodied palm against the stone.

The crowd continued their chants, the air continued to be free of power, and the wards remained completely intact.

She pressed her palm harder.

Not a flicker of light, a tether of power. Nothing.

Useless.

The stone shimmered reluctantly, pulsing dully then quickly returning to its static state.

Unworthy.

But a click sounded, and there was a lessening of one heavy feeling and the descent of another, just as powerful—the wards shifting slowly. Unlocked.

Shaking, she raised her hand and wrapped her fingers around the staff. She expected a tingle—to feel the power flowing up her arm and through her body—the experience that the others had spoken of, the feeling of having the world's forces at your fingertips, spreading through your veins. Power and might.

Nothing. She felt nothing. Nothing except the vaguest hum of immaterial recognition.

The scepter was dead under her bloodied hand.

I bet you lift it and it does nothing.

She took a moment to push that inner voice back down before gripping the scepter harder and pulling it from its stone sheath. She held it aloft in tribute and the crowd's chants went wild, and light...

Didn't shine.

Because you are useless. Lorsali's voice cackled madly from her memories.

With her blood dripping down the shaft, Nin slowly lowered the scepter back to eye level.

Nothing. It was as any other decorated staff held in her hand.

She gripped it with two hands and pushed at the power she knew lurked beneath. The pictorial descriptions had shown a figure pulling the scepter and light shining as the figure lofted it into the air.

Nothing happened. The most compelling of all rejections.

She felt absurdly like Etelian ul Fehl for a moment, wanting to shake the thing.

You will never wield a scepter.

She gave a stuttered laugh and released the shaft from her right hand, staring at her bloodied palm. Blood from the House of Scepters.

"Nin?" Taline called anxiously from above.

"I don't know why I thought—" She shook her head and wiped her hand across the square rag hanging from her waist. "Stupid. Stupid, silly girl," she murmured.

"Is it fake?" Kaveh asked, voice tight.

She grimaced, wishing it were so, and forced herself to look up. Kaveh's expression was grim. Taline's was tense. Rone looked relieved.

"It's real." Nin stared down at her hand as the blood started to bubble up again. The scepter was real, and she would never wield it.

"Why...isn't it doing anything?" Taline asked hesitantly.

"I don't know." She looked up again with a tight smile. "But that is for the empire to discern. Let them find someone worthy."

She wrapped her bloodied hand around the shaft again and took a moment to absorb the moment—disappointment, relief, failure, liberation, and bitter acknowledgment swept through her, but no flicker of power or further acceptance from the scepter.

Unworthy.

She let out a final breath. It didn't matter whether she was worthy or unworthy. She had *rejected* the Carre legacy. Yet it still ruled her—it would always rule her—because she had given it the power to.

She took a deep breath, then let it out slowly. Not anymore. This...this would be the final piece. She and Taline would forge a new destiny—a free destiny—and leave Tehrasi in another's hands.

She slowly ascended the stairs with the dormant scepter laid across her palms. The stone steps disappeared behind her with every step she took, and it would look to the crowd as if she was ascending once more to the heavens.

"Your Imperial Highness, the Scepter of Darkness." She offered it forward to Kaveh as she ascended the last step, scepter still dead in her hand.

Unlit—forever unlit, like any scepter she might claim.

She stepped from the top stair onto the antechamber's floor, and light—brighter than any she'd seen—burst everywhere in one, blinding pulse.

She barely had a chance to look at the suddenly glowing scepter in shock—the scepter was *lit*, its power shooting through her—before an outside power thrust the scepter from her hand. The scepter skittered across the floor. The power abruptly shut off within her, cutting her down like a sheaf of wheat under a scythe. She fell to the ground.

"Nin!"

Then the chamber exploded in sunlight flames.

SPELLS OF THE DAMNED

NINLI
TEMPLE OF THE SCEPTER

Sunlight flames encircled their position. The flames trapped the four of them inside, and blocked Kaveh from diving through. Even his corporeal shadow companion disappeared beneath the dark stripping wrapped repeatedly around his chest. Nin threw up a shield alongside the others to block the sight and heat of the flames, though the crippling agony of the scepter being torn from her made her hand motions sloppy.

Her body ached with the ripping of the scepter. Hunching on the stones, she tried to repair her magic.

Thirteen cloaked figures wearing pins drawn with five waving lines stepped forward. The antechamber's spells had been paused by the opening of the plinth, so the traps were currently dormant in the room they were within.

"Passage between world layers is forbidden. No one should wield that which evil shaped. We are here to destroy the scepter that should never have been wrought."

The pin, the words... How had pentalayerists gotten here? No one could have gotten through the first chamber without following Nin and Rone directly. It would have been impossible.

Unless...

The foot spell, duplicated. Nin closed her eyes. She'd known the betrayal was coming, but not what form it would take—definitely not in the form of people who wanted her kind eradicated. Pentalayerists were a secret sect of magi who believed that the split of the world into five equal layers was sacrosanct. The pentalayerists' sworn duty was the protection of the split—separating the non-magic world, where the scepter had been stored—from the magic layers.

The pentalayerists had killed gatemakers before. They had long tried to neutralize any magi who held the power to disturb that which they had sworn to protect. Nin had been raised on the tales and the price of being a gatemaker without royal protection. Their assassins came for magi whose special abilities affected the layers. The Carres had held an uneasy truce with the group and that truce had tightened Tehrasi's anti-imperialism and isolationist tendencies.

The cloaked figures moved forward, and the proximity and sunlight spell made it easier to see inside their hoods, and to further answer the question of how they were here. The two at the front were the workmen who had been the last to flee. She'd memorized their faces when she'd seen Taline staring at them with a frown.

Kaveh was already in motion, cloak flaring as he, too, realized what had happened, and was turning to obliterate the betrayer. Rone whirled around Nin, a knife already in his hand.

"Valeran," Taline hissed, shocked understanding and horror mixing in her voice. "What have you done?"

Rone pressed his blade to Nin's throat, ignoring Taline. "Now, now, princeling. Careful."

The only thing that mattered now was what Rone had planned—he would never have done something like this without forethought.

Kaveh advanced, his own blade unsheathed. "Kill her. The oath only covers her death by an imperial hand."

Rone chuckled against her hair. "All children of the emperor are covered by the imperial oath, of which I'm still a part."

Which meant if Rone killed her, Kaveh would die. Nin's heartbeat picked up speed. Taline looked caught between horror and fury.

Kaveh's fingers tightened around his knife, but his steps slowed. "I tire of oathbreakers."

"Kill the Shadow Prince, if you have a way to do it, Rone ul Valeran," the pentalayerist leader shouted, voice urgent and ecstatic. "And we will gift you whatever you desire."

Kaveh's gaze fastened on her. *Kill him*, whispered through her mind. She could feel the way he expected her to follow through on the mental command immediately, since his focus was already returning to the wider room and back to the pentalayerists.

If they managed to escape, the pentalayerists would know their faces—hers and Taline's.

"Remember your promise," she murmured to the man holding her at knifepoint as she tried to heal what had been ripped.

"Worry about yourself." His grip tightened.

"Kill her. Kill the prince. Destroy the scepter," the pentalayerist leader shouted.

Nin held still and Rone shrugged. "I suppose it cannot be helped."

Kaveh whirled back around, feeling something in her emotions that spiked his into returning magnified disbelief. Taline ran toward them.

Nin would die twice over—from an oath broken on both sides. She could *feel* Kaveh's incredulity concerning why she wasn't moving, while Taline's expression was a rictus of fury.

Nin had expected betrayal from Rone, though—she knew how his mind worked—and while Rone was many things, her killer, he was not. Not even to kill Kaveh ul Fehl.

Rone thrust her forward and dove for the scepter as Taline dove for Nin.

Kaveh's knife collided with Rone's two paces from his goal. Rone's eyes flashed and his mouth curved in a sadistic grin. "No magic, princeling."

"I don't need magic to kill you."

"And I don't need magic to make certain an unlit scepter is destroyed."

A dozen screams and an overwhelming pulse lit the space, halting the fight before it began. Rone and Kaveh instinctively sprang paces apart to deal with the unknown threat without losing sight of each other.

Where there had been thirteen standing figures, there was now one.

"Now, now, I can't have you ruining my plans, Valeran, more than the Fehls already have." The figure who had killed all the others looked up and the enchantment on his face fell. He smiled. "The pests proved themselves useful for once."

Nin felt fury light across the bond. Crelu ul Osni stood beyond the flames, face lit by unholy light, the Third Scepter of Tehras in his hand. He reached out and *pulled*.

She knew the enchantment, and it was not *his*. He had no right to it.

The island and bridge between the worlds started to burn with the force of the retrieval spell he'd raised—a spell powerful enough to try and cross the null field. On the top stair, the unlit scepter teetered. Taline dove into a somersault across the stones and pinned the scepter beneath her sandaled foot, not touching it with her skin.

The chanting of the worshipers grew more fevered as the world link crumbled, and the stink of their fervor grew worse. Anticipation and glory: Nin recognized the sight and smell well—the Carres had most loved the festivals where crimson ran down the steps of Tehras's temple, where sacrifice was its own due. The Feast of Sustenance and Renewal, the Festival of Blood...

Glorious sacrifice to rulers touched by divinity.

"Remove your foot and kick the scepter here, girl, and I'll allow you to live." Crelu ul Osni stood in the haze of light, fingers curled around his ceremonial scepter—a scepter capable of producing ceremonial spells like those associated with bringing light, darkness, and ambiance—a scepter capable of performing rituals.

"Never," Taline said furiously.

Rone was slowly moving behind Nin once more.

"Don't be exceedingly stupid, girl," Osni said to Taline. "I will get it no matter if you live or die."

"You shouldn't have enough magic for this, Osni. The emperor drained you." Kaveh's sharp gaze tracked the edges of Osni around the solid circle of light as it thinned and turned into an unbreakable clear field with a wave of the Third Scepter.

Nin had not been the only one to underestimate Osni.

"For someone who relies on sheer power, Shadow Prince, you discount what others are forced to do to compensate. A null field holding the scepter and a spell to trap you within that field? All it took was one whisper of a discovered spellbox that could create absolute sunlight to excite the pentalayerists. The temple and zealots did the job for me." Osni smiled. "It's too bad that the thirteenth prince mysteriously disappeared on a secret task for the emperor and was never found. Aros, always plotting, might even take the fall for your disappearance. Enough of a fall, even, to be permanently dealt with. I do hope so. Now kick forward the scepter, girl."

"*Never.*" Taline leaned her weight on the dormant scepter trapped against the ground.

"You are a dead man," Kaveh said, outward dispassion hiding his internal fury and resolve.

Osni smiled and touched the locket at his neck. "I've known that for a while. But I think I might last longer than you anticipate. I will have the scepter, whether one of you throws it or not. And as for the four of you, you will never see the light of day. Or, maybe it is more pertinent in your case to say, 'the dark of night.' Amazing what one can do when one plans an assassination so far in advance."

Osni waved a hand over the flames. "I've been waiting to use this spell against you for *so* long, Your Imperial *Highness.* The lapdog assassin for all Sher Fehl's needs—every time one of your shadows slipped around my neck, I dreamed of this day."

"And I gave you no further thought each time you dropped, gagging from my spells."

Osni's mouth went flat. "I will be pleased to rid the world of you."

"Where is my death then?" Kaveh sneered, arms going wide in graceful arcs. "My flesh is still upon my bones. My blood still in my veins." His expression went dismissive once more—as if Osni was a sand-ant pretending at being a flesh-scarab. "You stand there speaking of my death, and yet

I stand here alive. Come, Crelu ul Osni. Come kill me and put your words to deed."

Osni's smile went tight.

Nin could feel Kaveh's fury, but he looked *cold*.

Osni had them penned in, though, inside the null field. They had the most powerful relic in existence, but no magic to call to use it.

Unworthy.

No. Concentrate.

"Oh, your death comes. And I will remember your screams." Osni pulled jars from a large pack that he began placing in neat little rows.

Her chest grew cold. She knew what those jars were for, each with a brain, stomach, liver, lungs, and intestines squashed together inside with a *heart*. For there to be a heart... And in the numbers that he was placing...

She hadn't seen revenants since the days of sacrifice. Since blood ran through the streets of Tehras to feed the bloodlust of the Carres.

"Necromancy is illegal in the Sunlight Empire," Nin said, breath coming too quickly. "The emperor outlawed it."

Osni's smile turned barbed and horrible. "Much is illegal for those who are caught."

"A truth that is so often forgotten," Rone murmured.

"Silence, *betrayer*," Taline hissed at him.

Nin shifted so she was blocking sight to Taline. If Rone wanted them actively dead, she'd already have a knife through her throat or heart, but she had to play outside of him in this endgame. She knew Taline's strengths, and she could feel Kaveh's shifting emotions indicating an active thinking state, so she took a deep breath and focused on Osni and the part she could play.

That she *wanted* to play. "*Murderer.*"

"I have been known to dabble." Osni placed five more jars.

It wasn't enough. A shuddered breath ran through her. "Murderer of all that is holy," she spit at him.

"Holiness is granted to those deemed worthy."

"You were never worthy, Crelu ul Osni. *Betrayer.*"

"I'm beginning to think there was someone special to you who I killed," he mused without pausing his task.

"*Oathbreaker,*" she said harshly, forgetting herself in her sudden fury. "*Kinslayer.* Murderer of that which is held *sacred.*"

He froze. His eyes narrowed sharply and everything about him went on point as his gaze traveled her cloaked figure. "Who are you?"

Too much, too *soon.* Nin forced herself to calm. It was like trying to stop a churning water wheel with one bare foot.

"People talk, Scholari. Necromancy is a dying art—practitioners know each other. And their *crimes.*"

She had to keep his attention—just for a few seconds more, she needed to keep her anger from overwhelming the gambit.

"Your voice..." Osni cocked his head, gaze faraway—fear and excitement curling within it.

She forced her voice lower. "Even should we die and you

survive, the necromancers will come for you. They don't like such exposure."

"Dabblers. *Let* them." His mouth twisted and he set back to work—shaking off whatever memory had taken hold. "I will twist and rend them as I did those before, as I will do *you*—turning you into nothing that you desire and all that you will fear."

His hand flashed and the first row of jars burst. Misshapen, malformed bodies lengthened and grew. Claws and fangs, eyeless faces and dripping jaws.

The first revenants shifted forward on fledgling legs. Each additional moment gave them added strength—it was the risk if they couldn't get out of the trap: the revenants gained form the longer they stood conjured. Long, sharp teeth, daggered claws—the ability to rip and tear, even cutting through stone as though it were bare flesh caught in a crocodile's jaws—all grew more deadly the longer they stood in flesh form.

But the spellmaster, the necromancer, grew weaker with every moment and every revenant. She looked steadily at Osni, gauging his state. The scepter in his hand—never supposed to be taken from the palace—was an unanticipated impediment.

"You grow weaker, Crelu ul Osni, and the scepter won't save you. You will die here."

Certainty shook her as she said the words, and with it, relief. Relief from a task gone a decade too long. She looked at the unlit scepter clasped under Taline's foot, at the lip of the stairs above a slowly disappearing crowd gone wild with fervent sway. Osni would die and Nin... Unworthy, but complete, Nin could truly rest.

"You speak like the Shadow Prince, the favorite of the emperor and leader of all armies. So confident of success. But I've taken down the House of Scepters, and I will take down the Fehl Empire and Crown of Sunlight." Osni motioned sharply to the revenants. "They won't be gentle with you, and I will bring you back in an even more grotesque form. The beauty of embalming is the casting away of the shell. With only the five organs as a base, I can remake your bodies into anything I want. Won't the emperor be surprised when his favorite consumes him whole."

"Go for their hearts," Nin said to the others without looking away, her voice wavering only the slightest bit. "When they come, heed nothing but a heart strike."

Osni smiled tightly. "Someone who knows the craft. I find myself increasingly *put out*. Your *name*?"

Nin ignored him. "Revenants have a specific weakness," she repeated from hard-earned memory, fingers grazing her side. "Because they can't be fully returned to human state, it takes time for commands to process. There will always be a pause in their movements when they switch a task."

She drew the blade from her pocket and inhaled through her nose, then exhaled through her mouth, focusing. It wouldn't be her first time fighting a revenant.

Osni's smile tightened. "Interesting. But ultimately useless. The *truly* interesting thing about revenants is that they can survive a null field just fine. And I can make hundreds. You will fall beneath them, no matter how many you take down."

A dozen rose, then a dozen more.

They started to push through the unbreakable barrier. Sunlight blasted around the edges of each as it penetrated. Jaws snapped, bodies broke; some died as they burned in flame, but others continued behind, pushing over their comrades' bodies, eager to take their place. Soulless.

Without magic, the four of them wouldn't survive against two dozen monsters in such tight quarters. There was nowhere to flee for a higher or thinner vantage point, and no mass weapons to even the odds.

She had never fought a horde, but she would concentrate on one, then another, until she could no longer draw her arm.

"I hope you know what you are doing," she murmured to Rone, fingers clenched around her knife.

He looked at her. "Why do you trust me?" he demanded. "You know what I am."

"If we allow ourselves to be defined by our blood, we will never be free."

RONE

Sehk *damn* her and grind her to dust.

Rone stared at the scene as the first revenant broke

completely through. He shifted position in the tiny space as the world slowed to slices of movement—a claw ripping through the air, wet fangs snapping. Rone rotated the dagger in his palm, view shrinking to the pulsing heart inside the revenant's heaving, misshapen, marshy chest.

Step, rotate, pierce. The revenant burst forward and Rone's body started to move in rote form.

Darkness streaked past his peripheral view and Rone twisted at the last moment to let the shadow take the creature. Did the thirteenth prince have access to his power again?

The dark slice of malevolence twisted around the neck of the revenant like a whipped rock cord and sheared it free. The body of the revenant fell to the floor in a writhing mass, and the creature dropped, hissing with it. Rone realized that all of them except the Shadow Prince had forgotten they had a fifth combatant in this whole mess. The Shadow Prince's familiar: a creature with its own mind, apparently, separate from the Shadow Prince's powers or call.

"The heart," Kaveh ordered calmly.

The shadow didn't even pause, diving through the heart of the downed revenant—piercing it like an arrow—then lunging upward to dive through the next revenant pushing through the barrier.

Rone heard Ninli's breath catch. And he felt his own heartbeat shift. He shifted his feet to match.

There was an opening here. The creature could get through the flames in a way they could not—for the shadow could dive through a beast as it entered the sunlight barrier—forcing the revenant to act as its shield.

Rone could see from the Shadow Prince's expression that he was already counting on it.

Osni swore and scrambled. The shadow dove. Sunlight blasted.

When Rone could see again, the shadow was nowhere to be seen. The Shadow Prince looked as if he would kill everyone through his dead gaze alone, and Osni was laid out on the floor, panting. The scholari looked overwhelmingly ill—magic sickness.

"Your creature is *dead.*" Osni pushed himself upright with difficulty. "And you are depleted of power, *Imperator.* You will die here."

"You will die here as well, Crelu ul Osni."

The dark certainty in Kaveh ul Fehl's voice lifted the hair along the back of Rone's neck. And he saw the darkness curl behind Osni—the limping husk of it—as it lunged. Osni raised an arm to shield himself, but as he wielded the ceremonial scepter in his hand, its aim was wild and panicked.

The shot went wild.

The barrier started to crack.

Revenants screamed.

Osni screamed.

And the plinth started to pull inward, rotating again, closing in on itself.

The null field started to tilt wildly, breaking apart in sections.

Taline stumbled and the scepter spun across the floor, landing at the feet of the Shadow Prince.

Power rippled over the chamber and cavern, splitting between them and wildly rotating throughout.

The null field was cracking in sections large enough for the Shadow Prince to use his power to rip apart the revenants that grew too close. But like pockets in space, he had to wait for precise moments to strike, and that left him unable to control the battlefield in the way that he was used to.

And his neck, usually guarded by his creature, was exposed. Rone flipped the knife in his hand and drew his arm back.

Kaveh ul Fehl ripped Ninli from the path of the revenant that was lunging for her. The band around his wrist flashed gold in the motion.

Rone paused.

Ninli's own banded wrist cut through the air as she pierced the dripping flesh of the revenant with her blade—plunging it through its back and piercing its heart. His eyes followed the movement, zeroing in on where the band peeked from her overly long sleeve.

She would die if Kaveh ul Fehl died by Rone's hand. He knew that. He gripped the knife. Ninli had connected herself to a man who would follow the emperor's every word. And with Ninli and the scepters at hand, the empire would be unstoppable.

Rone would get to see the Valerans fall—a powerful

incentive in and of itself to sit on the sidelines and eat karo meats wrapped around slices of figs.

But the empire would be consumed from within, and the lure and song of the scepter would overwhelm all else.

He had no love for the empire. He didn't much care about the world either, but the lesson of the Carres was enshrined in blood. The scepters had powers that few understood.

With the Scepter of Darkness in the emperor's hand, all the scepters' powers would be unlocked. Rone would be located and caged, never free again—caged to a destiny he did not and would never want.

He looked at Ninli.

She had saved him, again—in the fight with Kaveh ul Fehl, and again during the plinth spell—and Rone knew her well. For her, there had been no other choice but to complete the deal with the thirteenth prince. She had needed to save Rone and Taline. And she wanted the best for Tehrasi, constrained forever to her guilt-stricken cage. She would sacrifice herself easily for the endgame that would buy her that goal.

And she would think that she could save everyone else by dying with her secrets.

He had never understood her, even with his lineage just as poisoned. *Especially* with his lineage just as poisoned. Had never understood why she *cared*.

Why she thought others were worth saving. That bad people could be *good*.

The null field fell over them again on its twirling axis, and deprived of power again, Kaveh ul Fehl reached for the scepter with a bare hand.

Osni, Ninli, Taline, Kaveh, Etelian, the emperor.

Freedom. Death. Choices. Promises. Betrayal.

Rone's feet acted on their own as he leaped through the air and twisted to land crouched in front of the Shadow Prince, boot atop the scepter's staff.

"I won't let the scepter be wielded by the empire," Rone said harshly. He watched a look of utter horror bloom across Taline's face. Watched acceptance settle on Ninli's.

The null field tilted once more, rippling across the Shadow Prince and Rone. A band of magic tingled across Rone's skin.

Kaveh ul Fehl raised his hand.

Powered once more in the tilting magic, Rone lifted the scepter with a gust of wind from his toes, pulled his knee to his chest and kicked the scepter sideways through the air.

He used the kicking momentum to lunge out of the way of Fehl's death strike but couldn't completely miss the blow. The skin across his chest ripped open. He turned in a burst of splattered red to see his own aim strike true.

The scepter flew through the air as if weightless, before smacking into the person he had kicked it to.

Taline instinctively curved a hand around the shaft of the object that smacked into her chest. The momentum drove her upper body back to teeter on the edge of the crumbling island, hanging over the abyss. The null field passed Taline, passed over Nin's blood on the shaft, and magic sparked like lightning.

Piercing light lit around Taline. Pulsed *through* her, connecting her mind to heart to right palm. Her palm lit with unholy light and she screamed.

"Taline!" Ninli's terrified voice exploded as she pitched herself toward her sister.

Taline fell to her knees.

The Shadow Prince pulled a throwing knife from his sleeve, gaze fastened on Taline.

"No." Ninli scrambled, shifting in midair to throw herself at Kaveh instead of Taline. She hit him in a flying tackle, but he didn't budge. She wrapped her hand around his throwing fist, as if that would stave off whatever he was going to do. Blood slid through her clenched fingers. "It fused to her. You can't."

Rone pulled himself painfully along the floor as the world tilted.

Kaveh looked down at Ninli, at the blood that seeped from her hand to his. "Separate her from it or she dies."

"Yes! I will do it! But I need time. It has bonded to her. Give me three moon rises to—"

Kaveh ul Fehl grabbed her chin. "It started glowing as soon as it left the null field. *You* were the one who pulled it from the stone. It was about to fuse to *you*. She is no one in this. Separate it from her now or she *dies*."

Rone continued dragging himself toward where Taline was staring emptily at the sparking scepter fused to her palm.

"She is the master of the scepter now," Ninli said. Passion, regret, and fear mixed together in her shaking voice. "It takes more than simple *desire* to undo that. There are spells and enchantments. Why do you think I didn't want Osni to touch it? Those who seek it blindly have *never* understood the real reasons the scepter was hidden so carefully."

Rone had never seen Ninli look so wild. Blood flowed rapidly down her arm, squeezed out from her clenching fist around the blade.

And her eyes...her eyes perfectly reflected the dripping blood.

Ice spread suddenly through Rone's chest. Ninli's ocular enchantments had broken. He'd only seen it happen once, but he'd never forgotten the sight.

Kaveh ul Fehl would never forget it either.

Rone closed his eyes. *Ninli ul Summora* was dead. There was nothing Rone could do for her now, whatever she would be forced to become.

But he could keep his promise to her. He pushed himself forward as Kaveh's fingers tightened on Ninli's arm.

"Separate her from it, or I kill her to get it done."

Ninli's genuine, wild, bright-red eyes slid to Rone and there were a thousand things there that he never wanted to contemplate—promises, debts, regret. "Yes."

Rone reached forward, and Kaveh shook free of Ninli, following her gaze. "Valeran, don't you da—"

Osni stretched out on the floor, and sent his last revenants diving toward them.

Kaveh stepped forward, hand outstretched.

Ninli grabbed the prince with her dwindling magic to stop him from whatever he was about to do.

Taline, who stared in blank horror at the scepter that lit brightly and painfully in her hand every time magic crossed over her, stood completely frozen to anything else that was going on around her.

Two worlds crumbled. The vortex swirled downward, collapsing. A hundred shadows flew.

And Rone grabbed a fallen stone for purchase, swinging himself sideways and drawing his knees to his chest. He kicked Taline into the vortex.

All hell broke loose.

He could hear her screaming; he could hear Ninli screaming. He could see Kaveh ul Fehl pivot to grab Ninli in one hand as he crushed the throat of the oncoming revenant with the other.

Rone grabbed the stone and threw himself forward in the same driving arc he'd sent Taline.

Wind rushed and magic stuttered in the shifting field of the abyss. Taline's mouth was open in terror and anguish as she looked up, free arm extended to her sister far above. Power circled her like a living thing, sparking from the scepter to everything around, further fusing its power to the person holding it.

Rone caught her roughly, still falling, the scepter breaking one of his ribs as it was crushed between them—sparking along his ripped open skin, whispering of the *power* it could give. The vortex pulled them in faster, whirling them around wildly.

"You have twenty-five days to bring me the scepter, Valeran, or I will make death the preferable option for her," the Shadow Prince said.

And Ninli, far above, in a stationary patch of light, looked straight at him, acceptance of her own death settling in her eyes, mingling with terror for her sister. "Keep your promise. Free her," she said. "Do right for Tehrasi. Do not come for me."

Then they were swallowed in purple.

SPELLS OF THE DAMNED

NINLI

TEMPLE OF THE SCEPTER

The vortex sucked downward, stripping the other world from view in a whirling tornado, pinpointed at the center as the plinth rotated back outward, remaking itself. A streak of movement surged past Nin with an unnatural speed and a deformed form threw itself into the last pinwheel, leaving two sliced-off toes behind.

Osni.

Then all was still.

Nin closed her eyes. Taline was gone. Rone was gone. Osni was gone—hopefully dead in that last crack or bleeding out, instead of hunting Taline, Rone, and the scepter.

The *scepter.*

Irrational amusement flooded her—hysteria forcing down her far more normal emotions of horror and fear.

Taline was now the master of the Scepter of Darkness.

When they'd entered the temple, no plan had included this outcome.

The irony of Nin's hand being the empty one appealed to her bitterest sense of justice. And the ghosts of the past whispered—*You survived when we did not. You do not deserve it.*

But the ghosts were easily shut away. Fear for Taline was not.

There was a price to pay as the master of the scepter. A terrible price.

Let them be safe. *Please.*

Magic burst to fill the room—the null bubble popping with the departure of the gate. Angry shadows wrapped her instantly. She instinctively fought the binds. Even depleted of any semblance of the power she'd possessed not an hour before, she still tried.

She had no one else to transport anymore; maybe—

Kaveh's fingers tightened around her neck and he pulled her back through the temple chambers, remembering the mazes with a mental retention she could only wish for. She could see the limp husk of his shadow companion tucked inside his cloak—a bulge of dying darkness that he must have collected when she'd been staring at the floor.

The oath band shifted beneath her sleeve and she could *feel* part of it dissolve and reform. She closed her eyes. No one else existed within their oath now. It was just the two of them and she was by far in the weaker position.

"If I thought you had any power within you," he spit. "If

I could *feel* that you had, I would make you open a gate to the non-magic layer this instant and make you watch as I kill your friends."

He could do it now—he could kill the others without consequence. The oath recognized that part of their arrangement had shifted and had compensated for it.

"I cannot open a gate to the other temple," she said. "No one can."

There were specific and overwhelming enchantments against such a thing—for the Carres had known that if a gatemaker outside the family found entry, they would be a danger to the secret of the scepter's location.

"I do not know where they are." She let the truth of it infuse her. The truth of the scepter's location had died with the king, queen, and crown prince.

She had no idea where Rone and Taline were, or where they would go, or how they would survive. But... If anyone could find a way back, it would be the two of them working together.

Or... Maybe the scepter would detach from Taline in the non-magic world, and they could *stay*. Live. Form a new life. Be free. *Be finally free.*

Her band slid along her wrist, a silken reminder of the chains that would bind her soon.

Soldiers dotted the forest hills as they stepped outside. Imperial boots and pins swam through her sight. A death squad stood before her. And she, with no power to call.

She physically reacted to the feeling she'd only

experienced in her endless nightmares. Lined up, stripped of power, exterminated—

"You will want to stop struggling," Kaveh ul Fehl said into her hair, voice tight and furious as shadows swarmed around the two of them—as if desperate to reconnect to their master. "For we are going on a little trip, and if I free you in these shadows, you will fall for an eternity in darkness."

His hand slid to tilt her head, shaking her enough so she focused on him. There was something darkly angry, and utterly revealing, in his gaze. "So you might want to put your efforts into hiding your venomous eyes again and holding on, *Zehra Amanan Carre.*"

Nin's fingers flew to her spelless eyes, the world crashing completely around her. The name brought forth the devastating memories she toiled to shut away.

Stuffed into a chute by a dozen sets of servants' hands, face stolen from her by a person who had always loved her—her guard, her most loyal handmaiden—looking back at her with Zehra Carre's own blood-red eyes. The signature eyes of all Carres who carried the gates in their blood. "They have breached the sanctum. Your magic is not yet attached. They will not know. Live, my beetle. Be finally free."

A shut door. A release of trash. Pain and darkness.

A release of all that Zehra Amanan Carre ever was. Onto the streets of a city that her family had ruled with an iron fist.

Blood in the House of Scepters. Blood in the streets of Tehras. The Carre rule brought down in one swift blow.

Terror, unlike any she had experienced since that day, shook her as Kaveh ul Fehl's shadows wrapped her in their grasp. The disintegrating temple landscape disappeared, along with her last secrets.

RONE

Rone woke to the tip of an infused dagger digging beneath his jugular and the sounds of zealous chanting reaching crescendo. There was no magic to call to his aid or to fix his flayed torso. But infused weapons would still work against flesh. His fingers inched along his cloak as his gaze rose to lock with the fierce golden-brown one above him.

"You will give me an oath," Taline spit, unlit scepter pressed against his chest.

The stench of hundreds of magicless humans grew as they repeatedly pressed sweaty bows to the ground around them.

"Will I?" He felt the blade press into his throat and smiled. He slowly palmed his closest knife. "We are in a non-magic land. You won't get anywhere without me."

"I won't get anywhere *with* you," she hissed. Her facial enchantments were eroding, revealing the real beauty beneath. "At least I won't have to watch over my shoulder with you gone."

Her skin tone remained the same medium brown, and her features weren't drastically different, but it was in all the fine tuning that a pretty face became beautiful—thinning or broadening, carving or smoothing. Blemishes melted away, and her eyes, still golden brown, were unhampered by the charms that usually radiated with dampening enchantments.

Fury brightened her usually cold and reserved eyes, making them alive.

Hair, always tightly coiled, was spread around her face and shoulders, like a veiled circlet lit by candlelight.

There was nothing outstanding about any one feature on Taline ul Summora, which was how she got away with her pretty disguise. It was in the combination of her features that she was remarkable.

It was in the way he was always drawn to her, despite the plethora of pretty faces across the kingdoms, that made her *dangerous*.

"Is that any way to treat your savior?"

"Savior?" Fury made her cheeks red and her eyes feverishly bright. "You have *killed Nin*."

"Killed? No. The Shadow Prince is bound under oath. And he's not stupid."

Rone didn't *like* Kaveh ul Fehl, but he'd never underestimated his abilities.

An ordinary prince could not become head of the imperial forces through brute strength or favoritism. An ordinary prince could become the ceremonial head of a country, like Etelian. The active leader of millions of soldiers? No.

Kaveh ul Fehl was far from stupid.

"He'll enslave her. He'll..." Taline's magnificent chest rose and fell with her heaving breaths.

He'd likely broken a few of her ribs in the kick. He kept his body loose, ready.

"He'll what?" he taunted. "Reveal her? He has already figured out her birth name."

As Taline froze, Rone seized the opportunity he had purposely created to flip their positions, gripping the wrist of her hand that was fused to the scepter against the ground, and her own knife pointed at her magnificent chest now. He leaned forward painfully, just enough to dig in the tip of the knife. "Lax of you, Taline." Blood seeped sluggishly from his mouth with every word. "Perhaps now we should speak of oaths."

"I'd rather die."

A brilliant burst thrust him from her. He threw his hand out to catch himself before he could be tossed into the fiery abyss of oil the worshipers had lit into the crevasse below.

The rapture of hundreds of voices grew to a fevered pitch.

Taline looked just as shocked as he felt, but she scrambled up and into fighting position.

He touched his scorched chest and looked at the scepter, fused to her hand but dormant once more. Unexpected. And something to think on.

"I wonder"—he flipped his knife—"should I stick this knife through your throat, narsumina... What would happen?"

She bared her teeth at him. "Come try it."

"The Scepter of Darkness just protected you, its wielder, in a non-magic space. It seeks to keep you alive."

"Sorry to *disappoint*."

He flipped the knife between his fingers a few more times, watching her, contemplating, then flipped it into his belt. He pulled Ninli's bag into his lap and began looking for poultices. At least his flayed skin had been cauterized. He eyed the prince's cloak—everything that had been dropped near the plinth had been sucked inside with them. He decided to leave searching anything of Kaveh ul Fehl's until he was well enough—when he might not immediately die from touching it.

"What are you doing?" she demanded.

"Not dying. What are you doing?" He watched her carefully as she violently waved the most powerful relic in the known kingdoms.

"I'm going to use this blasted thing to get back to Nin."

He waved a negligent hand. "Go on then. Open a gate."

He kept a close watch with his peripheral vision, while appearing to concentrate on his injuries.

Her eyes narrowed, and her fingers clenched in pain. She repeated the constipated motions, then did it again.

He released the tension in his shoulders. She couldn't access the scepter, then, not even in the temple of its host. Good. Trying to separate it from her would likely get him killed at the moment, but if he played things right...

She bared her teeth at him. "I'm going to figure out how

to use this blasted thing and get back to Tehras, while you rot here, Valeran."

"Or you will go mad in the attempt," he hummed. "There's a reason the Carres were mad—a reason Ninli was reluctant to wield that stick, even while she longed to do so with her tainted blood."

"Speak *not* of her."

He looked at the scepter. "If she had held it any longer in that space—"

"You *betrayed* her."

Betrayed *me*.

His eyelids slid half-closed and he peered at her with a self-satisfied smile. "Did you start to believe in me, little dove?"

She lunged at him and he let her tackle him to the ground. The knife at his throat stayed steady, but he felt the meat of another sink into his left lung, pinning him in place. He laughed, blood spraying from his mouth to paint her chest. "You did."

"A mistake I will not repeat."

He let his laziest smile curl as he kicked out from beneath her. She scrambled up immediately, ready.

He pulled a healing pad from Ninli's bag and a potion to fix broken bones. He threw the potion to Taline and watched through heavy lids as she gritted her teeth before drinking it.

He pressed the pad over his punctured lung and sucked in a breath as it worked. Items imbued with magic worked until the magic was gone. Only the imbued items they had brought with them would give them any magic to use here.

They'd have to rely on *other* things.

"We'll see," he said.

TALINE

Oh, *he'd* see. She'd make sure of that. Taline's fingers curled, then abruptly loosened, still feeling the shock of what rested there.

She looked at the scepter fused to her right palm. Cold, dark, and powerful—so unlike the ceremonial scepters that were strewn about the palace. She curled her fingers around the shaft and felt the echo of its power run through her blood—raw power, the kind that ran through Nin, that Nin struggled with every day—the kind that was far too potent for most to control.

A barely Level Five magi, she stood with the power of the gods in her hand. She looked at the figures bowed and still all around them, the chanting at an end. Waiting.

Like Valeran, they were watching her, weighing his next move, and hers.

They'd *won*. The *stick* in Taline's hand proclaimed it so. The scepter wasn't in Osni's hand or in the empire's possession.

They'd won. But she'd lost something far greater.

The power echo running through her dulled, and she curled her fingers harshly along its shaft as reality descended. They were in a world layer without magic—exiled there by Valeran.

Temporarily exiled. She looked at the hundreds of bowed figures, then at the scepter.

She'd find her sister. And if it meant she'd have to burn down the empire and the worlds around them to do it, so be it. That's what she'd do.

The story continues in

CAGE of SHADOWS

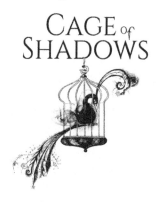

GLOSSARY

beldrake: a type of dragon.

blessed child of the emperor: an imperial child, who is blessed by the emperor in a ceremony that bestows upon them the ability to control imperial oaths. Imperial children given this designation may also be selected to serve as padifehl of an imperial territory someday. The blessing ceremony takes place when the emperor deems it time—usually when a powerful child has come into their powers, generally upon an Awakening from age 10-17. Children, like Kaveh ul Fehl, who come into their powers at an early age and show rare amounts of power or extraordinary gifts are blessed at a very young age and are raised accordingly. There are hundreds, perhaps thousands, of imperial children residing in the imperial palace and living in far-flung streets and lands, but the honor of being "blessed" means something far more elite and powerful. The emperor has been decreasing the number of blessing ceremonies and increasing the requirements as more and more of his children are born with great power.

Chrimoa: an elite crafter of decorative glass and ceramic pieces.

crouel: a person with little or no magic.

croupa: a sickness not unlike croup.

farhani: a necklace worn in imperial territories that signifies a magi's power level and has the magi's imperial fealty oaths embedded within. The investigorii can use the oaths to detain individuals in their territories for questioning.

fehlta, fehltan: a unit of currency used across the empire. Prior to its use, "measures" were used: five measures, three half measures, two quarter measures. Fehlta are similar to the Magahda coins used in Ancient India. In the Fehl Empire, there are 5 magi coinmasters keyed to the treasury whose responsibility is to create the coins using personal, magical stamps. When a coinmaster dies or retires, another is keyed to take his place. The five stamped signatures have to be correct for the coin to be legitimate. Counterfeiting coins is extremely difficult and punishable by death.

gate medallion: an object which has been imprinted with coordinates to transport a person to a specific place and contains a one-time activation. They are incredibly rare and expensive because they can only be created by a gatemaker or gate relic.

gatekeeper: a magi who cares for and repairs already created gates, and who is able to switch internally embedded coordinates to open through other created gates (connecting already created gates together). A rare ability.

gatemaker: a magi who creates ripgates and who is capable of tethering ripgates to physical objects and locations—making an arch or object with an open interior into a semi-permanent gate between two places. An extremely rare and coveted ability. **See also: ripgate**

imperial names: names given to citizens of the empire. The census requires all magi in the empire to receive designations based on the following name scheme: First Name **al** Power Level **el** Occupation **il** Birth City **ol** Oath Temple **ul** Family Name. These get shortened in informal use to First name **ul** Family Name.

Example formal: *Ninli al Six el Healer il Tehras ol Gomen ul Summora*

Example informal: *Ninli ul Summora*

For people living outside of the empire, individual society naming schemes prevail.

imperial professional titles: the professional designation that precedes one's imperial name. Professional titles eschew many of the imperial naming scheme elements brought by the census. Title + Family Name is most often used. If there is more than one person of the same profession with the same family name in the room, the power level is given in the middle. The first name would be added as well if the power level is also the same.

Examples:

Healer Summora

Healer Six Summora and Healer Four Summora

Healer Ninli Six Summora

investigore: head of the law enforcement, similar to a director. Investigore Malik ul Malit when formally addressed.

investigorii: a law enforcement unit or an individual officer (singular and plural).

imperator: title for the head of an army unit.

karogi tiles: tiles used in karogi (a game).

khursifa (khursifas): a spell-woven conveyance mat that can connect and use wind enchantments in a city and through its own woven magic. A type of flying carpet. Under the hands and skills of a specialist, they can be made to do wondrous things as a mode of transportation.

layer, layers, layer split: The split of one world into five, each duplicate existing on top of the next. Three creation magi (worldchangers) working together split the Earth into five identical layers of land. Four layers have magic, while one layer (sometimes referred to as "the first") is without. This first layer contains all the humans and creatures born without magic and is protected from the magical worlds by ruthless groups of devout magi. **See also: pentalayerists.** The Fourth Layer was created specifically for beasts, creatures, and hybrid beings and is sometimes referred to as "the land of the beasts." Five layers of the same world, existing each on top of the next. Four steady layers and one of chaos—not fully settled during the event that produced them. One of no magic, two of plenty, one of beasts and power, one of chaos.

magi: a user of magic.

mancaleh: a classic board game, sometimes referred to as mancala.

majex (imperial majex): the wife of the emperor. The high imperial majex is the ruling wife.

narsumina: a pet name Rone calls Taline (used in much the way someone would call another "princess"). The reference is to the beautiful, vestal temple attendants of Narsum, the god of beauty, youth, age, and time.

padifehl: the leader of an imperial territory, usually a child of the emperor.

palmera: a palm spring drink that is highly intoxicating.

pentalayerists: a group who seek to protect and preserve the layers as they were designed. This includes protecting the non-magic world from magical influence. Their goal is to eradicate magi and relics that can open gates between layers. As a precautionary measure, and if given the opportunity, they will also destroy *any* relic or magi deemed too powerful, who may disrupt the status quo.

Polingsa Manuscripts: manuscripts and scrolls that contain powerful spells created and kept by the Polingsa family. Qara ul Polingsa encourages Nin to steal them so that they can be added to the library for the masses, while still giving Qara a reasoned voice among the elite.

revenant: one of the undead.

ripgate: a temporary gate created by a gatemaker or relic. It is different from a gate, which is a permanent or semi-permanent fixture.

sandrake: a type of sand dragon.

sandpronga: a large worm-like sand creature with immense teeth.

scholari: the head of knowledge or science in an imperial territory.

scepter chamber: a curved chamber at the heart of the Palace of Tehras that holds the twelve scepters of Tehras. Four per "wall" in the curved chamber.

shadowshaper: one who can use and craft shadows to enhance sensory perception and who can control shadows by pushing their own sensory output through them. A shadowshaper can connect their senses through a shadow to affect whatever the shadow is touching. In this way, shadows become extended limbs of the shadowshaper and are able to do whatever a regular limb can. A thousand shadows could become a thousand separate swords when wielded by a magi whose mind is able to control a thousand different limbs at once. Only two shadowshapers are known to exist. Neither is fully human. It is speculated that a regular human mind is incapable of wielding as many separate entities as shadowshapers have been observed to wield.

stormbrewer: a magi who controls storms.

string: a signature, the feel of a person's magic—how one magi sensitive to it can identify another.

sunmaker, sunchaser, suncatcher, suntaker: a magi who manipulates sunlight or light for specific civic tasks (enforcement, agriculture, leisure, etc.).

windcatcher, windmaker, windchaser, windtaker: a magi who manipulates the winds for specific civic tasks (chasing people using wind spells, crafting directional breezes for city travel, routing weather for agricultural means, etc.).

CHARACTERS

Ninli ul Summora, Ninli, Nin: (age 19) healer and thief, gatemaker. Incredibly powerful magically and physically gifted in movement. Is unable to read (pure alexia) due to brain trauma at age 9.

Taline ul Summora, Tal, Tali: (age 20) healer and thief, spellcrafter. Highly intelligent with an excellent memory, but magically weak due to repeated stripping of her abilities when younger. Can recreate the bases and glyphs for spells she sees even a single time but is unable to power them.

Rone ul Valeran: (age 21) relic hunter, gambler, and trickster. The bastard son of two magically gifted lines, Valeran and Fehl. He is blessed/cursed with a distinctive hair color that cannot be magically or physically altered.

Kaveh ul Fehl: (age 22) thirteenth "blessed" child of the emperor, head of all imperial armies, and the emperor's favorite. A shadowshaper who is undefeated in battle, he answers only to the emperor and has ties to no other. He is known as the Shadow Prince, Imperator General, Imperator General of the Empire, Terror of the Battlefront, Nightmare of the Empire, and He Who Has Never Failed.

Sher Fehl: (age 52) emperor, The Fehl, Great Fehl, Emperor of All He Touches.

Nera ul Fehl: (age 48) High Imperial Majex, favorite wife of the emperor. Born Nera Erias.

Aros ul Fehl: (age 32) first born of Nera, first blessed child of the emperor, no current territory.

Etelian ul Fehl: (age 31) Padifehl of Tehrasi, second born of Nera, second blessed child.

Shiera ul Fehl: (age 30) Padifehl of Cuipsin, eighth blessed child, beloved by her country.

Baksis ul Fehl: (age 27) imperial prince, twentieth blessed child, no current territory.

Simin ul Fehl: (age 26) imperial prince, eighteenth blessed child, no current territory.

Ifret: corporeal creature of shadow, companion to Kaveh.

Irsula of Denz: Night Terror of the Land of Darkness, Mistress of Shadows; mother of Kaveh ul Fehl. Born to Darkness and a human woman, she is half-human. Imprisoned, and with no oaths taken, she has no imperial census designation and no surname. Denz is the place of her birth.

Barrini: a deceased family line of gatekeepers and gatemakers.

Governor Nunde: governor of Lyndel.

Crelu ul Osni: Scholari of Tehrasi, worked for and betrayed the Carre Family; now rules Tehrasi from the shadows and hunts scepter lore.

ssss

Farrah: Osni's deceased wife.

Malik ul Malit: Investigore of Tehrasi. Head of the investigorii—the law enforcement branch of Tehras.

Qara ul Polingsa: an elite of Tehras, politician.

Larit ul Polingsa: bondmate of Qara, healer.

Madame Forsa: head servant in the women's quarters of the Palace of Tehras.

Healer Amura: palace healer, Level Eight.

Healer Tenzig: Healing Guild head.

Gantres: brothers who sometimes act as the Hand.

Madame Yates: a Tehrasian woman about to have her third baby.

Lansson: a Tehrasian seal maker whose spellwork has become obsolete.

Carre Family (in order of age):
Giran Carre: former King of Tehrasi.
Jisarek Carre: brother of Giran, kidnapper of Nera ul Fehl.
Salare Carre: former Queen of Tehrasi.
Savvan Carre: former crown prince.
Lorsali Carre: former first princess.
Fein Carre: former prince.
Allit Carre: former prince.
Memni Carre: former prince.
Jolan Carre: former prince.
Zehra Amanan Carre: former princess.

PANTHEON

Sehk-Ra: two-faced god of death and chance (shadow wielders, undertakers and embalmers, death rite clerics, touch killers, gamblers, thieves) and god of the sun, rule, order (rulers, head of households, judgment/truth speakers).

When face names are used individually: Sehk for death and chance, Ra for rule and order.

To be Sehk-Ra-blessed is to be in total control = the god of dominion.

Ferra: goddess of birth and health (healers).

Akkan: god of winds, travel, and travelers (port mages, paladins/finders, some weather mages).

Gripna: goddess of domestic matters/hearth/estate/money (homemakers, merchants).

Narsum: god of beauty, youth, age, and time. Depiction varies—sometimes shown genderless, sometimes shown possessing all genders, sometimes shown as an infant, sometimes stooped with a cane. Narsum is the representation of all things experienced in a lifetime—change both physical and spiritual. Narsumina is the title given to the vestal tenders of Narsum's shrines and temples—usually beautiful, young women.

Marsk: god of war and victory (warriors, rulers, politicians, etc.).

Oceana: goddess of all waters, the seas, rivers, rains and snow (fishermen, some weather mages, etc.).

Verdis: god of flora and fauna, forests (hunters, herbists, farmers).

Called upon by imperial citizens, prayer usage varies:

A healer might pray to Verdis to find herbs, but to Ferra to bless a procedure.

A sailor might say: May the winds of Akkan bless us and the waters of Oceana hold us.

Godly names are used as swear words often, especially Sehk-Ra, Sehk, and Ra with any combination of descriptive terms attached. Sehk-Ra-be-damned, Sehk-damned, etc.

AUTHOR

Anne Zoelle has loved books about fantasy, magic, math, wit, and imagination since devouring A Wrinkle in Time, Phantom Tollbooth, Alice in Wonderland, and the Chronicles of Narnia as a child. She loves writing about college aged protagonists who get embroiled in complicated adventures.

Split between the midwest and west coast, she writes books for all ages that feature sentient libraries, rock guardians, and people finding family. Normally nestled deep within her writing cave, you can sometimes find her on Instagram or (elusively) elsewhere online.

Sign up for her newsletter on www.annezoelle.com or send her an email at anne.zoelle@gmail.com

Made in the USA
Coppell, TX
26 January 2021